SEARCH

by D.K. BOHLMAN

To Charlie,
Enjoy.
Best Wishes
Deche

First edition in the United Kingdom 2015.
A catalogue record of this book is available from the British library.
Paperback edition ISBN: 978-0-9934262-0-9.
Kindle e-book edition ISBN: 978-0-9934262-1-6.

PROLOGUE

Cold steel sometimes traces out a tortured death. In this case, maybe it wouldn't be too bad a thing.

From beneath the mattress came a red silk bag, embroidered with angular images of small, colourful birds.

Inside, a knife.

The future perpetrator of this murder curled warm, thin fingers around the bone handle and withdrew it from its sheath. The sharp blade gleamed silver-grey. It was engraved along its spine with tiny pictographs, which seemed to lend an authority to the use of the blade; a story which justified its purpose.

A brush of a finger along the knife, testing its edge, drew a small droplet of blood and a light intake of breath.

Held high against the fading light it became a symbolic shape, carving whispers of intent in the air as it rehearsed the movements of assassination.

A life for a life.

PART I

ENGAGEMENT

1

A middle-aged woman sat drooped over her desk. Her pale grey skin was matched by the high cloud outside. It had been a momentous decision and she felt worn out but, equally, strangely excited. She leant back into the leather swivel chair with a weary sigh and picked up the two photographs in front of her.

She looked intently at the picture of a young man. He wore faded blue jeans and a rock band's t-shirt. She thought about him again. His laughter, his touch. Her memories had faded over the years, which hurt her. She'd always felt it would have been perfect, she'd never doubted that. But now, with today's news, it had become too late. Some words from an old song drifted into her mind. The time of our lives has come and gone...

That caustic old feeling of jealousy burned at her, tightened her insides.

She tilted her head to look at the other photograph, almost for relief from that bitter feeling. Two fair-haired toddlers. They were so beautiful. She wondered about their lives, what they may have made of themselves. It hurt badly that she hadn't seen them grow up.

Now she had been dealt her final card. She stood at the top of a darkening helter-skelter of decay. She felt anger and resentment well up inside her again. At least she had the energy for that, hadn't completely given up yet. That inner well of emotional power would help her over the coming months.

She slid the photographs back into two separate white envelopes and placed them inside the old walnut desk's letter compartment.

So much for the decision. Now she had to create the plan.

It needed to be someone with discretion. Tactful would be good. Open to influence was an absolute necessity. A track record would help speed things up too of course: now she had made her mind up, she needed to have this dealt with quickly.

She picked up the telephone and dialled an old, nearly forgotten acquaintance.

He answered briskly.

'Hi Paul, remember me... it's Glenda Muir,' she said softly, initiating the next episode of her life.

2

The two-carriage diesel train clattered its way into the station, laying an acrid oil stench across the narrow platform. Calum Neuman wrenched his black rucksack down from the overhead luggage rack, pushed his way past two day-tripping Americans blocking the carriage door and stumble-dropped onto the damp concrete. He rubbed his chin: the day's stubble was rough against his hand as he moved out past the tiny station building. There were no station staff: those days were long gone.

As the diesel fumes cleared, he breathed in the clean Highland air. He set off down the harbour road towards the village, reflecting that today's trip had been a lot more interesting than most during the last few months. His new client was deep, for sure and he sensed a faint aura of darkness around her. Intangible, but there somehow.

He was followed by a cool, moist breeze, even though the sun was shining and summer was well underway. In this part of the north-west highlands, genuinely warm days were a rare luxury and his light raincoat came in handy again today.

A gull slipped overhead, screeching its agitation across the startlingly blue waters of the loch and diving down the contour of the slope which led to a white-washed inn. As he neared the village centre and the row of palm trees that belied the true nature of the local climate, he was illuminated by one of his, somehow now less frequent, light bulb moments. For all of their slowly increasing rarity, when they did happen it was like switching on the searchlight in a prison camp.

The inn came slowly into view. He could almost smell his first glass of Talisker: it was his comforting promise to himself at the end of a long day out - a sweet, strong warmth which instantly unwound his coiled mind. The lure of the alcohol vied in his mind with the emerging realisation of who he may have met during the day. He dismissed any thoughts about dropping into his office first and tilted his head to squeeze his tall frame under the inn's low wooden door lintel.

He chose his usual table: a slightly rickety affair in the corner near the bar, with a wooden spoke-back chair and enough space for a drink and a newspaper.

'Bad day at the office, Calum or just your usual gloomy self?' queried the severe looking woman behind the bar.

'Hi Gill. Bit of both. Well just me probably... nothing a double won't fix.'

Gill Gilzean walked over with his personal tumbler dosed with a hefty slug of whisky. It was etched with the Talisker distillery logo and flashed an amber sparkle as the low sun crept through the open door and shattered on its cut-glass faces.

She managed him a faint smile. He'd known Gill since he was a child. She'd never been the most welcoming of people - he thought it was an odd career choice, running an inn and serving the public. Maybe she had few choices: lots of people in the village just wanted to stay in this idyllic place and had a number of jobs to make ends meet.

'Anything to eat?'

'Mmm, some pan-fried herring would be good,' he said. His instinctive cholesterol counter told him this wasn't too bad a meal, so long as he chose potatoes over fries.

'Ten minutes, ok?'

He nodded.

The bracing smells of salt and malt twisted together in the sunlight as the first dram sank into his throat - now he could think over what was ticking through his mind again. Glenda Muir was already beginning to intrigue him.

3

Glenda stared out of the large south-facing window of her house, onto the backyard, wondering if she had made the right choice.

She felt the need for tea, so wandered through to her kitchen and boiled the kettle.

As the water started to bubble, she thought Calum Neuman was going to have an interesting time finding John.

John Coulson.

They hadn't spoken for so long... though at times, when she pictured his face, it could feel like it was only recently when she last felt the overpowering pull of his arms, hugging her closely to him.

Never again.

The kettle clicked off. Her eyebrows flinched, awoken from her imagination and she grasped its handle, thus starting the ritual she carried out many times a day.

Her parents had been professional nomads, trailing her brother and herself around a succession of exotic overseas locations - and one of the enduring joys of her daily life had been discovered in their time in China: the art of making tea. Green tea was her favourite, but jasmine was a delight on a warm afternoon: not that there were too many of those in a Scottish summer.

She pretended to follow the Gongfu method, though she knew that in China it wouldn't be done with green tea. She let the water cool for a few moments before she poured it from a height over the fresh leaves, sourced from a specialist delicatessen in town.

She swilled the water around a little, before discarding it down the sink and refilling the teapot with fresh hot water. Precisely three minutes later she dispensed the tea into a jade green patterned cup, one of a set her family had brought back with them from Shanghai.

She sat down at the kitchen table, the quiet of the room only broken by the soft ticking of an old wooden clock that had also belonged to her parents. She took a sip, rolled it around her tongue thoughtfully.

She so needed this search to be successful, but her old flame Paul Proudson had spoken highly of Calum, who'd seemed shrewd and had asked some insightful questions about John, her motivation and the boys' background. He was also quite attractive - but that was something that would take a separate course.

She mused as to whether he found her interesting too, but he'd given little away. Time would tell. She didn't have a lot of that commodity left though, at least not with any quality. She thought she might need to give it a push if there was any chance.

Triggered by the faint possibility of a dalliance, she let her mind drift into fantasy. One in which sex with a new man would hammer another blow at her rotten past. Yes, that would feel good, if only for a while. She smiled, blankly, at the prospect and sipped some more tea.

For the time being, all she could do was sit back and wait for results from him. She hoped it wouldn't be too long. It would be best if this could be concluded before summer got properly underway; she had plans to travel in the long university holidays if things worked out well.

Turning her head slightly to peer out of the window onto the street, she thought about her children, first wistfully... but then angrily. This was no easy task ahead and she knew it was unlikely to be without some unexpected problems: especially where John was concerned. Her mind was set though and she resolved to think about the future as optimistically as her somewhat unstable mind would allow.

The postman walked up the path to her house with a late delivery and the letter-box snapped sharply as it disgorged his consignment into the hall. She broke away from her abstraction and went to see whether there might be something interesting amongst the junk mail.

The postman ambled away down the front path and she watched him with narrowing eyes, through the small window set next to the door frame. With her thoughts already primed in that direction, after pondering on the topic of conquests, she wondered whether she might invite him in for some tea one morning.

4

It had been an early start to the day. The train to Inverness pulled sleepily out of Plockton at 6:33 a.m.

The guard sway-danced his way down the carriages, checking the tickets. It was generally a peaceful run at this early hour. Sometimes, the biggest problem was rousing the travelling sleepers. Like this guy in front of him right now. Here was the fun bit.

In a very loud voice.

'Morning sir, tickets if you will.'

Calum jerked backwards and looked up at him, with eyes like puffy clouds. He scraped his hand clumsily inside a jacket pocket and slowly produced £40.

'Return to Inverness please.'

After his rude awakening, he finally roused himself properly to buy a cup of tea and a hot bacon roll. He pulled the fatty rind off the bacon before devouring it hungrily, washing it down with the hot, amber liquid. Amber liquids were important to him - tea and whisky were his per diem props.

The train trundled through a succession of small halts en-route to Inverness, the view taking in vast expanses of mountains and loch and then replacing the pretty shorelines with scrub and mud-flats as it approached the destination. Its arrival in Inverness was heralded by bursts of sunlight through the glass sections in the old iron station roofing, creating a strobe effect in the carriage as it came to a lurching halt.

Calum blinked slowly in the bright light and hauled himself out of the airline-style seat. There was something exciting about arriving in a city early in the morning, the day afresh with possibilities: he wondered if this particular assignment would repay his optimism over the coming weeks.

He shrugged his coat on and made for the end of the carriage, glancing at his wristwatch, the wind-up old Roamer that once was his grandfather's.

His mobile bleeped at him - flagging a missed call. It was Cassie. He wasn't in the mood. Calls from his ex-wife often created hassle so he left it for later.

His appointment with Glenda Muir was at 2 p.m. There had been no more convenient train to catch, so he walked down Union Street and busied himself with a rare visit to his bank: he was travelling to Italy soon and took the opportunity to collect some Euros.

He wondered if one of these days Scotland might adopt the euro, especially with the issue of separation from the UK. He wasn't sure he cared: which was slightly ironic given how much he disliked England. It wasn't the English - just the place. He'd worked as a solicitor in England for a while, after his graduation from Aberdeen university. First in London, then Leicester, before taking the life-changing decision to move back home and enter the world of private investigation.

He looked back on it as a slow migration to the north and home, a realisation that England and the law weren't for him.

With plenty of time to spare, he sauntered down to Bank Street and sat on a bench overlooking the River Ness. He gazed at the hotels and bingo hall opposite and speculated that the water that flowed past him might have borne a mythical beast only minutes earlier, further up the loch. He'd never believed the legend about the monster, but it was more amusing to think it might be true.

The weak warmth of the morning sun on his face was pleasant and his mind relaxed.

He started to ponder on what might be awaiting him. The initial contact from the client had been brief. Some words about an urgent task and a brisk discussion about when it might be convenient to meet. She had mentioned that she worked at the University of the Highlands and Islands in Inverness. That was all.

He wondered if he should have brought Jenna with him to make notes and get up to speed more quickly with any potential research required - but as usual he rejected the idea. Often on these first meetings there was some personal issue that clients were a little reticent to disclose - and having a young girl with him might not help create the right mood for soul-baring.

He decided on an early lunch. A sandwich and coffee at an old family-run cafe on Margaret Street seemed to fit the bill, so he wandered up through the town and ordered a tuna melt. He sat down on a plastic window seat and chewed it, with no particular rush, staring out with disinterested eyes at the shoppers drifting up and down the street in the bright sunshine.

Glenda lived in a small detached Victorian house on Old Edinburgh Road, a short walk from the small city centre. He didn't want to be late for this first meeting so he set off with plenty of time to spare and at a brisk pace towards the south side of the city.

He'd worked up a light sweat on his forehead by the time he approached the address. He checked the house number in his notebook, then instinctively looked up when he felt he was being watched. He caught sight of some movement in an upstairs window - a curtain flicker or a reflection, he wasn't sure. Maybe it was her, impatient for his arrival. He rang the brass doorbell of the old stone house and waited to be greeted, admiring the original timber door.

The door opened and Calum was immediately struck by the height of his prospective customer. Glenda Muir was nearly six feet tall and her thinness accentuated the impression of height. Long fair hair, tinged with the first signs of grey, cascaded down around her head and was held together by a single band at the back. She was dressed in tight blue denims and a cheesecloth blouse reminiscent of some long gone hippy summer.

'Welcome. Calum I presume?'

'Indeed. Pleased to meet you, Mrs Muir,' said Calum as he offered a handshake. It was met with a warm, dry hand that grasped him firmly and shook gently.

'In fact it's Miss - but let me show you in first. And please call me Glenda.'

He was ushered into a large room, evidently a study. It was lined with a collection of different sizes of bookshelves at varying levels on each wall. There were two large leather chairs in the centre of the room and a desk at one end.

'Do sit down. I should explain, I use this room sometimes for private clients. I'm a psychologist by profession and I sometimes do private work outside of the university,' she smiled. 'But I promise not to analyse you today.'

'Tea?'

'That would be great,' Calum answered enthusiastically.

'I have green or jasmine, which do you prefer?'

Calum suddenly felt less eager. A good strong cup of English breakfast tea or even one of the pretentious single variety blacks was in his mind and now he felt disappointed. He didn't want to upset his client on a first meeting so settled on the jasmine.

'Back in six minutes then,' she said as she disappeared, presumably towards the kitchen. Six minutes struck Calum as being unusually precise. 'Must be a Virgo,' he thought to himself.

As she busied herself with making the tea, Calum stood up and took a good wander around the room. There were a lot of books on psychology - and some on hypnotherapy. A fair range of fiction as well: a sprinkling of classics, some fantasy – Stephen King seemed a favourite and lots of the psychological-emotional soft thriller novels that Calum didn't really like. All in all she seemed well read. It was generally untidy, with books laid haphazardly across the tops of the shelves as if they had been dumped there once read.

He stepped over to the desk. It was an old-fashioned bureau type with slots in the upright section for correspondence and lots of little cubby holes. It was uniformly stuffed with papers and envelopes.

Around the room, in between the bookshelves, the walls were adorned with some pieces of what looked like African art: wooden pictures of people and animals. Nothing aroused his immediate attention. It looked like the home of an academic or professional.

Glenda returned carrying a black lacquered tray on which were set two small oriental tea cups and a beautifully patterned teapot. She poured a pale brew out into the two cups and sat down. She looked directly at him, fixing his eyes without blinking.

'Just having a look at your books... hope you don't mind?'

'Well, no I suppose not.'

Calum sat down, feeling as if he had been slightly scolded.

'So I suppose I should begin with an outline of what I need you to do?' she said.

Calum nodded. 'Please.'

'Have you heard of Huntington's Chorea?'

He raised his eyebrows and pursed his lips.

'I have, though I'm not sure I know much about it. Why?'

'I've recently tested positive for it. It's a serious disease which will degrade and shorten my life... but it also has implications and consequences for other people who are related to me and that's where you come in. I need to find someone - well, two people in fact - and I want you to do that for me.'

No holding back so far then, he thought.

She twisted her mouth a little and mock winced.

'However, it's somewhat complicated. The people I need you to find are my children.'

Her expression became blank, distant.

'I know. It sounds ridiculous, but I don't know where they are.'

Calum held back his natural inclination to jump in with a barrage of questions, instead letting a short silence prevail before Glenda continued. Experience had taught him over the years that understanding the personality of the client themselves could often inform and help the eventual success of the brief. He was already beginning to feel that this particular client had some depths he needed to dive down into.

'I was with someone back in my university days, a man called John Coulson. We never married, but we had two children, twin boys. It's a long story but John and I broke up a year or so later and the boys went to live with him. We never kept in touch. I know it sounds odd and well, cruel maybe, but there were reasons why at the time it suited me. Then it became too late to change things. But now, as you may know, now things are different.'

'In what way?' Calum prompted. The name John Coulson seemed to ring a distant bell in his memory, but he shelved the thought for now.

'Huntington's Chorea, or Huntington's as it usually called, is a disease that's handed down the generations. Whilst it's not certain that my children will carry the defective gene, if they do then they will almost certainly succumb to the disease in the future,' Glenda replied, in a tone verging on monotonous.

'If it's not too painful a question, how serious is this? How might it affect them?' It was a risky question, he thought.

'Pretty nasty. Neurodegenerative. In simple terms, your brain decays fast. What follows is any combination of unsteady gait, jerky body movements, psychiatric issues, general mental decline, all of which degrade further until you can't really co-ordinate your movements and fall into dementia. All sorts of other complications too, heart disease, pneumonia, brittle bones, wasted muscles, that kind of thing. You just die of it. Slowly and badly.'

Too brutally honest for Calum. He swallowed hard, trying to clear his softly choking throat for another question.

17

'The boys have a fifty percent chance of having a mutated gene, which is the thing that leads to them developing the condition. If they have it, the mutated gene will dominate, in other words it will override a good copy: I suppose you know we have two copies of each of our genes? So between them there's a three in four chance that one or both of my children will develop it. I think you can see therefore why I need to find them.'

Calum nodded.

'What's even more worrying is that they are now seventeen years of age. At that age they are clearly capable of being fathers themselves. Whether that's a real possibility I have no idea about of course. But it *is* possible, so they must be tested soon.'

'So you have absolutely no idea where they now live? Or their last known whereabouts?'

She looked at him as if he were questioning her word.

'No, none at all. I had an address for John and the boys originally - he went to live in Lincoln, which is where he first got a job - part of the reason we split in fact. But I know that he moved on. Letters started to come back marked as "addressee unknown".'

'And you have no more information for me to start to work with? What are the boys' names?'

'Nope, that's it. It's Ben and Gordon, they kept my surname: just a sentimental thing I insisted on at the time. I knew I was going to give them up so I wanted to leave something with them,' she explained, as if it needed justifying.

'I do have one other thing, though I doubt it will help.'

Glenda rose quickly from her chair and walked over to the bureau desk. She slipped her hand into the letter compartment and withdrew a crisp, white envelope and handed it to him.

Calum flipped the envelope open and pulled out a colour photograph: two small boys, sitting in a pram together. They were sunny looking little things, fair-haired and smiling - and around twelve months old.

He pulled his lips into a tight smile.

'They're bonny looking kids,' he declared. 'But surely you must have more photographs than this?'

Glenda shook her head, vigorously.

'No, I'm afraid not. John took all the official stuff, you know birth certificates and the like - he'd need them. And for my part, well I chose to keep just the one photograph, the last one we took of them. At the time, it seemed right not to remind myself more than was necessary. I wish I'd kept more now, but life's like that isn't it? It comes back to bite you.'

She threw him a faint smile. He didn't get any warmth from it.

Calum nodded slowly. 'I suppose so,' he said. 'All right, I'll start with what you have then - but can you fill me in on John's age, birthday, physical attributes etc... and do you have any photographs of him?'

'He's a Virgoan, Sept 24th. Same age and birth sign as myself, 41,' she said, with a hint of unexpected playfulness. 'I had some old photographs, you can have them if you wish but to be honest you can probably find more up to date pictures of him on the web. It seems he's become quite a celebrity in his own circles in recent years. I'm sure you can research those.'

Calum had started to make some notes. He smirked internally at having guessed her birth sign, then looked up.

'If it's ok with you I'd like whatever you have. At least I can corroborate them with whatever I find on the internet, even though there's been a large time gap. What is it he does for a living?'

'He's a criminal psychologist. He works for various UK police forces from time to time, as well as lecturing and I believe some private work. I'll get the photos I have for you.'

She stood again and reached up to one of the higher book shelves and brought down a small photo album.

'One other thing,' she said, handing it to him. 'It's important to me that John doesn't know about this, so please do not under any circumstances make yourself known to him. I want

19

to talk to the children myself. So please locate John and the children and let me know where they are, and how you think I can best approach them without John being present.'

She hesitated, enough to make Calum to look up again and wonder why, and then went on.

'Clearly, I could have tried to find a way to get to John directly myself, but I just don't want any contact with him. It's going to be a hard enough message to give, without having to worry about meeting John too. To be honest, looking at his material on the internet, there doesn't seem any clue as to his location or how to contact him. I'm assuming that's something you can overcome.'

'Does John know you were a potential Huntington's candidate? I presume if it's handed down that someone in your family must have had it in living memory'

'That's right, my grandfather had it and I believe two generations before that someone from the female branch of the family tree. John did know this... but it's been over sixteen years since we've spoken so I've no way of knowing if he's mentioned it to them. At the time we split, my mother hadn't been tested for it but she was later found to be positive too. She's pretty ill now.'

Calum nodded, sympathetically.

He twisted his lips a little, to begin phrasing a question.

'So why now, why haven't you wanted to tell the children they were at risk earlier?'

'Good question. I suppose a combination of things. It was always a risk for them: but I didn't really want to re-establish contact with them, or John, until absolutely necessary. It's also possible the disease may not affect them. I didn't want them to grow up through their young years worrying about it all the time. But now they are coming to the time when they may conceivably have some offspring of their own, planned or otherwise, so I felt I needed to have the test myself and talk to them about it. In any case the law says that they can't have the test themselves until they are 18.'

She looked down a little.

'And, well, I don't know how fast the disease will affect me so I suppose - maybe - I just want to see them before it becomes too hard for them or me?'

Calum nodded. It seemed a reasonable answer, but there was another question he was trying, and failing, to form in his head. Her words were cold, clinical - as if there was a heart in them that had been precisely cut out. It created an uneasy atmosphere somehow.

He set out his usual business terms and conditions whilst his brain whirred in the background, trying to dual process: but the question still wouldn't come to him.

Glenda straightened herself and looked squarely at him.

'So, is there anything else I can tell you, Calum?'

He returned the gaze and paused a moment.

'For now no, I'll do some initial research and be in touch if I need any more direction.'

'Well if you'll excuse me then, I have to be back into college this afternoon to run a seminar - always busy.' She laughed lightly.

Glenda rose and motioned Calum towards the hallway.

As he approached the front door, Calum turned towards her and fixed her face with a direct gaze.

'One final question. How did you choose me for this search? I always ask my clients - helps with the marketing strategy.'

'You came recommended,' she replied. 'I'd prefer to keep the name of the recommender private,' she added, after a slight hesitation.

He nodded.

'Fair enough. I like to keep my sources private too.'

'I'll be in touch once I've any news and I'll let you have a written update each week, just so you know where we're up to.'

Glenda nodded back and shut the door behind him and on the conversation.

Calum pondered on the interview as he walked down the garden path: it had been very brief. Glenda was clearly a determined and single-minded woman. In fact, the sort of woman he rather liked. He looked down at his belly and wondered how attractive he was. He was approaching middle age, but reasonably fit he thought: his small overhang probably just about passed muster.

He wandered back to the town centre. He had time to kill before the train home, so he sat on the same bench overlooking the river, making some notes and thinking over his next steps. He would drop Jenna some research tasks via email later that night.

For some reason Glenda's name still seemed familiar but he couldn't quite put his finger on why. He knew from experience that if he let his brain run free without his conscious pushing, it would eventually sieve through the information repeatedly until it told him the answer.

His mobile phone rang. It was Cassie. He answered it with the usual apprehensiveness reserved for his ex-wife.

'Ellie hasn't been too good the last couple of days. Thought you'd like to know. I tried to call earlier.'

'Oh, how bad?' His shoulders tensed upwards. He felt guilty for not returning her call earlier. She hadn't left a message though.

'Well, you know how it is, the same as usual when she gets bad.'

That didn't tell him much. He wondered if she was being purposefully vague. But her house was only ten minutes away.

'Ok. Look, I'm in Inverness right now. I can pop over for a little while now if that's ok?'

'Yup, sure. Come on over.'

She clicked the phone off promptly.

He walked back up from the riverside and hailed a cab.

*

From the back of the car he gazed absent-mindedly at the buildings sliding by, as he reflected on his daughter's condition.

It had been a brief marriage, his and Cassie's. He had felt such a bastard leaving Eleanor alone with her battle with cystic fibrosis. He reminded himself, once again, that she hadn't been diagnosed before they parted ways. Cassie had seen the sense in splitting too though, thankfully, which had helped keep things calm between them over the years. She was a strong woman. She had to be to deal with Ellie: he admired her for that. Love, however, had faded from the equation almost since Ellie had been conceived.

As he arrived he peered up at Ellie's window. She was peeking out over the window sill, propped up in the chair she sometimes used when she was having a bad spell. She waved weakly at him. He gave her his best smile, paid the cab driver, and rang the doorbell.

Cassie opened the door.

Her gaze said 'so you occasionally do turn up then'.

He knew that was unfair but didn't rise to the temptation to react: it was just too much effort.

'Go up and see her. I'll be up in a few minutes. Want some tea?'

'Sure.'

At least it would be real tea this time.

He padded respectfully up the stairs of the small terraced house, not wanting to appear too pleased with the hospitality. He had no idea why he reacted like that, but it irritated him.

Ellie's door was open and he caught sight of her face peering into the doorway, looking for his entrance. She forced a tight, restricted smile at him.

She was a brave girl in the way she had dealt with her illness: somehow that made it even more poignant when he saw her suffering. She was breathing in quick, shallow scoops of air. An inhaler mask lay by the side of her chair. She seemed to have even more pictures of boy band hunks plastered around the room.

23

'Hi my love. Mum says you've not been too good. Using the antibiotics?' He passed her a copy of a girls' magazine he'd picked up on the way.

'Yeah, Dad. Thanks'

Another weak smile.

It was always difficult for him at times like this. It was an effort for her to speak, so he couldn't ask her too much. On the other hand, what would she want to know about his work? There wasn't much else in his life that might interest her either. He smiled back, then leant over and hugged her, kissing the top of her head. He sat down on her bed, looking around the room for something that could spark a question or an observation.

He was saved by Cassie entering with two cups of tea.

'That was quick.'

She shrugged her shoulders and smiled.

'The physio has just been. She was here for an hour, doing her lung exercises. You seem a bit better than this morning, don't you love?'

Ellie nodded as vigorously as she could.

'How long have you been on the antibiotics?' he asked.

'Started today,' Cassie answered for her. Calum hated people doing that and gave her a flickering, dismissive look before returning his gaze to Ellie.

'So is it helping?'

'Yeah it does Dad. Just takes a while to kick in.'

She held up the magazine, for her mother's benefit.

'Dad bought me this,' she said, smiling.

'The man in the shop told me it was for teens, so is that ok?'

'Yeah Dad, but I am nearly a teen now remember!'

And so the conversation went. He found it impossible to get beyond the clichéd politeness that flutters around any ill person, particularly with Cassie in the room. Calum put it down to a lack of family time together. That was never going to be possible now, but he knew it was a reason for their stilted triangular relationship.

As soon as he had drunk his tea, he made the train his excuse to leave and hugged Ellie once more before making his way down to the front door.

He turned to Cassie, who had followed him down the stairs.

'Let me know how she goes?'

'Of course. You can always ring too, you know that don't you?'

Of course he could: but he rarely did. Mostly because the conversation was even more awkward over a telephone line than face to face. He just didn't know how to close off those kind of calls either, in a way that would make Ellie know he cared.

He left feeling a wholly unsatisfactory mixture of relief and frustration. Relief in escaping from the awkwardness of the bedroom: frustration at not feeling close enough to his daughter when she was ill. And, worse, annoyance with himself for being relieved to be leaving and in being so useless for Ellie.

5

After some final arguments with herself, centring on whether a neon-orange sweater decorated with yellow suns around the neck was going to provoke a worthwhile reaction from Calum, Jenna Strick pulled her waterproof jacket on, grabbed her packed lunch, and ambled out onto Harbour Street.

She felt the need for more coffee - it had been a good evening at the pub, it was local music night and Gregor had been on fine form with both fiddle and charm; which always ended up with her drinking more beer than she'd planned.

Turning the corner away from the loch side, up a narrow passageway, she pushed the key into the front door of the office, shouting a slightly muted hello as she threw her coat and lunch onto the sideboard in the hallway. No response. Maybe Calum had got back late, or maybe the Talisker had got the better of him again.

She sat down at her scuffed oak desk in the corner of the sparsely furnished office and logged on to her laptop. At least Calum had seen the sense of a new computer for his research assistant - after a number of heated exchanges.

Her email inbox had a single new message - she always cleared out her email before she left each night. It was from Calum. He must have been in the office later on or logged on from home last night.

She opened it and sat back to digest the contents.

Hi... got back a bit late so didn't call. If you're in before me, can you start researching everything you can find on a John Coulson: search tags might be criminal psychologist, Lincoln, Lincolnshire ... think he moved there about sixteen years ago. Key thing is where does he live/contact details ... Glenda Muir is an interesting one: might be an unusual case for a change ... will fill you in later. Keep the coffee nice and hot for me :) Calum.

Jenna liked this work, which was why she'd agreed to stay on working for Calum, following the temporary arrangement in the summer she left the local high school.

She'd intended to go to university in the autumn but, well, had ended up agreeing with Gregor when he suggested she defer for at least a year or two and follow her heart. That was a synonym for himself mostly: though he'd also baited her with her work with the local wildlife conservation group, knowing she adored helping with the seals and dolphins. Now she was getting on with it - but she knew a further decision point would come for her soon.

She clicked open her browser and set to work.

*

A rattle at the front door roused her from her concentration an hour later and Calum bounded through from the hallway and over to his desk.

'Morning,' she said vaguely in his direction, whilst continuing to peruse her screen.

'Yes I worked that out from the position of the suns on your sweater,' he retorted, with a mock scowl on his face.

Good choice she thought as she purred internally - same old Calum, same predictable reaction.

'So what progress have we made this morning?'

The 'royal we' annoyed Jenna - he meant what had *she* done that morning. She pressed her lips together and rose above the irritation.

27

'Well, trawls for John Coulson didn't come up with any address references in the usual search engines and nothing significant in the local press archives that I can access: just a string of minor articles about his involvement in national crime cases, starting about a year after he arrived in Lincoln judging from your email.'

'Mmm, we're going to have to tread a bit gingerly with this one Jenna, there's some sensitivity in it,' said Calum.

'And are you going to tell me why then?'

'Err... well, this John Coulson is a criminal psychologist. He works for police forces around the UK from time to time and has become a sort of minor celebrity in those circles, so I've heard. Given the police aren't generally madly in love with us, we need to watch how we approach finding him.'

Calum decided he didn't want Jenna to know what else he had remembered the previous evening. In fact there was still something bothering him about the interview, some detail that didn't fit with the rest or an obscured familiarity with some of the data that he couldn't quite identify. He let the thought drop again, for the moment.

Jenna gave a shrug of her elf-like shoulders.

'You'll need to watch yourself then - as usual,' she said, with a slight smirk. One of the benefits of growing up in this village was knowing local people well. Though she hadn't worked for Calum that long, she'd known him a long time, almost all of her life. It was a comfortable relationship and Calum seemed to enjoy the barbed repartee they often exchanged. He'd be a better investigator if he tried that bit harder though. He was a bit too comfortable with his life she thought.

'How was the music last night?'

'Yep good, lots of people turned up. Ended up being a pretty late one.'

'So you'll be needing some coffee then? Make mine a tea,' he gently chastised.

On the other hand, there were times when he was just as annoying as her father.

A little later, with hot beverages in hands, they clustered around Jenna's computer and looked through what she'd retrieved to date. There was a distinct lack of leads. Glenda had given Calum little information: John's date of birth, some old photos, his last known address in Lincoln dating back sixteen years - and a photograph of her children when they were around one year old. It wasn't much of a start and given Jenna's lack of progress, he decided to visit Lincoln and try to track him down through local investigations.

'OK Jenna, can you get me some train options for Lincoln for tomorrow? Let's see what else we can come up with today, but I think I need to go and sniff around the old address and see what turns up.'

'Yes boss: will that be a first class or second class ticket?' she said somewhat sarcastically.

'Second... I don't think Glenda Muir will run to luxury - and find me a reasonable B&B in the city please. Book two nights.'

Jenna decided to try hard to find somewhere interesting for him to stay: after all, it was more fun for her to look for a place she might like to try herself. One of these days Calum might actually take her with him, client budgets permitting.

She leaned back into her chair, yawning from a shortage of sleep and lazily began digging into a couple of accommodation websites.

Thirty minutes later she started to feel quite proud of what she had found for him. She hoped he would too.

*

Calum spent the rest of the day looking through the detail behind the web references they'd found on John Coulson. There were actually quite a lot; some referring to his seminars on criminal psychology, but most described criminal cases he'd assisted the police with in recent years. It looked like he must have been successful with his initial engagements: he'd been involved in a fair number of cases, particularly over the last five years.

Calum was also waiting for a call back from an old friend. Paul Proudson had studied Law at Aberdeen university with him. After a fairly successful few years in private practice he'd returned to his alma mater for the softly padded cut and thrust of academia. He'd called Paul last night, and left a brief message.

He wanted to confirm what he'd suddenly suspected: that Glenda Muir was in fact the same Glenda he recalled Paul having a brief fling with in their university days. If he was right, she was a fresher: he and Paul had been down at the weekly Friday night disco in the Student's Union building, when they both zoomed in on a couple of likely looking girls who looked like fun.

His date had ended in nothing, but Paul and Glenda, if indeed it was her, had a couple of months before their relationship petered out. He couldn't recall seeing much of either of them then, but there was something about the way Glenda Muir had spoken to him the day before, that triggered a recollection of that alcohol-driven Friday night many years ago.

He searched the web for Glenda Muir and found a website for her professional work. Ignoring the description of her services, he looked up the pen picture of herself on the homepage. There it was: a graduate of Aberdeen university in 1992. Now he just needed Paul to confirm it: not that it necessarily meant anything, but all information *might* be good.

Having found what he was looking for, he browsed the rest of the site. It wasn't that extensive, just brief details of her services, some references and contact details. She offered psychological support services: psychotherapy, counselling and hypnotherapy. That seemed to tally with the contents of her bookshelves. Nothing else caught his eye, so he closed the web page. He turned his attention to planning how he might start to use John's old address in Lincoln, to trace his movements from sixteen years ago, to wherever he had ended up now. He'd printed off a couple of recent photos of Coulson from the web articles to help him start.

Jenna interrupted him with a beaming self-satisfied smile and a piece of printed paper.

'You're going to love this place I've found you Calum,' she said. 'Not exactly your average B&B but I'm sure you can pack some cornflakes. And it was a bargain since I booked at the last minute.'

She handed him the accommodation details. He scanned it.

It looked like he was going to be staying in some sort of converted self-catering apartment adjoining the castle at Lincoln.

'Yep that's right, a real castle!' Jenna exclaimed. 'Wish I was staying there too.'

She blushed as she realised the ambiguity - fortunately Calum was still studying the details and didn't notice.

'Actually there's a small breakfast room with a buffet too, if you don't fancy making your own.'

'Ok you did good there Jenny babe,' said Calum, in the mock American accent he annoyed her with sometimes.

'Looks fun - and at least it's not too pricey. Well let's hope the person search is as fruitful too. I'm going home now Jenn, pack some things and stuff. Lock up behind you?'

'Don't I always?' Jenna replied with false indignation. She gave him a wink and resolved to leave no more than ten minutes after Calum went. She still hadn't quite recovered from last night's excesses and needed to doze.

6

Calum flopped down on his sofa, switched on the television and yawned loudly. He wondered whether he could allow himself a small pork pie. He usually kept a tight rein on his fat intake, but his time in the east midlands had left him addicted to the traditional, lard-laden, delicacies.

Keeping a watch on his cholesterol levels had become a daily obsession, a need he felt multiplied by a family history of heart disease. His father had died young. The visions of hospital visits, seeing his father wired up, pale and lifeless, was his memory's wallpaper.

His decision-making was interrupted as he noticed the message waiting symbol flashing on his home phone. He turned down the television and pressed the glowing button to listen. It was from Paul Proudson. 'Good to hear from you Calum-o... catch me tonight? Talk soon.'

He convinced himself that the conversation would be best fuelled by a mouthful of pie, so having raided the fridge he sat down and dialled Paul back. He answered immediately with a pleasantly soft Scots accent.

'Hi friend! How are you doing?'

'Not so bad Paul. Been too long since we spoke - but listen, I have a trip tomorrow and wanted to just check something out before I left.'

Paul confirmed Glenda was indeed Glenda Muir. No surprise then.

'Scotland's a small country: our social circles really aren't that small either are they mate? Something else Calum, she actually called me and asked for advice on choosing an investigator to help her. Guess who I recommended?!'

Calum pressed his lips together in a faint smile. 'Ha, now it all falls into place. She wouldn't tell me how she'd picked out my name. But why ask you for advice?'

'Hmm, well I suppose because she knows me; though we've not stayed in touch we're both in academic circles, so we're vaguely aware of each other's situation. Since I work in Law, maybe she thought I might have some contacts in the world of private investigation. In fact I don't, apart from you being my friend. So I didn't have many to choose from,' he teased.

'I didn't mention we knew each other and I don't suppose she'll connect you to that Friday night twenty odd years ago.'

'Well thanks Paul, I owe you one.'

'Actually you can make that two pints... one Friday night soon.'

'Heh I will, it's been too long, but I'd better go now, I need to pack before tomorrow. One more thing though... what's Glenda like as a person, from what you can remember?'

There was a pause before Paul answered.

'Well, fun in a twisted sort of way. Lots of energy but I always felt she was a little too intense for me. Not much else to say really, it was a long time ago.'

He sounded wistful. Maybe his mid-life crisis was in train. Calum nodded.

'I do remember someone saying she'd gone off the rails a bit just after we graduated. Not sure how and why but she seemed the sort that might, you know - full of ideas, energy, a bit erratic, tended to exaggerate things, including emotions. She always seemed slightly nervous, on edge.'

'No wonder you disappeared from our nights at the pub for a while after you snared her eh?'

'Well, yeh. She needed my full attention Calum. I guess she saved me from your many beer dens for a while, though not sure my liver really remembers that holiday now.'

Calum laughed with his friend at the distant shared memory.

He said goodbye and put the phone down - then finished the pork pie thoughtfully.

7

John Coulson found his porridge somehow didn't really taste that good this morning. He took another mouthful and rolled it around his mouth before swallowing, with less than his usual appetite.

His medium height frame was half-sprawled on the sofa in the lounge, balancing the cereal bowl on his slightly portly belly.

'Want some more coffee?' Suzi shouted from the kitchen.

He didn't register the question: he was still thinking through last night's phone conversation and half-watching the breakfast news on the lounge television. He focused onto the reflection of his angular, lightly-stubbled face on the surface of the screen. He thought he looked worried and tried to relax.

He eventually realised Suzi had said something though. He raised his voice above the morning presenter.

'Sorry, what did you say? Couldn't hear over the news.'

'More coffee?' she said, somewhat louder this time.

'Oh yeah, please. A quick one, then I'd better be gone.'

Suzi walked into the room with a cafetiére in one hand and a milk bottle in the other. She topped his half-full cup up and stared at him.

'You look miles away. What's on your mind? Want to tell me?'

He wasn't in the mood to share his thoughts right now. He used his usual defensive ploy, for when he didn't want a conversation.

'No. Thanks but it's client details. You know I can't talk about them. Just been on my mind that's all.'

'Uh uh.'

'Nothing a good prosecution won't sort out.'

'Well, let's hope so. Maybe we should go for a walk tonight - looks a nice day. Drink in the pub later?'

'Yeah, nice idea, maybe we can if I'm home early enough. Let's see later, eh love?'

That was probably a no then, she thought.

She pecked him on the cheek before retreating to collect her jacket and bag. He looked up and smiled, grunting goodbye through a mouthful of porridge.

As the front door clicked shut behind her, he let out a sigh, relief from having to protect his thoughts from others.

He looked out of the kitchen window at the clear blue sky and thought it would actually be a nice day for an evening walk: if he was in the mood later.

Coulson walked out through the front door of his stone farmhouse and took a lungful of the fresh rural air. Evidently the farmers had been manure spreading again this week - still, it made him feel in touch with nature and good to be alive. He needed that jump-start after the tense discussion he'd suffered last night. He'd lain awake for long periods, wondering how he would deal with it. Coffee wasn't enough sometimes.

He jumped into his red Volvo and crunched his way down the shingle drive to the metalled country lane and turned onto the route that would take him to his office in the village. The journey was less than ten minutes down the quiet, narrow road: most city commuters' idea of heaven. The route was bordered by huge seas of yellow rapeseed fields, gently swaying in a light breeze this morning, curtsying to his passing.

Despite the serenity of his surroundings, another day on the trail of some deranged mind was in store for him. It had brought him a good living. Nonetheless, at the core of it all were violence, misery and death. Not the kind of stories to tell the kids when you came home each day.

He parked the car beside the small cottage he rented and entered his office. He had no permanent assistant.

There were some phone messages waiting for him, which he listened to first. There was only one requiring his immediate attention. A request to quote for leading a seminar: lucrative work and he always dealt with sales enquiries first these days. It wasn't that he set out initially in his career to make a lot of money: but whilst it was on offer, well, best make hay whilst the sun shines.

He settled down on a plushly padded leather swivel chair with a mug of tea in hand and pulled a cardboard file off the top of his in-tray. He reviewed the analysis he'd done on his current case for the Greater Manchester Police. A string of violent attacks had been committed, mostly with knives. None of them had turned into murder, though one had been close: perhaps a miscalculation on the attacker's part. All had been against women. He had drawn up a psychological profile of the perpetrator, whom the investigating team believed was one person.

He was feeling sure he had a good fix on the sort of characteristics this person, almost certainly a man, would have. As he started to write up his findings for the investigating officer, he was interrupted by a call from DCI Alec Bridge, a detective who had led a case he'd assisted with some months back.

Bridge relayed some news to him which caused him to become intensely irritated.

'But you and the press guys involved knew very well how important it is that my home and office locations are kept completely private. How did this happen?' John snapped.

'I know John, we're really sorry, it seems a junior reporter prepared the story and the senior guy on the case just didn't read it thoroughly enough. They would retract it of course, but since the cat's now out of the bag maybe the least said the better. It simply said you were Lincolnshire-based, so no details,' Bridge replied.

'Well I don't think we need to say any more, other than that I'll be making an official complaint. As you say, little more we can do now.'

He clicked the phone down sharply, his hand trembling slightly as it lay resting on the receiver. He licked his lips, a nervous habit he'd developed as a child.

This was bad news. If anyone *wanted* to know where he lived, of whom there were a few, and had read the story, they had a start. Criminals with a grudge against the person who had chiselled a way into their minds were always likely to be nagging potential menaces.

The weather had deteriorated since he arrived at work and a steady beat of rain started to thrum against the window behind him. Together with the darkening skies and the events of the last twenty four hours, life had suddenly started to throw on a cloak of gathering gloom.

He spent the rest of the day struggling to concentrate on finishing the report, interleaving writing with flipping his thoughts between the two pieces of bad news he'd received over the last day. He felt he needed to act in response and he knew that on one of the issues he could. He put the finishing touches to the analysis, wrote a few routine professional phrases in the covering email as a summary, added the cut and pasted legal disclaimers and hit the send button.

He closed the office and walked across the village green to the pub, where he ordered a pint of bitter. *Time to create a plan and some tactics.*

8

Jenna entered the office late. She had let herself oversleep a little, knowing Calum would be on the train to Lincolnshire and was looking forward to a quiet day on her own.

A few minutes later, with a mug of steaming Colombian parked on the desk by her keyboard, she logged on and decided to finish the searches on John Coulson, before starting the relative drudgery of report writing.

There were more results around links to police investigations, so she delved into each one to try to find some reference to his home location: to no avail. It was pretty clear John Coulson was keeping his whereabouts private. The final page of results had a different complexion though. As well as crime case references there were a couple of links to odd-looking headings. One was a web-site for a Scottish witching organisation - and the other a newspaper article on a related topic. She leaned back and clicked in to them.

John Coulson appeared to be the head of a Caledonian witches' assembly, which oversaw the organisation and operations of covens throughout Scotland. Weird things people do in their spare time, she mused.

She read further on the web-site: there was a generic contact email address for enquiries but nothing else. Out of curiosity she read a number of the web pages about the assembly and its aims: it all seemed quite benign and well meaning: not quite what she had been led to believe based on children's storybooks and typical folklore. They appeared to be individuals who didn't have a single God, amongst other attributes, and their general aims seemed cool with her.

But... there were some weird sounding snippets that a brief sweep of the internet threw up:

> *a witch is a fascinating or enchanting woman*
>
> *in Tanzania, about 500 older women are murdered each year following accusations against them of witchcraft*
>
> *witches still go to cross-roads and to heathen burials with their delusive magic and call to the devil; and he comes to them in the likeness of the man that is buried there, as if he arise from death*
>
> *in the 900s... church authorities tortured and killed thousands of women, and not a few men, in an effort to get them to confess that they flew through the sky, had sexual relations with demons, turned into animals, and engaged in various sorts of black magic*
>
> *warlock - a male witch or demon*

So was John Coulson a *warlock*?! The word seemed too ancient in Jenna's modern world.

It struck her that that there was a perhaps a bit of truth in here mixed in with a lot of superstitious nonsense but it was hard to get to the truth for the casual reader.

The second John Coulson reference was also interesting. It was the minutes of a witches' organisation meeting. It described some tensions in the witches' 'management' hierarchies about future direction and how the public perception was dealt with:

> *... Minute 9: JS proposed a vote of no confidence in the current public relations approach. After debate, the question of the vote was deferred until the next meeting, given the late hour. JS requested this be a formal agenda item at the next meeting...*

It struck her as not the sort of item that anyone would want on public display: maybe it had been a simple publishing error.

She pulled her attention back to the screen and thought she probably ought to let Calum know the latest position on the search, so called his mobile. No answer. Probably out of range on the train. She left him a brief message and dropped him a short email.

The witchcraft angle had caught her imagination. She wanted to find out more, both about witches and Coulson's involvement: it helped put off the dreaded report writing too. But, for now, she thought she might just do this bit of research without telling Calum.

9

Calum settled down again on the early train from Plockton and checked for emails on his smartphone. There was one from Jenna. It was hard to work out exactly what to make of it. The witchcraft thing sounded a bit far-fetched and he wasn't sure whether he needed to follow it up. On the other hand it might provide an alternative route to locating him. He elected to call her once he'd arrived in Lincoln in the evening.

The taxi rank at Lincoln station was quiet and he stowed his rucksack in the boot of a Skoda estate car before he directed the driver to Lincoln Castle.

'Robin Hood convention is it?' joked the taxi driver.

'Yeah, I'm all a-quiver,' Calum quipped back. His time in the east midlands had helped him learn the legend.

'Where do you recommend for some outlaw food tonight?'

The only thing he remembered from the taxi driver's list of recommendations was a curry house at the bottom of Steep Hill. That would do.

The taxi sped over Pelham Bridge, where he was greeted with the glorious spectacle of Lincoln's medieval cathedral, already lit by floodlighting in the fading light, staring majestically out from atop the high limestone ridge which bisects the city.

The entrance to the apartment was in a very old stone building adjacent to the castle, fronted by a massive wooden door set on gleaming brass external hinges.

He checked in at a tiny desk inside the dusty stone-floored building lobby and after a quick look round the apartment, he called Jenna. It was 10 p.m., much too late to call his assistant - but he was sure she'd had a pretty easy day.

'Hi Calum. You there yet? How're the rooms?' Jenna chirped.

'Yes fine and a nice view out the window of the castle and cathedral. You did well,' he said. 'I got your message and email... did you look for contact or location details for Coulson in the "witchy" leg of the search?'

'You make it sound childish: these are quite serious people really, they have some good aims.'

That left him amused and confused, as she often managed to make him feel.

'Of course I did. Dug two or three layers into all the rest of the links. Nada, mi amigo.'

It was what he had expected: John Coulson was obviously ex-directory in every sense.

'Never mind then, let's see what I can turn up here tomorrow. Thanks Jenn. How are you getting on with those reports?'

'Oh fine. Look I need to go now, I'm out with Greg at the moment. Good luck tomorrow.'

Calum smiled wryly. He expected she had gone home early and taken advantage of his absence. He didn't pay her much though and she was a great help so he didn't want to push her too hard: everyone deserves a break at times.

He strolled down the hill to the curry house, which turned out to be worthy of the recommendation. Whilst it was entirely delicious, he decided he had eaten too much out of boredom, and resolved not to be so greedy next time.

He soon regretted the amount of alcohol he'd drunk too: it was a surprisingly hard haul back up the cobble-stoned hill and he wasn't quite fit enough to take it without a stop. Steep Hill was aptly named.

Stumbling somewhat breathlessly into his apartment, he undressed quickly and fell into a heavy sleep, snoring loudly and waking no-one.

10

Jenna was waiting with bated breath now. If this took the wrong path it might trigger a great deal of wrath from Calum. If it worked though, she might actually prove to him that she could do a bit more than basic back-room legwork and travel arrangements.

She'd emailed the Caledonian witches' organisation the previous afternoon, saying that she was a reporter who wanted a phone interview with the organisation's head, relating to the recent web article about a power struggle. Jenna had figured that they would probably be quite keen to play down such talk, so there may be a chance of her request being welcomed.

She'd taken the precaution of sending the email from a separate account, which Calum reserved for when they wanted to be anonymous.

She was still surprised when she received a reply the following day, accepting her request. She was asked for a phone number to call and given a time: 4 p.m. and told she would be given only fifteen minutes. She had another hour to go till then. Her mind raced with the implications of getting it wrong, Calum's face kept flashing into her mind's eye and she had to keep telling herself she wasn't afraid of him: which she knew was slightly untrue.

She dashed off a brief acceptance.

The phone rang on the stroke of 4 p.m. She let it ring at least eight times and her heart rate increased with each ring. She began to think she wasn't going to be able to answer it: then she grabbed the receiver and gabbled a brief hello. After a small pause a quiet, pleasant man's voice spoke his name: 'John Coulson here. Who am I speaking to?'

'Hi Mr. Coulson, it's Susan Black from Local News Syndication: we have an interview arranged.'

'Yes I believe we do,' came a very measured and precise answer. Preciseness with a little charm wrapped around it.

Jenna was nervous. Her breathing was ragged and quick. She tried to concentrate on speaking slowly. His apparent confidence wasn't helping. She hoped her tension wasn't transmitting down the copper wires.

She asked some of the questions she'd prepared. It seemed the issue around the organisation's strategy was quite simple: should they spend time and effort explaining their very innocent and benevolent aims to the public, to help the general perception of their creed, or should they not.

'So why are you opposed to a more public face and transparency?'

'It's really about free choice,' he explained, after some tangible hesitation.

'We have a set of beliefs and a way we go about living our lives. Why should we have to explain this any more than any other body who has a particular set of beliefs? There is no reason for us to advertise ourselves, we recruit like-minded individuals into our covens very well.

The risk is that whilst we spend what would likely be many years trying to get the general public to understand what we do and what we stand for, many of our members would become more visible in the process. In that interim period, they would likely be subjected to a lot of ill-informed and unnecessary ridicule. I simply believe that's an unreasonable position to put people into.'

She nodded.

'Yes, I can see that.'

'Let me put it another way... what do *you* think of when you hear the word "witch"?'

Jenna smiled nervously to herself.

'Hehe,' she replied, 'well yes I can see your point. I guess we tend to think of women in pointy hats with long noses!'

'Exactly so, young lady.'

'... and cauldrons, funny dancing and being boiled alive.' She was almost enjoying herself now. She leaned back on the chair slightly, relaxing a little.

'Well my coven wouldn't boil you. We're far too civilised. Gentle poaching is so much more refined and it preserves the flavours better, don't you think?'

OK. Time to be serious again. She leaned forward.

'All right, I get your point! Sorry. So the "challenger" to your view, a Mr. Jack Sorenson, believes you should invest the time to educate the public. What sort of support does he have in the organisation?'

Again, some hesitation. A suave answer nonetheless.

'Some. However I believe I have enough credibility in the assembly to head this off. Our voting members will see the sense of what I am saying as the arguments mature.'

Jenna probed the strength of his arguments a little. She'd been prepared for what he'd said, based on what she'd read - and all in the cause of appearing to be a genuine hard-nosed news hound.

She found him resilient and well-versed in defending his point of view. It appeared the crunch time for this power struggle would come later in October when the organisation's general assembly met around the time of their most important celebration: a festival known as Samhain.

'Well young lady, I believe our fifteen minutes are up,' he announced, somewhat triumphantly and earlier than she had expected. Time had flown too quickly. She cast her eye down the questions she hadn't asked: she knew there was one she really needed to ask somehow.

'This has been really interesting Mr Coulson. Once I've drafted the article for approval, I'll send it to you: is there an email I can use to do that directly?'

John Coulson licked his lips with a flicker of his tongue and agreed.

'If the article generates interest, would it be possible to do a personal interview later, maybe at your office or home? Would that be ok?' she said, as her heart skipped a beat.

'I'm afraid not. As I've explained, I don't want any of our organisation to get unnecessary publicity: and that includes me, sorry.'

They exchanged the usual pleasantries before Coulson ended the call.

Jenna lent back in her seat and exhaled very deeply. Ultimately it had not been successful. She hadn't located him. Nonetheless she would contact him with the draft and try to think of another way to take a step closer. For now, it might be best to get on with what Calum had actually expected her to do whilst he was out of the office.

On impulse, she dialled 1471, to hear the last caller's number.

*

John Coulson's view of the conversation was rather different. For one thing he hadn't been anything like as calm and confident as he'd appeared to Jenna. He was intensely irritated that Sorensen's desire to lead the organisation has been made public. This had all started at the last group meeting, when there had been an argument about how to drive the organisation forward: numbers were dwindling a little and Sorensen wanted to open the group up more publicly so he could recruit more quickly to fill the gaps.

He found the article on their website, stuck away in a corner not obvious to the casual reader, but a search had clearly come up with it. He didn't have the technical wherewithal to delete it so dropped an email to Steven Ingleby, the secretary, requesting he pulled it off the website immediately.

And not just that. Once he saw the interview request arrive at the generic assembly email address, he became immediately suspicious. It was unusual for an email not to have some indication in the email address itself of the company or organisation it was coming from. Given the events of the last 24 hours he was on his guard even more than usual.

Having successfully elicited a phone number to call, he had used a reverse number lookup service - not legal in the U.K. he was sure - but he needed to know. And it worked: he now knew that the number belonged to the offices of a private investigator in Scotland.

John flicked his tongue over his lower lip and dialled the number, determined to maintain the conversation as it was diarised: an interview. He would maintain that stance unless things took an unexpected turn. The phone at the other end began to ring. Just as it started to seem it wasn't going to be answered, he suddenly remembered he had forgotten to dial the code in front of the telephone number, which kept the number private to the call recipient. He instantly panicked but the number answered at the same second.

Damn. He felt he had no real choice but to carry on. His heart rate went skywards and he hesitated before speaking. The woman (or girl?) at the other end of the line sounded somewhat nervous. He knew why and wondered how often she'd impersonated a journalist.

The conversation had gone pretty smoothly though, she'd asked some good questions and he thought, ironically, that she could maybe even make a journalist. What she didn't sound was dangerous, deluded, or remotely like one of his criminal profiling targets. What did worry him though, was how and moreover *why* she had found out there was a power struggle going on. He had no idea what would have driven her to do that.

There was no hint of anything *really* obviously worrying though, until the end of the conversation, when she asked to visit his offices or house for a follow-up interview. He refused of course. He wondered why she wanted to visit: to carry out something other than an interview? Or simply to find out where he lived? He hadn't found the phone call directly threatening, but he still didn't know why a private investigator was trying to engage with him.

He thought about the problems in the assembly he'd talked about, which were quite real: was someone trying to rake up something from his past to use against him? There were two people whom he might suspect could have the motive and character to go down that route.

Somehow though, he couldn't believe that they would go to the length of using a snoop. There must be some other motive at play.

He cast his mind back to some of the more dangerous individuals he'd helped convict over the years. There were a number of those that might now be freed from their resultant incarcerations. One name in particular kept dropping back into his thoughts: Alan Butler.

Butler was one of the first police cases he had worked on and had been convicted of a series of stalking episodes. He had also attacked two of his victims. Finally, he had attempted to murder the last of his targets. It had proved a difficult case for the police to solve: Butler had displayed great cunning and skill in covering his tracks. He was an intelligent man, yet a complete psychopath. He'd had children very early in his life, though they seemed to have been adopted. Children often smooth the sharp edges of a character: not this one.

During the trial, he had been called as an expert witness and endured two separate appearances in the courtroom. Those occasions were the low point of his police work; he had a particular aversion to seeing the person he had profiled.

Whilst there was some kind of pleasure in observing whether the criminal's appearance was anything like what he'd imagined, the physical proximity to people whose innermost mental malformations were known to him, was often a deeply disturbing experience. Especially for someone who usually lived his daily life in contact with what he considered to be normal, balanced citizens...

He had felt a distinctly evil menace emanating from Butler in the dock and at times it had seemed very personal. He stared at you in a detached sort of way: but somehow that gaze searched your soul for weaknesses. He just made you *feel* that stare inside.

He was usually made aware of when people he had helped convict were due to be released from jail. He'd heard nothing about Butler though - he did a quick mental calculation and concluded he might well be close to release now... if he had behaved himself.

He pulled out a leather notebook from his desk drawer and looked up the investigating officer from the case: Bryn Dunne. He recalled him as a young, newly-promoted detective inspector with an energetic and cheerful personality. He smiled to himself and wondered if the subsequent years of experiences had dampened that exuberance. He just knew it would have: eventually the misery of these types of cases poisoned the outlook of everyone involved.

He dialled his number and waited for the phone to pick up. To his surprise he got straight through to the detective. They exchanged the usual pleasantries, then Coulson asked him if Butler had been released. After a quick check Dunne had told him, 'No.'

'Ok,' said Coulson.

'But he will be released in a few days, John. Your notification is probably on its way to you through the usual sausage machinery.'

He pondered on the consequence of the answer. He wondered if it was possible Butler had started a search for him whilst still behind prison bars. He also began to think he might be turning paranoid: there were other people out there with a reason for a grudge against him, there was no reason to focus just on Butler.

He pulled out an opened bottle of Shiraz from the cabinet behind his desk and poured himself a small glass: he wasn't normally a day time drinker apart from socialising with business clients, but he needed one to calm his nerves right now. The wine had been open for a while and he winced as he took the first couple of sips.

When he remembered his mistake over the caller ID his heart sank a little further and he poured himself another. He realised now that if he had hung up and re-dialled quickly with the prefix, in all likelihood the previous call number would have been overwritten. Probably too late now. On the other hand, there were two possibilities, the first that she didn't bother checking it before the next incoming call overwrote it and secondly that she wouldn't be as scurrilous as himself in using it to track back to an address. He hoped those two barriers would be enough to protect him.

He dialled her number again, this time with the prefix and let it ring only once before putting the receiver down. Now he might be safe.

He was wrong.

11

After an early breakfast, Calum set off directly to the address Glenda had given him. He'd hoped to observe someone leaving the place after devouring their own bacon and eggs. It was twenty minutes brisk walk but it turned out to be a fruitless investment, other than in his own fitness.

7, Kensington Avenue didn't exist anymore - or at least not where the clearly out of date street map, which Jenna had found for him, had indicated.

Instead, it looked as if the whole of the street had been re-developed. It must have been relatively recently as there was a show home at the end of one of the neighbouring streets. Calum noted down the name of the developer and retreated to a cafe he'd passed on the way.

He searched the developer's telephone number, as well as that of the local planning authority, on his smartphone. They both confirmed to him that Kensington Avenue was no more. Nonetheless, a helpful young man in the developer's office did find references to number 7 having been rented out and passed him the name and number of the landlord, which was probably more than he ought to have done.

Calum told the landlord, when he managed to get hold of him, that he was an old friend who had recently returned from ten years in Australia and had lost touch with Coulson.

Off the back of that lie, he rather easily agreed to disclose John Coulson's forwarding address to Calum: it was lucky he could still find it from some old files, as it appeared Coulson had left the address a good few years ago.

He caught a taxi to Coulson's next address and spent a few hours surveying the suburban semi-detached house from a distance. It was a pleasantly warm day and so he managed to sprawl casually on a grassy bank nearby without, in his opinion, looking too suspicious. The house looked particularly old-fashioned, its paintwork slightly peeling and boasting original window frames in what looked like a 1920's build. Most people would have replaced them with double-glazing by now, he thought.

There was no sign of life through the few windows he could see into from his position and no car on the tarmac drive. Time dozed for a while. He lazily surfed the internet on his phone to pass the time. After an hour or so his patience was rewarded, as the wooden side gate of the house swung open and through it padded an elderly couple. They were dangling a couple of empty shopping bags from their hands. Not a promising appearance.

He decided there probably wasn't much point continuing to watch the property. John was Scottish, it was unlikely at his age he would be living with his parents in Lincolnshire: this looked either a dead end or another staging post in Coulson's travels. He considered whether to approach the couple for information, but thought better of it. It looked like they were going out shopping so he decided to return at a better time when they may be more relaxed about talking to him. Maybe he could find Coulson through association with this address somehow, maybe it would point to some other aspect of his life that would lead to him, but an initial search on the address returned absolutely nothing.

His stomach whispered to him that it was approaching lunchtime. The thought of a fresh pork pie and a bottle of ale on this lovely, sunny day enticed him down towards the old centre of the city. He found what he wanted close to the Stonebow, an impressive Tudor stone archway which stood at the head of High Street.

Carrying his lunch, he went and sat on a bench by the Brayford waterside, awash with office workers on their lunch breaks. According to the information board on the water's edge, this stretch had been a Roman harbour at one time. Now swans ruled the waters.

The bottle of brown ale went nicely with his pie and he felt very content with the sun warming his upturned face. He did a rough mental tally of good and bad food he'd eaten over the last few days and reckoned he was a bit in deficit.

His peace was shredded by the intermittent screeching of his mobile phone. He made a note to admonish Jenna, again, for the annoying ring-tones she kept setting up on his phone when he wasn't looking.

Talk of the devil. It was Jenna checking in and asking a few questions about the draft reports she was writing up.

It stirred him into action for the afternoon though. He decided to take a slow walk around the town for an hour and then go back to the address, in the hope that the elderly couple had returned from their shopping trip. He wandered up Steep Hill: it felt more comfortable without a stomach full of beer and curry.

At the top the cobbled road widened into a square with the Norman castle on the left and to the right an ancient stone archway into the courtyard surrounding the city's towering medieval cathedral.

Having felt lazy this morning, he'd eaten some breakfast from the buffet in the small communal area in his apartment building. He'd asked the manageress for some ideas on how to spend a free hour or so in Lincoln, anticipating he'd have some down time.

'Well, looking for the Lincoln Imp might take you a while,' she'd retorted, with a mischievous grin spreading across her face.

'At the cathedral, used to do it when I was a kid! There's only one mind you...'

Calum sensed a tricky task but strode onto the cobbled yard around the cathedral. He halted just inside the small entrance of the west door. A brief glance around the central nave confirmed the teasing in his landlady's suggestion: this indeed might take some time.

Half an hour passed quite pleasantly, slowly pacing the stone-flagged floors. Now, however, with no sight of the elusive imp, it had started to become tedious. He stopped in the middle of the Angel Choir, an open rectangular area lined with intricately carved wooden stalls with a gleaming lectern at one end. He was approached by a bespectacled and besmocked man, as he stood looking forlornly around.

'Enjoying our cathedral?' he enquired.

'Well, yes, though I might enjoy it more if I could find a cross-legged fellow!'

'Ah the imp. Yes. It's hard to find. You know he was thrown up high by an angel and frozen into place at the top of one of the main pillars: his punishment for annoying them. Look in the V-shaped pieces of stonework at the tops of the pillars around the Angel Choir here: clue's in the name!'

His interest renewed by the rector's words, he thanked him for his help and turned his face upwards and resumed his search.

Two minutes later, high up in one part of the cathedral, lodged at the bottom apex of a pair of the ceiling vaults, he spotted a cross-legged stone gargoyle with the appearance of an imp. He felt slightly foolish once he'd found it, especially as there was a small spotlight picking it out.

It had passed some time pleasurably though and he set off again for the semi-detached house he'd observed during the morning.

He was in luck. The old man answered his knock on the front door. He again rolled out the story of having been out of the country for a long while, to explain why he didn't have his supposedly good friend's address.

The response was not quite so positive. The old gentleman, who introduced himself as Jack, had at least agreed to talk to a perfect stranger on his doorstep. However, he was not clear about whether he could help or not.

'Well, It's bin a long time, ten years o' more,' he said, in a broad Lincolnshire accent. 'Ah remember the chap, he'd rented the 'ouse afore we bought it from 'is landlord, a chap who lived up the rord.'

'What number did the landlord live at?'

'Won't help ya: he died a few years back, someone else there nah. Thing is, we 'ad a forwardin' address for Mr. Coulson I think, but ah've no idea if we can find it, it'll probably take me and thu missus a while to search for it.'

Calum reflected on the answer for a few seconds. Maybe the old chap needed an incentive. If he did find the address it *might* be the one that took him directly to Coulson.

'Maybe I could offer you something for your trouble,' he asked.

The old man nodded and took his time to answer. 'Orright, I'll let ya sen know if ah farnd it, let's sare twenty pahnds,' he said, with a sparkle in his eye.

Calum celebrated silently with himself: it was good to meet people who weren't always greedy to make the most of their advantage. He gave the man his mobile number, impressed upon him the importance of it and expressed his wish for a call later that day. Then he began to wait.

He didn't have to wait long. After turning away down the path and walking no more than fifteen yards, he was recalled by the man who had suddenly 'remembered' where the address was. Obviously keen to seal the deal before I get my answer elsewhere, thought Calum, with a wry smile.

He was ushered inside as the man went into another room to find the address.

He returned after five minutes.

'Well it turns out ah remembered wrong. It was a phorn number we 'ad to call if anythin' turned up unexpected. 'E forwarded the post 'imself - that's what the missus said.'

He looked at Calum expectantly, clearly wondering if their deal was still on the table. Calum pulled a twenty pound note out of his leather wallet and offered it to the man.

'Good to do bisness with ya,' he said as he handed over a slip of paper with the number written on. It looked local at least.

'Likewise,' replied Calum, wondering if that would prove to be the case.

Calum walked back to his apartment via a different route, which took him through the Roman arch at the start of Bailgate. As he walked under the side arch, he imagined a Roman soldier standing guard on the stone flags here and wondered what it would have been like to grow up in a town with as much history as this. Pretty cool, he thought.

It was still very warm, so he picked up a couple of bottles of soft ginger beer from a grocer's shop for later. He'd had enough alcohol for today he decided. He arrived back, made some tea and sat down on the sofa, wondering what to do with the number. Glenda had been very specific about contact with John. She'd asked that he didn't make himself known to Coulson: that didn't necessarily mean that he couldn't have any contact at all, but that his identity and purpose shouldn't be disclosed.

He came to a conclusion and acted immediately. He called the number. There was no answer, instead an answering machine clicked in. It gave no clue as to identity, just requested a message be left. He said that he was looking for John Coulson, whom he needed to speak to and left his mobile number.

If the number called him back, he could ask if he was speaking to Coulson without giving anything away, other than a cover story: which he'd decided would be a false enquiry over an old case he read about on the web. He could also ask for an address to visit him: and not turn up. He was feeling smart.

*

Coulson let the phone ring and picked up the message straight away. Someone else with a Scottish accent wanting to speak to him. This was becoming more worrying. He put the mobile number through reverse look-up and found it was registered to a Mr. Calum Neuman. On searching that name on the web he found it linked back to a private investigators' firm in the West Highlands: the exact same outfit he had identified via the conversation with 'Susan Black'.

Calling back felt risky. He wasn't sure he could carry off a second conversation with someone from the same company without getting into a situation he couldn't control or understand - or both.

He clearly needed to do *something* though, before this went down a route he couldn't predict and didn't want. He thought through his options. He'd met some unsavoury characters in his work with the police. Maybe one of them could actually be useful to him now: he wasn't sure he wanted to go that path - on the other hand he was beginning to feel personally threatened. Doing nothing just made him feel more vulnerable.

He wondered how he had got into this position, with more than one thread of his life starting to feel dark and threatening. All he had wanted to achieve in his life was some professional success, a pleasant lifestyle and his hobbies. He started to feel he was becoming involved in things beyond his comfort zone and absolute understanding.

He wasn't even sure if there was anything threatening at all out there - which was the most unnerving part of it. There was someone else in the back of his mind too - always had been when his thoughts turned dark. He pushed away the image it conjured up.

He left the office and drove home deep in thought. There was a heavy scent of mayflower in the hedgerows after the recent rain. He breathed it in and exhaled with a sigh, his arm trailing out of the open driver's window. Turning up into his drive he almost drove into the back of Suzi's car: she was home early. She was a part-time receptionist at the local doctor's practice; on this particular weekday she usually worked late. He was hoping there was something already being prepared for dinner: the nervous tension was making him hungry.

Suzi welcomed him with a hug and asked him about his day. Too nervous to recount everything, he simply said 'Fine'. Today, he *really* didn't want to go into detail, he just hoped there was something he could lose himself in on the television that evening: a good war film washed down with some red wine ought to help do that.

12

Calum watched the news on TV and chilled out for a while. The ginger beers weren't chilled at all, so he put them in the freezer to cool down quickly. He mused on whether to eat out or in and eventually chose to order a pizza delivery. Whilst he waited for it to arrive, he logged on to his laptop and passed the time catching up on emails, browsing some shirts for his holiday and playing an on-line game.

His thoughts drifted between the case and his daughter. Sometimes, his conscience was pricked about how remote he was from her at times. Times like when she was in hospital the other month. Maybe he should do something regularly with her, like when she was smaller and he used to take her cycling around the local parks. She'd fallen out of love with that for some reason, but her condition didn't help. When she was in a good phase, she could do most things kids of her age did. The rest of the time was unpredictable.

Perhaps something non-physical that she could do in her own time with him... maybe... a little help on some non-urgent bits of his casework, something he could make anonymous. She often asked him about what he was working on. Yep, that was a good idea. He could work on that.

The pizza was good and he brewed some coffee. He seemed to tire more easily these days, the fresh air and exercise walking around this hilly city had taken its toll.

Despite the caffeine kick, it wasn't long before he was feeling sleepy again.

He needed a bright start the next day: he had a quick bath, rolled the duvet round himself and read for a few minutes before nodding off to sleep around 10 p.m.

*

He wasn't sure whether he had actually been asleep or not when he suddenly found himself sharply awake. He thought he had been awoken by a noise: but couldn't be certain. He lay awake, listening acutely, aware his heart was suddenly beating very fast. He pulled the duvet slowly away from his ear to listen more clearly. *Nothing.* He glanced at the red LED clock numerals which told him 11:32 p.m. Too early for a night-time burglar he tried to convince himself.

Then he definitely heard a slight creaking sound, from the living area on the other side of his bedroom door. It repeated itself, but with a different tone. The LED clock cast a faint glow across the room, which would have made it more difficult to see any light source creeping under the door. It looked as black as coal around the door edges.

Adrenaline started to pump into his bloodstream fast. He scrambled to think about what he could use as a weapon, scanning the room quickly with rapidly focusing eyes. There was a heavy looking table lamp at the other end of the bedroom, on a dressing table.

He very slowly slid out from under the duvet, holding his breath as he put his weight on the floor and hoped it didn't creak. It did a little. He sat motionless, half in and half out of the bed, listening for any reaction on the other side of the door.

Nothing again.

He moved carefully across the room and grasped the base of the table lamp. The power cord led away round the back of the dressing table it was placed on. He would have to move the dressing table slightly away from the wall to unplug it.

He lowered himself virtually to the floor and eased the table forward with one hand, holding the lamp in the other. As he reached to grasp the plug, a sharp and very loud cracking noise came from behind the door: it sounded like glass was shattering in the aftermath.

He yanked the plug out of the socket, launched himself upwards, grasped the door handle and opened it a fraction, virtually in one movement.

There was a light spreading across the floor on the other side of the room, in the kitchen area. There was something glittering on the floor in the light - glass.

His heart was hammering very hard now.

The fridge door was open - and the freezer compartment door inside the fridge was also open.

He suddenly slumped to the floor, with total understanding.

'Shit! Jesus!'

He started a nervous, staccato laugh.

That would teach him - he wouldn't forget to pull the ginger beer bottles out of the freezer again in a hurry. They'd exploded with such force, the glass pieces had knocked the small fridge door open.

He sighed hugely, still infused with adrenaline, trying to slow his breathing.

Twenty minutes later, he finally felt calm enough to sleep and rolled back under his duvet, after he'd carefully picked up the dozens of glass bottle shards that had slid across his kitchen floor.

13

The prisoner sat down in the assistant governor's office for what he hoped would be the last time. Freedom always has its price and in this instance it was a heavy session of form filling, checking, and signing. He felt ill at ease in the fresh shirt, tie and suit he had changed into five minutes previously. Years of prison clothing had left him forgetting that more formal clothes were not the most comfortable. He fidgeted around on his seat, stretching his shirt collar slightly with two fingers. He checked his personal belongings one last time, then signed for them: he hesitated, he felt there was something missing but he couldn't quite put his finger on what.

He mentally walked through the occasion many years before when he had signed his possessions over to the prison.

A mobile phone: that was it. He enquired as to its whereabouts.

The assistant governor shifted his gaze slowly up from the desk that separated them. 'It was taken away as further evidence: do you really think we would give you that back after what we found in the photo gallery?' he said flatly.

It wasn't entirely unexpected. The prisoner chose to say nothing. He had more substantial issues to worry about than a phone. The prison resettlement service had helped him rent an apartment in advance of his release but he had a lot to do in terms of settling into it. His, now, ex-wife had sold the marital home and he needed to get his share of everything that entailed. He had people to contact, years of the city's development to explore and catch up on, *maybe* some sort of employment to search for - and now a mobile phone to buy. At least his personal bank account was likely to be pretty healthy.

He signed the final piece of paperwork and stood up, holding a suitcase full of belongings. He was proffered a brief handshake which he surprised himself in accepting and then he was ushered out of the room, down the corridor to the main prison gates. He was taken into an ante-room to the main gate entrance and had his papers checked again.

The door, heavily barred, was shut and locked behind him. Then another, similarly protected door was opened to the gate room. Again it was locked behind him, before the warder opened the main gate's pedestrian door and he was allowed to step out through it.

He took two steps forward into the street. The door was closed behind him very quickly, with a resonating metallic clang. Was that a movie scene he'd just been through?

The feeling of freedom and fresh air was overwhelming. He stared at the road ahead of him and the cars that sped past - one a family saloon he'd never seen before - he was going to have get used to seeing things that seemed alien.

He stood on the edge of the pavement and breathed the air deeply for a minute or more: it smelt of traffic fumes and wet pavements.

He then became very still, collecting his thoughts. To any bystander, he had become a pavement mannequin. A brown-haired, medium height, rake-thin mannequin, modelling the previous decade's suit fashion and sporting a fashionable amount of stubble.

His mind drifted over two faces that were important to him - in very different ways. Both hauled up vivid and strong feelings. Soon, he'd be able to give vent to those feelings. The fogs that surrounded his head when he thought about them would clear over the coming days.

He drifted back into the reality of the street with the sensation of water crawling, slowly, down his shirt collar.

It was raining very softly with the kind of large droplets that only seem to appear on calm summer days. The air was surprisingly warm for northern England and the raindrops were evaporating soon after landing on the concrete pavement.

Ten minutes later, he was still looking at the very same part of the free world, water soaking his head and shoulders now, taking in the sights and sounds of the passing traffic and people and starting to wonder just how good his first pint of beer was going to taste. He finally crossed the street and walked into the first pub he came across: one no doubt frequented by many releasees before him, and the regular prison visitors: not that he'd seen many of those.

He ordered steak pie and chips and a pint of bitter and sank the pint within two minutes whilst waiting for his food to arrive. The impact on his body was unexpected: the time of day, lack of food over the last few hours and his years of enforced abstinence, made him feel quite drunk and faint. He bought some peanuts to fill the gap and try to sober himself, as he made a mental note to drink alcohol slowly for the first few occasions.

The food tasted good, mostly because it was a free choice. The music being played through a pair of tiny wall mounted speakers was starting to irritate him though. Much of it was completely unfamiliar: he started to feel like an outsider in a holiday town, rather than the place of his birth.

He pushed the plate aside, settled up the bill and walked outside to hail a taxi. It was still raining and he had to wait a while for one to pass him. Fifteen minutes later he was deposited at the entrance of a suburban apartment block. It looked decent, if grey and cold, a jigsaw of unpainted concrete facias. He turned the key he had been given into the front hall door and walked up the unheated stairwell, gripping the plastic handrail to steady himself against the weight of the suitcase. His footsteps echoed eerily in this concrete tower.

The door to number 9 stood blankly to attention opposite him. He opened it and entered the first room off the interior hall. It was his bedroom, housing just a bed frame with a bare mattress and a single wardrobe. He sighed as he launched himself onto the mattress and fell asleep for a couple of hours, still suffering from the effects of the beer.

*

When he awoke, slightly dizzy, on his new-found bench of anonymity he slowly picked himself up and sat against the bedstead, and stared at the sparsity of his room. He felt unstable, physically and mentally. Well, on the latter count, he knew he wasn't *normal* in the way other people viewed the world. But he had to do what he needed to do didn't he? If that meant doing things that upset *normal* people, then... well, he would do whatever he felt he had to. It *had* got him into a lot of trouble though.

He shook his head violently. He needed to speak to people more than anything. He went into the bathroom, splashed some cold water on his face, searched around unsuccessfully for a towel and so wiped his face on a t-shirt. He clearly needed a major shopping trip tomorrow, but for now he'd go out and buy a mobile phone and some food.

An hour and a half later he was back at the apartment with chilled pizza, more beer and some things for breakfast. He'd been able to get his old number transferred to a new mobile phone, so he put the phone on charge, the pizza in the oven and the beer in the fridge. At least there was a television in the apartment, so he could amuse himself this evening by watching all sorts of new, unseen programmes and the news: what might that contain? The regime in his jail had been pretty conservative in terms of the amount of inmate entertainment.

After twenty minutes he served himself the pizza and the phone started to chirp that it had some new messages.

He flicked through them: there were the usual network welcome messages and a few which had got stuck in his old inbox by the look of them. There were a couple of out of date texts from friends and a voice message notification which looked like it had been left during the afternoon.

He dialled the voice box number. The message was in a voice he knew well; the one he'd hoped for. It was brief, but it was clear that the years in prison hadn't necessarily lost him that friendship. He would make contact soon.

Before then, the plans he had been fantasising over for more years than he cared to remember, could finally be executed. He had the most exquisite motivation to carry them out.

Revenge.

He let the pizza, beer and television win the battle for his attention for the evening. Tomorrow would be soon enough to start. He switched on the television, where the opening credits to Big Brother were rolling - it would be peaceful to watch TV without a couple of dozen or so other inmates clustered around the set...

PART II

SORCERY

14

Jenna wrestled with herself over what to do with the information she now had. By being very smart, at least in her opinion, she had the address of an office in a small village in Lincolnshire.

She pondered the idea of taking a train there herself and confirming John Coulson was indeed there: but discounted that as a step too far, even in pursuit of impressing Calum. No, she knew she needed to bring Calum up to date - it was just a question of when.

She would call Calum in the morning, she decided. She had found via a quick scan of Companies House that there was a company registered to that address and she would research that first.

It seemed it had been incorporated around nine years ago. There had been no movement in company directors etc. She wondered whether it was worth paying £1 to get detailed accounts information, then quickly chided herself for quibbling over such a paltry amount. It might throw up something interesting. She ordered the data and spent the rest of the afternoon scouring the web for further information: it proved futile.

She wondered if she should think wider than John Coulson to find out more about him - colleagues, friends, love history and - of course the two children. She drew a halt to this train of thought. She had an address, Calum could observe him there and follow him home. The next step after that, in terms of finding a way to contact the children without alerting Coulson, was up to Calum. He was the boss after all.

*

Drawing a deep breath, Jenna dialled Calum's mobile as soon as she reached the office the next morning: she had made sure she was in work early, to catch Calum before he left the apartment and could plan his day on the back of her information: which wasn't much.

He answered with a mumble, smothered by a mouthful of toast and lime marmalade.

'Gotcha,' Jenna said cheerily. 'I guessed you be eating breakfast by now. I've some good news for you oh mighty one!'

'Oh yeah,' said Calum with some difficulty as he chewed his mouthful more rapidly so he could speak. 'Tell me more m'lady.'

'Well, I've been super sleuth and searched out an address for John Coulson. Got a pen?'

'Hang on,' Calum said in some surprise, as he balanced the plate with toast on his lap and reached over to grab a pen from a nearby table. 'Go ahead.'

'I'm not sure if it's just an office or his home too, but here you go... '

Calum scribbled the address on the edge of the newspaper he was reading.

'How did you get this Jen? I spent all day yesterday trying and I ended up with nothing.'

'Ah, this and that,' she said mischievously before relenting. 'I made some further investigations into Coulson's involvement in a Scottish witches' assembly. I got a number through that route and back traced it... you know, the illegal way you do Calum.'

'It's not illegal to do it, just illegal to provide the information in the U.K.' he replied.

'Or at least that's my understanding. Here's me spending £20, bribing some old guy for similar information: good job the client's paying.

Well, the girl did good - again! Thanks Jen, I'll call you later if I need anything - in the meantime can you get a car delivered to this address pronto? For a day at first... and check if we can extend the apartment here for another day or so if I need. Thanks, we'll talk later.'

Back to the mundane, Jenna thought and started to search for car hire companies in Lincoln.

Calum meanwhile resolved to take some chocolates back to the office for Jenna; she had done well again: he really should think about how to make sure he kept her as long as possible, assuming she eventually decided Gregor wasn't going to be enough of a reason for staying in Plockton.

He finished off his breakfast smartly and dressed. He picked out his favourite, anonymous, tracking clothes: blue jeans, dark tee-shirt and a grey windbreaker. It was quite likely he would be stalking the target for a while and didn't want to stand out in any way. In that respect, he could never decide if sunglasses were good or bad.

Jenna sent him a text with the car hire company name: they would be outside in thirty minutes with a VW Polo: he sighed and hoped that he could push the seat back far enough to accommodate his frame. He always forgot to remind Jenna about things like that.

The Polo arrived on time. He did the paperwork and drove off towards the address Jenna had given him, armed with a rudimentary area map routinely dished out by the hire company.

He had started to like Lincoln: the towering spires of the cathedral towers were viewable for miles around the city in all directions, a beacon for home coming. Together with the castle and the many Roman relics around the city, it gave the place a real sense of history.

His destination was Nettleham, a small village three miles from the north east of the city centre. He parked on the far side of the village green from the house and took a brief walk to the adjacent grocery shop, to give himself a better view of his target. It was a small end-terraced cottage, but there was a side door with a bell-push and brass plate: which usually signalled an office.

From the shop he headed back to the car. He'd made a mental note of the lunch options at the shop's cold counter and firmly crossed pork pie off his potential list. Such trivia passed the time in what could well be a long day.

It turned out to be just that. No-one emerged from the office until later afternoon: but the silver lining was that the person appearing from the doorway was, judging from the photographs Calum had seen, clearly John Coulson. He started his engine after Coulson jumped into his red Volvo, and followed him as closely as he dared.

15

John couldn't believe how quickly this was moving. Suzi had handed him the post last night: one envelope had stood out, one with an address hand written on it. Reading it had put him in an even worse mood all evening. Even a televised Champion's League match couldn't lift his spirits.

Jack Sorensen had gone further than the phone conversation of two evenings ago and written to him formally.

Coulson shook his head. He could have seen this coming but he still couldn't quite believe it: Sorensen had asked him to stand down.

The timing was odd too, just a couple of days before their gathering for Litha, the midsummer celebration. He wondered whether Sorensen was planning some kind of coup attempt there.

Sat in his office, leaning back in his leather chair, he ground his teeth together and snorted: this was just preposterous. Further on in the letter, Sorensen explained that he felt it was in the best interests of the organisation if Coulson stood down and avoided a leadership battle: Sorensen implied he had already gathered enough support to make the vote a formality...

... and by doing this now it will save internal tensions and enable the new approach to begin as soon as possible. It's what the majority of assembly members want John - I have a lot of support for this...

He immediately judged this to be a bluff. There was no way his oldest friends in the organisation could have deserted him in enough numbers to enable Sorensen to succeed. Or was there? He thought through the list of assembly members. Many of them had grown up in the movement with him over fifteen years or so. He was sure he knew they had the same desire to keep their affairs private as he did. There were perhaps two or three individuals who might be bent to listen to a different point of view. Two, three, or even four or five votes, would not unseat him.

On the other hand if he resigned, then the old guard *might* split under pressure. He was decided: he would rebuff this request immediately.

He logged on to his desktop and drafted an email to Sorensen. He wanted to explain that he felt this was a bluff and that he wouldn't be taken in by it. He also wanted to get himself on the front foot and take away some of Sorensen's impetus, whatever that was. That was it: that was enough, no need to be particularly aggressive.

Jack,

I received your letter today thanks. I really do think that this is unnecessary. I do understand you have different views to my own on the future direction of our assembly. However, I'm sure we both have its best interests at heart: and that's best served by resolving this difference of opinion in a proper way. I'm happy we table it at Samhain in the autumn and debate and vote on it formally. In the meantime, let's enjoy our midsummer's day celebrations. Happy Litha!

Best Regards,

John.

An email reply chimed its way onto his screen only ten minutes later, interrupting some research he'd started. He waited a moment or two, took a deep breath and clicked it open. His heart sank on reading it through.

John,

Sorry but it's time to change our approach and we need to crack on with it. You need to understand how to bend with it. If you won't, then you should worry. I do have the best interests of our organisation at heart, but I won't accept the status quo and will be single-minded in striving to change our strategy sooner rather than later. I do have support, it's real, not imagined. I'd rather you were not embarrassed by the way the change will come about. Let's discuss soon, at Glenston for sure.

Regards,

Jack.

He dwelled on that response all afternoon and by the time he left the office it had taken its toll. On top of it all, he also knew he was being tracked by private investigators and that was now making him paranoid and very anxious.

He checked all the window and door security in the office before double-locking the main office door, and then checked around the side of the building for anything suspicious before finally walking to his car.

As he flopped into the front seat, he was overcome with a wave of relief and exhaustion. He didn't understand the relief element: maybe that was getting away from the office, the phone, the emails. But the more he thought about that, the less relieved he felt. He pulled away with a slight wheel spin on the loose gravel and headed in the direction of home.

Two turns out of the village took him onto the road that led him virtually to his house. His senses were on overdrive and he couldn't help notice the white VW Polo that had turned twice in perfect synchronisation with his exit from the village. It was following him at a respectful distance: exactly what you would expect if it was driven by a professional investigator he thought.

He decided he would try something out. At the next junction he turned left, onto a road that would eventually lead to his house via a long, circuitous route.

Sure enough, the white car turned with him. His mind and body suddenly prickled with a spasm of shock. He started to sweat. His mind raced as he struggled to think clearly of what he would do. He was on a small country road with hardly any traffic, which left him feeling pretty vulnerable.

As the adrenaline worked its magic it bought him clarity. He would drive past his house to the nearest pub, have a drink, have a meal, watch the TV there until it was past dark and hope his pursuer had given up by then. He realised that in fact if he went to the pub he had in mind, he could even leave the car there and walk home across a couple of fields if he needed to. His body relaxed, feeling reassured by his plan.

He swept past his house and drove a further mile or so before he pulled into the White Horse car park. He watched the Polo carefully through his rear view mirror. He noticed it slow to leave the same distance between the two cars and then drive past the car park as he stopped. But as it passed, he noticed the driver glance slightly - almost imperceptibly, at him. It was enough to convince him that he was definitely being watched.

He strode into the pub briskly and felt the warm glow of relief from the human company. There were only two people in the bar but he knew it would be busier later on and that it was likely he would have one or two familiar faces to talk to. He ordered a large whisky and sat down in an area where he could see the television. It was going to be a long evening, in June the sunset came late.

The evening passed slowly given his worried state of mind. He came across two of his neighbours and some normal chat about football and politics was slightly therapeutic - but he was continually darting his eyes over to the entrance area to check who was arriving. As the daylight started to fade he chanced his first proper look through the bar windows into the car park and adjoining section of the road. No white Polo there, although another small white car gave him a brief fright before he could clearly make out the manufacturer's front grille emblem.

He calculated it would be harder for his pursuer to follow him after it was fully dark: if indeed he was parked somewhere he couldn't see. He waited a further thirty minutes and then left just as briskly as he had arrived. He looked expectantly around the parking area and jumped into his car, but saw nothing to worry him.

He fired the ignition and drove hesitantly out of the car park and towards his home. All the way he scanned ahead and behind for signs of being followed but there was nothing. He hoped his stalker had given up for the evening.

As he entered his house, he threw a last look over his shoulder: nothing again.

He'd already packed everything for an early start the next day: the taxi was arriving at 6 a.m. to catch the first train out of Lincoln towards the Scottish highlands. He usually looked forward to Litha, the mid-summer celebration, looked forward to the bonfires that were lit to protect against evil spirits, worrisome beings which were believed to crawl the earth when the sun was turning southward. It was normally an uplifting kind of time and when the weather was good the outdoor bonfires and their accompanying light-hearted frolics were a joy.

He had mixed emotions this time though, given Sorensen's interference.

Nonetheless, he felt like he might actually be able to sleep, especially in view of the four pints of bitter he'd drunk on top of the whisky. Suzi had gone off to her mother's house for a few days since he was going to Scotland: without anyone to disapprove, he walked through the door, locked everything he could think of and fell onto the bed without undressing. He slept like a log.

16

Calum cursed his luck when Coulson turned into the pub. He parked a little further down the road, waited a full hour and drove slowly back. The car park entrance was on a blind side of the building coming from this direction, so he turned in and parked immediately, before he could be seen through the rear bar windows.

He walked into the pub, ordered a pint of beer and scanned the bar's denizens while leaning on the counter. It was a typical English country inn: half a dozen rooms, some with open fireplaces, though none were lit at this time of the year. The windows were composed of squares of bottle glass separated by wooden cross-spars and the jaded traditional feel was completed by a threadbare floral design woollen carpet.

Coulson was sitting down in the main room with a drink, watching the TV and exchanging comments on the game with two men sat nearby. Calum thought he may have glanced back at him: maybe he was looking to see who else had arrived. Hard to be sure.

Calum wasn't sure how to play the rest of the evening. He lingered over his pint, had an extra half and then decided to go back to the car: Coulson was obviously here for the evening, having ordered food and more beer and settled into conversations with a couple of men who, judging by their welcome from the barman, were regulars. It might be difficult to follow him out later if there were only a few customers around, so he pondered his next move while he sat in the Polo, which seemed to shrink every time he hauled his tall frame into it.

He figured that since Coulson was talking in a pretty familiar way to pub regulars, then he might live fairly close to the pub. He drove along the road a mile or so until he spotted two detached houses not more than fifty yards apart. He glanced at them as he passed: they were both lit inside.

As he passed he noticed something on the roof of the second house, which struck him as unusual. It was a weather vane: it depicted a stooping old man with a big sickle over his shoulder and some stakes in the ground near him. Something about it made him think of witches, maybe it was the sickle: maybe he was looking too hard for something to help mark out Coulson. In any case he stopped and reversed into a field gateway, half way between the houses.

He scratched his chin and settled down for a wait. Then he realised there was no need. He'd just do a circuit around the local area very early in the morning and look for a red Volvo. Sometimes the simple options were too easily overlooked.

On his way back to the apartment, he remembered his plan to get Ellie more involved in something. It was late so he decided to text her. He stopped on a grass verge right on the edge of town and typed into his phone.

Hey, remember how you're always wanting to know about my cases? Well, can you help me on something? I need to know if there is a link between a weather vane made up of a stooping old man with a large scythe or sickle over his shoulder and some posts in the ground near him... and witches. Yeh, witches! Any kind of witches. Let me know if you can find anything as soon as you can? Love, Dad x

Well at least it *sounded* exciting, if that didn't work then the more mundane stuff he did was definitely a no go. Feeling satisfied he'd made a step forward with Ellie, he pulled away from the verge towards town.

17

Calum rose at 6:30 a.m. and was on his way to run the rule over the houses local to the pub half an hour later. The air was cool so he switched the heater on in the car. As he wound his way through the lanes around the pub, he wondered if he would be able to complete the assignment today. His holiday was looming large now and he'd like to get it all tied up before he left. He switched his phone on. A message from Ellie.

Hi Dad, sounds weird! I sat up last night for ages after Mum went to bed (don't tell her!) and looked all over the internet. Well, it isn't anything to do with witches as far as I can see ... but I found a picture of something I think you meant ... it's from a cricket ground called Lords: it's on a building at the ground. I read that the man is Old Father Time and that the posts are cricket stumps, whatever that is! Hope that helps you, sorry I couldn't find anything out about witches, that would have been cool :)

Lords cricket ground? Was Coulson a cricket fan maybe? He had no idea and couldn't think of an easy way to find out.
He texted Ellie back.

Hi love, great thanks for that, yes I guess you found where the original is then. Maybe it will help me with this thing I'm trying to find now. I'll let you know. Hugs, Dad xx

He really wasn't convinced it would help him, but he had to encourage her now.

He spent a full two hours driving up and down the lanes, looking for a red Volvo or some other sign of Coulson, widening his search, but it ended fruitless. He cursed himself for not sticking it out last night and remembered the old adage - "a bird in the hand is worth two in the bush". He wondered where this particular bird had flown to.

This was where his job became a real personal challenge: the drudgery of failed surveillances and the ensuing feeling that he was wasting his life in achieving absolutely zero, wore him down sometimes. He needed to make something of the day: he called Jenna to see if she had any more information of use. Nil return.

The obvious thing to do was to return to the pub and ask around after Coulson: it was still far too early for it to be open though, so he spent some time parked on the edge of a barley field, reading a novel on his electronic reader while he waited for the doors to open.

The lunchtime crowd was hardly that: three people in the first hour and a half: the barman had no knowledge of Coulson and Calum didn't recognise any of the drinkers from the previous night. He resolved to visit again in the evening: at least the beer was well-kept: cool, smooth and a nice hoppy aroma. It helped.

He returned to the apartment slightly drowsy from the effects of a lunchtime beer and felt it was time to drop Glenda a brief update: regular communication did seem to help deflect a little of the constant suspicion, which many clients seemed to have, that they were being charged for no action.

He constructed an email detailing the current status: that Coulson's office had been found and that he had been seen. He also suggested he was close to tracking his home address and he mentioned the witch's organisation angle: not that it was relevant to finding the children but it all helped convey the impression he had been working hard on his client's behalf. He finished with a summary of expenses to date - he usually billed for them every two weeks unless they were particularly expensive.

A short reply from Glenda pinged back within an hour: 'Thanks, good to know, keep me posted.'

He relaxed. Clearly she wasn't going to be the sort who wanted to ask lots of questions about every detail he mentioned: some people were a real pain in that respect, it was always a double-edged sword telling clients what he had found to date: in some cases the resulting questions seriously delayed him making further progress. Evidently Glenda Muir had more common sense.

He decided to doze a while since he'd had an early start and had no idea how long the night's task might take. He lay on the bed; it was warm so he left the window slightly ajar. He could hear the people in the castle square going about their daily business: it made him feel as if he was in their company and he soon drifted off into a pleasant light sleep.

*

He awoke feeling a little dizzy and dry-mouthed: as he usually did when he slept during the daytime. He made a cup of tea and sat drinking it with his head propped against a cushion until he felt more human. He turned on the radio - there was some cricket on. It wasn't really his thing but the slow, quaintly humorous commentary and the tea had a reviving effect.

Time passed and he soon felt hungry. He planned to eat in the White Horse, so he would have to fill the gap with some biscuits for now. He dunked a few ginger nuts in his tea, picking up with gentle fingers the ones which broke when he let them soak a second or two too long. After an hour, he splashed his face with cold water, smartened himself up a little and drove out to his target for the evening.

It was a balmy, sun-filled evening and as Calum walked from his car into the hostelry, he was surrounded by a shimmering mass of tiny insects. He waved his arms erratically and vigorously, closely resembling an insane Coco the Clown, as he hurried into the bar.

'Thunder flies,' said the barman who had noticed his agitation. 'Lincolnshire's answer to the Scottish midge. Your head will be tickling all night now,' he laughed.

Calum was already beginning to feel it: a faint itch on his scalp. He scratched at it and smiled ruefully at the barman. 'Let's see if alcohol helps then,' he countered and ordered a pint.

'Never seen anyone rub beer on their head.'

And so the banter went.

Time droned by. Whilst devouring some fish pie and another pint, he spotted a couple of men walk in, and he recognised them as the ones to whom Coulson had spoken the previous evening. He nodded to them politely, when one of them placed his hands on the bar as if he was going to start some press-ups on it and ordered their beverages. He engaged with them in a little chat about the thunder fly count. After a few minutes they excused themselves and went to sit down near the windows.

He judged it too rude to ask them about Coulson after a two minute conversation, so waited an hour or so before drifting over to them and enquiring about the man he thought he recognised as a moderately famous criminal psychologist. The men looked blankly at him. Evidently Coulson didn't discuss his work in here. One of the men eventually cottoned on to who he was talking about and agreed he knew roughly where he lived.

'Up on Scothern Lane,' he said. 'Just past the children's playground. There's couple of houses there on the left hand side, it's one of those, not sure which one though. You want to talk to him?'

'No, no I was just wondering if it was him or not and whether he lived round here, out of curiosity that's all,' Calum replied.

'Well he's here most weeks, doesn't give a lot away but he always seems ready for a chat. Think he lives on his own, maybe that's why.'

Calum ears shot up. 'On his own you say? No children then?'

'Not that I've heard. Mind you - as I said - he doesn't say much about himself: don't even know if he has a woman,' the man replied. His friend agreed.

Calum stayed ten minutes further and passed some more idle conversation about the weather and the news headlines and then made his excuses to withdraw back to the bar.

He leaned his elbow on the bar and began to think. The houses they had just described were where he had been the night before, so maybe his intuition about the weather vane had been correct: he needed to go back and see if a red Volvo had re-appeared. Strange they didn't know he had children - but he reminded himself that people all have very different lenses through which they view life.

He walked away to his car. His elbow was soaking wet with beer: they really ought to mop up the bar more often, he thought irritably.

A few minutes later he drove past the houses in question. No lights on at Old Father Time's house and no red Volvo at any on that stretch of road. He considered that Coulson could be away on business and decided he would chance a closer look at chez weather vane.

He parked the car a little up the road and waited a while until it was almost completely dark. Pulling a rubberised torch out of his rucksack, he closed the car door as quietly as possible and walked slowly and carefully towards the house. There was only very sparse traffic on the road and none appeared before he reached the driveway. He checked again that he could see no lights or other signs of life and then proceeded up the driveway, in the shelter of a row of conifers which shielded him from the closest neighbouring house and the road.

The garage to the side of the house was fronted with old wooden doors, glazed with frosted glass panes in the upper sections. He peered through: it was hard to make anything out so he chanced his torch for a few brief seconds: there was definitely something red in there, a car judging by the size and there was a symbol on the front of it that might have been a Volvo emblem - it was the right sort of shape, as best as he could make out.

He switched the torch off and crept around the other side of the house, inspecting each window he passed. All the curtains and blinds were drawn. He couldn't really make anything out inside the house, even by squeezing his torch's light down the side of the blinds.

Breaking and entering wasn't something he did normally: it was a last resort and at this stage of the investigation there was little to gain that wouldn't hopefully be arrived at by a little more patient stalking.

He walked away from the house down the drive and from this perspective spotted something he hadn't seen when walking up towards the house. A standalone mail-box. He checked the front: no name, just the house name and number. That would be consistent with Coulson's apparent desire to keep his location private. Breaking and entering a mail-box, as opposed to a house, was something he wouldn't be averse to.

He levered open the flimsy, rusty lock with his car key and found three letters inside. All were addressed to John Coulson. Bingo. He put them back and shut the door as best he could: it looked intact now but any close inspection would reveal a forced entry. He mentally shrugged his shoulders.

He returned to his car, wondering whether the children were there in the house: or indeed, if anyone was present. He'd have to return again tomorrow very early and stay around all day until he saw some signs of life: maybe Coulson would return too.

He was just about to drive away when his phone buzzed.

A text message.

He opened it.

I'm watching you. Won't be long now.

Calum's heart skipped a beat or two, then he re-read the text.

It hadn't changed.

He glanced urgently around him, to see if anyone was looking at him in the car.

Nothing.

What did it mean, watching you? Here? Now?

He looked at the number. It wasn't one he recognised.

He snapped the phone shut and gunned the ignition, making good time out of the area and back to Lincoln. He watched his tail the whole way back, but no-one remained in his rear-view mirror for very long. He needed a stiff whisky to settle his nerves, he told himself, as he parked the car and strode back up to his apartment's front door. It was a couple of hours before his tiredness finally overcame his mind turning the text over and over: even then he had only a fitful night's sleep

*

The following morning proved to be no more fruitful. He was watchful as he left the apartment but the cobbled square outside the front door was deserted when he left around five-thirty. Despite arriving near the house by six, there were no signs of life all morning. Calum was feeling pretty dispirited, even with the pleasant sunshine filtering through his car windows. The strange text message he had received last night was adding to his gloomy mood and putting him on edge. He wondered if someone was actually watching him here, though he very much doubted it.

Only Jenna knew he was here.

Didn't she?

Well, there were a few people at the pub here who knew he was looking for Coulson's house, but why would they want to track him? He'd only just left the pub before the text arrived and they couldn't possibly know his mobile number.

Weighed down with his thoughts, he took a break and returned at 3 p.m., watching for another seven hours. Nil return again. After that he was beginning to think it was time to return to Scotland. He was achieving nothing.

He still thought it was surprising that the boys were not around, but at the age of seventeen they may well have had June exams and be effectively finished at school for this term. That scenario could make the next steps more difficult if they had taken the opportunity to go travelling, or to stay with friends or family elsewhere. He wondered if he could persuade Glenda to let him ask Coulson directly where they were: or do it herself.

It was time to start acting like a modern investigator: he had some micro-surveillance equipment in his rucksack: a small wireless webcam with a battery pack and solar charger. Powerful enough to keep it running for a few days at least. He searched for a suitable place to rig it up and picked a telegraph pole about fifty yards from the house. It had a good view of the house and drive and also wasn't too visible from any other human presence: except that he had to look casually disinterested when the odd car drove past as he strapped it up.

Pleased with his handiwork and convincing himself that it would be very unlikely to be spotted on a country road with no footpaths, he tested the system from his laptop and managed to retrieve some initial images. The definition wouldn't be that great at night but it would be enough to show if anyone was back at the residence.

He called Jenna. She didn't pick up, not surprising given the hour. It was nearly midsummer's day and the late sun had deceived him as to the time.

'Jenn I need to come back in the morning. Can you cancel the apartment, I'll get my own ticket home. See you later in the afternoon maybe,' he said.

There was another message he needed to send. A text.

Hi love, well the cricket link worked, I found the man I was searching for. Brilliant! I'll have to involve you again, Sherlock - if you want??!! Love Dad x

A quick reply to his little deception.

Yeh anytime Dad, text me with stuff, I liked doing it xx

White lies definitely had their place, he mused, as he drove off in search of food, avoiding the pub in case his face became too well known. Despite the lack of sighting of the boys, he felt pleased to be getting back on the road to Scotland the next morning.

He was also pleased he'd made a little breakthrough with Ellie.

18

It always started to get dull after Calum had been out of the office more than a day or two. Their constant banter was amusing and the office clock ticked slowly and loudly when he was missing.

Jenna was done with all her routine work now, so had been racking her brains for ways to help Calum. She brewed some more coffee and sat with her chair facing the window, which afforded a partial view of the harbour. She absent-mindedly watched the gulls and boats dancing their endless waltzes in the choppy water, as her brain tried to break out of its current jelly-walled box.

She reflected on what they had done so far: which was centred on trying to locate John Coulson. That was not the desired end game of course; it was the children they needed to ultimately pinpoint, for Glenda Muir to be able to speak to them. She decided to focus on looking for *them* for a while.

Putting her coffee mug down by her computer she started to search the internet using their names.

Nothing came back of real interest, other than one reference for a Ben Muir aged 6, in a junior school sports day report last year. Obviously too young to fit the bill. A school in London as well, not Scotland or Lincolnshire.

She pondered on what other activities they may be engaged in that might provide a narrower search thread: a sports interest maybe. Probably too wide a search field and unlikely she would guess right: that line of investigation promised a very low rate of return she concluded.

She turned to her old standby: the social media that a lot of teenagers use to keep in touch: Facebook, Twitter, Snapchat maybe - she would try them all. Her personal favourite was Twitter and she had a Facebook account, but would have to set herself up on the other systems to be able to search them.

She started with Twitter. *Zero matches.*

Facebook, however, suddenly injected some excitement into her senses. Both Ben and Gordon Muir were easily found. Their ages matched, from what she could see from their birthdays. She surveyed their public details and friends. There wasn't a huge amount there, though Gordon was more "visible" than Ben. Neither of their locations were made public: she thought this could be read either of two ways. Whilst John Coulson wanted his location kept secret why would two teenage boys? Maybe their father had insisted there be no back door to trace himself. Or they could simply have not bothered to update that item.

She leaned back and considered how, and indeed whether, to use this new knowledge. She clearly had to remain anonymous as far as Calum's firm was concerned. On the other hand she didn't think that contacting the boys as a private individual would be a problem: whether it would actually help the investigation was another matter.

Gordon's "wall" wasn't that busy, just a couple of events he'd been to, some likes of bands and clothing brands: he seemed to have only a handful of friends.

She chose to make some contact with both of them. But she would make a direct approach to Gordon and set up a separate account to use with Ben.

An angle, a reason to contact was what she needed. Maybe she could somehow pretend to know someone who was already Gordon's friend, then make out she was curious about their "mutual" friend, or some fake common interests.

She chose a female intermediary named Sheila Burns, who was in his friends list, but had little activity as far as she could see, then ran through Gordon's personal profile. She clicked "like" on a few items both of them looked like they might be interested in. He had shared some music tracks: commenting on them seemed a natural way to approach him. She looked up the tour dates of a few of them and found a list of upcoming concerts for one band who were gigging around the country during the next few months.

First she sent Sheila a friend invite. Then she invited Gordon, passed a comment on a track he'd shared, mentioned Sheila and asked him if he had tickets for the Edinburgh gig. To make sure it sounded credible she listed the band as one of her likes in her own profile. Then she waited for a reply.

This all felt a bit crude and slightly implausible, but she couldn't think of anything better for now.

Then she set up a separate account under a pseudonym, sent out a batch of friend requests for it and thought through a plan to approach Ben in a similar, but different fashion: she needed the two approaches to be distinct as she assumed that the brothers might share some of their Facebook content. She would delay that approach a little too, so they didn't seem too connected.

She'd have preferred more time to set up the relationships more slowly, to make them appear that bit more credible. She wasn't sure Calum would allow that time though.

She searched other aspects of both boys' profiles, looking for further clues - nothing of any professional interest. She noticed their mother and father weren't listed as friends: perhaps not surprising, lots of kids had that marked down as the ultimate embarrassment.

She turned her attention to John Coulson's Facebook pages then; and thought she might look at Glenda's later too, if only out of pure nosiness. She gazed out of the window at the wavelets in the harbour, their small peaks painted with sun sparkle. It was a lovely summer's day. She would spend another half hour here, no more, then join Gregor out on the weekly dinghy race.

19

Jenna stayed over at Gregor's after the race and rose early, cramped by his small bed and sprawling testosterone.

She showered, ate some breakfast, made coffee and put a mugful on his bedside table. He didn't stir, so she wafted the coffee under his nose and stroked his feet which were dangling outside of the duvet. No response: such was the male waking habit she chuckled to herself.

Suddenly she was on top of the duvet and being pulled downward into its warmth, unable to breathe.

The duvet started to vibrate with the rumble of masculine laughter as she fought for air. 'Got ya!' Gregor yelped as she poked a finger in his ear to encourage him to release her. 'Come and drink it with me,' he said, with a mock wicked grin on his face.

She calculated quickly: Calum was out of town, she had a low workload today - the answer pretty much self-computed...

'Mind the coffee!' she shrieked as he rolled the two of them and the duvet over the edge of the bed and onto the wooden floor.

'Not to worry, I don't need any stimulants now.'

*

An hour later Jenna skipped briskly down the street to the office, smiling inside. She checked her mobile as she walked and picked up Calum's message: at least he would be out of phone signal coverage much of the day. Time to get a little more research done on John Coulson, to demonstrate her worth.

She logged on to her laptop and fired up email and Facebook.

Gordon had been silent. That was disappointing. She really ought to wait, any more prompting might result in her being ignored, especially as she was unknown to him. She decided she had to be patient. She logged on to the false account and sent an initial friend request to Ben, quoting his favourite author as a rather tenuous reason and started a separate wait. In the meantime, scouring Coulson and Glenda's Facebook accounts was enticing work: she settled down to that with lively expectation, having dumped the task for the boat race last night. In the event, it turned out Glenda didn't have an account and Coulson's was closed for general access which didn't surprise her.

A little later, Gregor texted, inviting her to lunch: something about finishing his coffee was mentioned. She agreed on a sandwich at the inn with a smile on her face, which put her in a good mood for the rest of the day.

When Calum finally walked through the office door at the end of the afternoon, he actually noticed she was looking in a good mood.

'I just realised I've missed your happy face,' he said, throwing his rucksack down by his desk. 'Now let me guess, some sailor boy been casting that smile on you?'

Teasing again - but she liked it.

'You might be right *Mr. Neuman*. Good trip?'

'Yeah fine, just long. Any chance of some tea for a weary traveller?'

'*Naturellement!* Then I'll tell you what I have on Coulson and the boys.'

She pouted enigmatically over her shoulder as she went into the kitchen.

Calum sat down and logged on. He had been wondering whether to update Glenda again. Maybe it would be better to go and see her face to face and see what latitude she would give him over them approaching Coulson directly. He would do that once Jenna had updated him. He found persuading anyone to do anything was always easier in person: it was more comfortable to say no when you weren't looking straight into someone's eyes.

She returned with a steaming brew and placed it on his Talisker drinks coaster. He looked at the mug and mat and some words formed in his head around a marriage made in heaven.

'So... any more progress yesterday, Calum,' Jenna asked.

'Not really. We know where he lives and that's it. He didn't re-appear yesterday, he may have gone away. No children or anyone else there either. I've set up a surveillance camera. You can help me track it if you like,' he replied. 'Anything on your side?'

'Some, yes. I've found Facebook accounts for Ben and Gordon and sent them both messages. I've just this minute had a brief reply from Gordon. He accepted my friend invite. I need to work on that now and see how much information I can get out of him,' she said.

Calum was silent for a moment. Facebook was a bit of a weakness for him. He knew he needed to get to grips with it, as the software was clearly useful in finding people and information about them. Somehow he was put off by what he perceived as the usage of the system by the masses: letting the rest of their known world see their latest goofy photos or what they'd eaten for dinner. He needed to wise up faster, whether he liked it or not. He didn't really know what question to ask next, he struggled to compose one that might be seen as half-way perceptive.

'What are the chances of more information then?' he asked, taking a walk into the dark, given how far his own understanding took him.

'I think I'll probably get there one way or the other but it might take days or even weeks, rather than hours. Depends on how active they are on Facebook and how open they are with their friends on the system. How long is a piece of string Calum, as you say quite often?'

'By the way, did you say Coulson was away?' she added.

'No, just speculating.'

'Hmm. Well it's midsummer soon. I'd expect a witch to be doing something to celebrate the midsummer event... maybe that's it?'

'Good point Jenn. In *which* case, if you'll forgive that pun, he may be away a few days,' Calum said, quietly impressed at her suggestion. 'Let's get a look at the webcam: can you spend half an hour looking through today's video quickly? In the meantime I'm going to call Glenda Muir and suggest a quick catch up tomorrow.'

Jenna got on with the video review: it was fun to do if they found something, deadly dull if not. She sipped her coffee as she fast forwarded from when Calum last looked at it. A few images slipped in and out of the monotonous, almost still, time lapse: just cars and wild animals.

Calum settled into his chair on the other side of the office and dialled Glenda's number.

'Hi Glenda, Calum Neuman here. I've just got back from Lincolnshire and need to chat through our next steps. Are you available tomorrow for half an hour?' he asked.

'Well, do we need to meet or can we just discuss it on the phone?' she said.

'I'd prefer to do this in person,' he replied. 'Any time after 9:30 is good for me.'

There was a slight pause. 'Very well then, will four in the afternoon do?'

He agreed, pulling a resigned look onto his face, thinking it would entail another late return to Plockton.

Jenna had drawn a blank on the video search. He decided to call it a day.

20

Coulson relaxed on the train. He was taking mostly the same route which Calum Neuman would soon travel. After a full cooked breakfast with lashings of hot coffee, he settled comfortably back in his first class seat, feeling content and alert.

Each year at midsummer the assembly met in Scotland. Somewhere remote suited their purposes and the long, light evenings also worked well with the outdoor events.

Usually they stayed at an old farmhouse, but this year they had made an exception and booked rooms in a small, privately-owned castle on the Isle of Skye, which had been part converted into a conference venue. Perhaps a sign of their increasing mutual wealth, as they all progressed in their respective lives and careers. It was normally a celebratory occasion rather than a formal governance meeting, though given Sorensen's approaches over the last few days, he wondered what tone the meeting would actually adopt.

He pulled his laptop out of a brown leather bag and flicked it on. He was feeling nervous as he loaded the webcam link for his home security cameras. He wanted to look at them given the events of the last couple of days, but was afraid of what he might find. The various camera scenes all looked clear at present so he skipped back through the archive to last night and fast forwarded through the night. There were a couple of forays up his driveway by a red fox but nothing suspicious showed up.

There had been no reply from Ingleby though, over the website deletion he'd asked him to arrange. He rang him from his mobile.

'Hi John, how are you doing? Not long to go now eh?'

'Yes Steven, indeed. I'm on the train now in fact, getting there a bit early to prepare. I'll see you there but just wondered... did you see my email about deleting a document on the website? The minutes of our last internal governance meeting. It seems to be publicly viewable?'

A moment of hesitation.

'Oh... well that's odd. Didn't see your email John. Maybe I set the viewing rights up wrongly... probably just a mistake I'll have a look. No worries.'

'Thanks Steven. Do it today if you can. I'm concerned it may get unnecessary attention if someone stumbles across it...'

'Sure, no problem John. I'll do it now. Don't think it will have been seen to be honest. See you tomorrow.'

The phone clicked off sharply.

Coulson relaxed again and went back to his newspaper.

Midsummer's day was still a couple of days away. After arriving at the castle in the afternoon, he would have the time there to relax and ample opportunity to prepare for the celebrations. He intended to return home the morning after midsummer and resolved for his own peace of mind to check the cameras a few times during his time away.

The train finally ground to a halt. He walked the short distance from the train station at Mallaig to the port. He was a little early, so sat on a concrete bollard on the harbour side for a while, sipping the remnants of a coffee he'd bought on the train. The town behind him was dour, streets lined with flaking cream painted buildings, tattered round the edges, lacking colour and bustle. Just beyond its perimeter, it was crowded by low hills, covered with olive-green scrub. It was clearly a working town, the train station and port undoubtedly providing most of its jobs and business. He'd read in a leaflet left on the train that the area had once been famous for fish smokehouses but that only one kipper firm remained now. It had that feel of a place that had to continually struggle to maintain itself.

It was a connecting, slightly choppy, half-hour ferry ride across to the port of Armadale on Skye and then another thirty minutes taxi ride up to the castle, which was situated on a rise, surrounded by a grassy estate, densely dotted with mature trees and bushes. The taxi pulled off the country road and onto the castle's private paved driveway. He caught sight of the imposing front elevation through the mass of pine and fir trees which screened it from the direction of the road. The drive snaked round and the full grandeur of the castle slowly rotated into view.

The taxi door was opened for him by a castle employee dressed in an old-fashioned footman's livery: a bit cheesy but paradoxically classy too, he thought. His bags were whisked away and he was led in to the check-in desk.

A smartly dressed woman in her mid-thirties greeted him at the desk and enquired as to his name. Once she realised he had booked a large party into the castle, she seemed to warm to him quickly. He was smugly pleased to be allocated the best room in the castle, presumably because he had made the booking himself: hotels always liked to encourage the party booker to repeat business and what better way than the bribery of a lavish suite.

'Don't hesitate to ask me if there's anything you need at all during your stay here, Mr. Coulson. My name's Shona, just ask for me and I'll try to help. James will take your luggage up for you. I hope you have a wonderful time here.'

He was shown to the room: it was dominated by two floor to ceiling windows, laced with leaded panes and set into solid stone surrounds. The bed was a four-poster, draped with a heavily embroidered cover and cushions. There was a distinctly medieval feel to the room, which he was reassured to notice stopped at the threshold to the bathroom, a dazzling cuboid of very modern grey and white enamel tiling, chrome fittings and a crystal clear glass shower wall.

The view out over the estate and surrounding woods was spectacular. He instantly started to envisage the midsummer evening rituals being carried out in the woodland in front of him. The chants would work especially well in a secluded glade. A natural setting always seems to make things more special, more spiritual.

He tipped the porter for his luggage and sat down to make himself some tea. He sat in front of the window and enjoyed the view for a while, sipping the tea, before unpacking and starting to plan out the rest of his stay.

His initial exuberance at arriving and the wonderful surroundings started to fade somewhat, once his thoughts turned, inevitably, to Jack Sorensen. The man's attitude was nagging away at him and irritated him to hell. He decided he just had to put the worry aside, at least for the rest of the time until people arrived.

He placed a small black velvet bag onto the dressing table and checked the contents. All of the tools he needed to conduct the rituals were inside it, without them he wouldn't be able to perform them properly. He examined them to make sure they hadn't suffered in transit: the wooden pentacle was a little fragile. All fine, though. He was careful not to cut himself on the sharp athame blade. He put the bag into the room safe and set up the electronic access code, locking it straight away. The last thing he wanted was the hotel maid finding odd implements in the room and local press headlines the next day declaring a sadomasochist convention had hit the town.

He would lead the event and he would lead it well. That was the best way to deflect Sorensen's tactics wasn't it? He liked leading the group for sure, he liked the big suite he got as recognition for that, but in the end it wasn't a big enough deal to get worried about, was it? He sighed, blew out his cheeks and thought not, then headed off down to the bar, happy with himself for deciding so.

21

The prisoner awoke with a hungry sense of anticipation and excitement.

As he ate breakfast he made some mental notes on how he would take the next step of locating the target of his hatred. Revenge is a dish best served cold he reminded himself, as he felt himself start to get impatient about carrying it out. It wasn't as if he hadn't waited long enough already - he just needed to get this absolutely right. He had no desire to be detained in Her Majesty's prisons again anytime soon.

He'd long planned to go into hiding afterwards. He had the ill-gotten funds to do that for a substantial length of time. He also had the skills to make a living somewhere other than the U.K. Well, so long as it was the sort of country where the administration wasn't going to be concerned about a British criminal who was was subsequently linked to a murder inquiry. There were a few of those places around the world, if you had the money.

He dialled directory enquiries and got the numbers he was looking for. After some nervous hesitation and rehearsal of his words he dialled the prime number. A young woman's voice slid down the phone line.

'Hello?'

'Hello, I'd like to make an appointment... this week maybe?'

'Well no, sorry, it would have to wait a week or so.'

There was a brief negotiation over a date before he agreed on July 10th and gave a false name and reason for the appointment. He also managed to discover that his target was away from the office and was given, after much insistence on the need to have a brief but urgent discussion before the appointment, a hotel name and phone number.

Perfect. In fact, the more he thought about it, the more it made sense to travel to his target's current location and move on from there.

He made some enquiries and booked some travel tickets. Now he needed to get some new clothes, sort out his finances properly and make firm plans for the getaway.

There was also the question of exactly how he would strike. The object of his anger was holed up in a hotel it seemed. To do it efficiently and out of the public eye, he realised he might need some helpful technology. He sighed, realising the one person who could help him wasn't someone he wanted to be indebted to.

But this was his chance, a great chance, one he couldn't pass by. He looked up Charlie's number and with a large breath dialled it and hit the call button.

*

A day later he pulled on his leather jacket and made his way into town, to a small cafe on the back streets behind Piccadilly Gardens.

It was one of a dying breed this place, locked into the Seventies by way of its decor and, by the looks of it, its menu too.

He ordered a buttered tea-cake and white coffee and checked his watch. Charlie would be here soon. Charlie Marsh: villain at large. A man with more connections than LinkedIn's central database. He'd been released six months ago, so no doubt he was already up to lots of no good.

He walked in, surprisingly almost on time, carrying a small holdall and a broad grin atop his substantial frame. Marsh's flame red hair reminded him of his volatile temper. Not a man to be messed around with, unless you were confident of handling the consequences.

'My man: good to see you!'

'Likewise, Charlie.'

Hands were shaken, a meaningful glance exchanged. Charlie nodded.

'Where's my coffee? I'll get some myself then, tight wallet!'

He nodded to the girl at the counter and mouthed 'coffee, white,' at her and assumed it done.

'So... just out eh? And already planning mischief? Bad lad. Some people never learn eh?'

Something about a pot calling the kettle black slipped into the prisoner's mind but he stopped short of repeating it back to Charlie.

'I've got your stuff. A thousand for the passport, two thousand for the door trip and its clever extras. Another two grand for the gun: you can pick that up in Verona. The address is in the bag. Bag's free.'

'Who's the contact in Italy? Don't tell me you're in with the mafia?' he asked, with more than a hint of sarcasm.

The prisoner thought that might have been pushing the boundaries a bit.

Charlie leant forward, until their noses almost touched. Neither man flinched. It wouldn't do to show any weakness with Charlie. He exploited it in others.

'I have friends everywhere. You'd do well to remember that.'

Charlie handed the bag over and glared expectantly. He was waiting for the money. They'd agreed cash. His customer slipped his hand inside the bag and retrieved the passport. It looked damn good. His late request for the door trip, well, he had no way of knowing in advance it was going to work. He had to take that one on trust.

'Heh, all looks in order. Thanks Charlie. Here's what I promised.'

He handed over a stuffed brown envelope. For a moment he felt like he was in a film set again.

'Good man. I won't count it - I know you wouldn't dare diddle a friend.'

The prisoner rocked his head in agreement and smiled sarcastically.

He was right. *But friend didn't come remotely near it.*

22

The train journey to Inverness was a bit more bearable this time given the later start. Calum nonetheless consoled himself with a de-fatted bacon roll and tea.

He found himself rehearsing the words to Glenda, trying to compose the right phrases to cajole her into allowing him to speak to Coulson directly. Given his experience of her to date, he thought she might be so single-minded that she may simply say no.

He knocked on her door just before four. He noticed that the plum velvet curtains downstairs were drawn.

Just as he was beginning to think she wasn't there, the door opened. Glenda looked down at his feet rather than at his face, shielding her eyes from the daylight.

'Come in,' she said slowly, 'I have a migraine so forgive me, I won't be able to talk for too long.'

They seated themselves in the same room as on his previous visit.

Glenda slumped backwards in the chair, keeping her hand slightly over her face.

'So what do you have to tell me, Calum?'

Calum felt a little anxiety rise into his throat and coughed gently to clear it. He passed her the file containing Coulson's address details and what they had found out about him in their searches, including the material on the witches' organisation.

'Well, I found John and located his home address. So far so good. However, it's been proving difficult to trace the children so far. I've made some contact with them via Facebook but I'm having to tread carefully and slowly, for fear of frightening them off. By the way, there's also some material in the file about his recent professional media entries and his involvement in a Scottish modern witchcraft assembly.'

'I see. Well I have time to wait. I'm finding myself wondering why I didn't think of Facebook myself though, even though I've never used it.'

'Yes, being truthful, it's only been a year or two since I've started to automatically use it as a tool. I think it's the younger generation that doesn't think twice to use it.'

Glenda looked slightly offended by the suggestion she may not be young herself.

'Maybe you should join and I'll hook up with you,' Calum said, attempting to recover from his remark, but in doing so creating a double entendre that he hadn't intended. Sometimes, he thought, he just needed to stick to an explanation of the facts.

'Well, maybe you could pass me anything you see on their walls?'

Calum hesitated, for a reason he didn't immediately understand. 'Of course. In fact I had been wondering how you would feel about me talking to John directly. I haven't seen the boys at the property, although he seems to have left the house himself now. We may know why. It would be quicker if I could talk to him and get you the contact details for them.'

Glenda sat up straighter and looked thoughtful, at least from the small part of her face he could see under her left hand.

'I don't trust John. If you asked him for the children's details he would want to know why you needed them, as anyone would. Once he has that information, I can't trust him not to tell them himself and keep me out of the loop. So no, I'd rather we didn't do that. Now I have the details of his whereabouts I could do that myself... but I'm choosing not to. It *would* be easier for me to talk to him through yourselves, but I'd really rather just keep him out of it altogether.'

Calum sighed a little externally, and rather more internally.

'I understand that. I think he may have gone away for a specific reason, so I'd expect him back within a week. I'll keep watch at the house, in fact I've set up electronic surveillance there. I need to establish where the children might be now though. It's probably unlikely he's taken them with him, given what we think he may be doing, so is there a friend or relative you know of they could conceivably be staying with?'

'I have no idea. As I told you when we first discussed this assignment, I haven't had any contact with John or the boys for all these years.'

She looked irritated by the question and flashed her eyes at him, making him wince.

'I really don't know if or where he would leave them if he was away... although they are old enough to be left on their own I'd say?'

Calum nodded.

'I suppose so. Well, if there's nothing else you can tell me then I'll leave you to suffer the rest of your migraine in silence. Thanks for your time, I'll be in touch with any news of course.'

'Yes, thanks, sorry for not being at my best. I get one or two of these a year, you chose badly today. By the way, you mentioned you thought you might know where John has gone. Where do you think that is?'

'Well I did think it may be something connected to midsummer's day given his role in the witching hierarchy, but that's just a guess. I've no idea where that might be, except probably somewhere in Scotland. I'll watch out for his return closely. I'm starting a week's leave tomorrow, but I'll be keeping of top of things. When I'm back I'll review the latest surveillance results and let you know if there's any news.'

He thought it better to sound as if *he* was keeping an eye on progress, rather than his assistant was. The same reason he didn't mention Jenna had dealt with the Facebook story; you continually had to justify your fees in this business.

'By the way, what do you know about his involvement in witching?' Calum asked, looking closely at Glenda for any reaction.

'News to me... I was thinking of asking you the same really. Didn't know he was interested in that kind of thing at all.'

He felt she was telling the truth.

'Ok, just thought I'd ask, may be of no use or interest to us anyway.'

Calum got up as if to leave and Glenda asked him to show himself out of the house.

As he closed the front door, he tried to catch the thought that was slipping through his mind. There was something that hadn't rung true in their brief discussion but he couldn't pin it down yet. Maybe a mind numbing train journey home would help.

The other thing that was worrying him was the text he'd received whilst scouring the Lincolnshire countryside for Coulson. The words were becoming increasingly present in his mind's backdrop and, try as he might, he couldn't think of any obvious reason for him to be under threat. Glenda was bothering him as well though. He pondered briefly whether the two things were connected before pushing that idea firmly back where it came from.

23

Coulson had always planned to arrive at the castle a little early. He wanted to get some golf practice in and unwind before the day itself.

The weather had been perfect and he'd tired himself out during the day on the links course and in the swimming pool. He rounded off the day with some hearty food in the hotel restaurant and a visit to a small hostelry just up the road that served his favourite bitter. In fact he'd managed to relax so much he hadn't really spent much time preparing for the assembly, until the day of the arrival of the rest of the members. Even his regular checks on his home webcam had failed to reveal anything to unnerve him any further. The country air really was doing him good.

Planning out the midsummer event was pretty easy in any case. It was a well-loved sequence of rituals, chants and blessings and only changed slightly each year with the addition of any specific help they might choose to give in the rituals to their friends and families.

Dealing with Jack Sorensen was a rather more difficult prospect. He gathered his thoughts on that topic and scribbled a few of them down, looked over them and sat chewing the end of a pencil for some time as he mused on the right words and approach to take. He chewed long enough to make himself hungry and had a sandwich sent up to his room for lunch.

In the middle of the afternoon, he wandered down to the hotel lobby to enquire on early appearances.

'Yes, there are a few guests from your party already arrived,' announced the receptionist.

'Any names?' he asked. There would be over sixty when all had assembled.

She ran through the list of guests so far. He knew them all of course: so far Sorensen was not there, which pleased him. He would make contact with a few of his friends and colleagues in an early drink at the bar and try to assess how far Sorensen's influence had really spread.

He went up to his room, threw his jacket on his bed, and started dialling the rooms of those who had arrived. He arranged to meet for a drink in the bar at 5 p.m. with the few he managed to make contact with.

Idling time away, he gazed out of his leaded windows. He could see down onto a large section of the castle walls and through the crenellations and arrow slits a small stream running alongside the eastern wall. It reminded him of Robin Hood: the legendary outlaw he had loved to watch in television series as a youngster. Wrong country though. The castle was likely to have been used during the inter-clan wars in Scotland's turbulent history: it prompted him to think about what skulduggery would unfold over the next day or so.

The phone rang. It was Jeff McLean: one of his closest friends in the organisation.

'A gin and tonic waiting here for you John, when you're ready!'

It cheered him to feel welcomed like this. 'I'll be there in two ticks,' he said brightly and immediately skipped down the wooden staircase to the ground floor bar, in a much lighter mood.

The bar was set in a large open area on the ground floor, filled with old oak furniture, wrought-iron light fittings and a surfeit of red velvet. Tarnished, crossed swords above the huge open fire place at one end of the space, completed the medieval feel. McLean was seated near the window, at a table with two other assembly members. They all greeted him enthusiastically as he sat down, clinking glasses together in celebration at meeting up once more.

The sun drifted in lazily through the window as they chattered about their lives since they had last met, around the time of the Samhain celebration the previous autumn. A few more arrived and filtered into the bar to meet them and the gathering spread out concentrically from their table.

Whilst most of his nearby colleagues were engaged in individual conversations, McLean leant towards John in a manner that suggested he wanted to say something quietly. He raised an eyebrow. Coulson moved nearer him in sympathy and dropped his head in anticipation of what he was about to say. McLean edged him a small distance away from the nearest attendees.

'How are you planning to deal with Sorensen then?' McLean asked, with a concerned edge to his voice.

'To be honest Jeff, I don't know. I was hoping to work that out partly through being here. I know it's not a life or death issue, but I enjoy leading this assembly and I really believe in the stance I'm taking on our forward plans.'

'Leading has its benefits of course.' McLean winked at him.

'Hmm of course, we all benefit from this union of belief. You think Sorensen has more material interests?'

McLean snorted softly. 'Of course, he has a lot of business interests and we all know the assembly helps its own members: in spiritual ways of course, but, well, in other ways to which we usually turn a blind eye. So long as it's not illegal. The leader of the organisation has much more influence over how far and deep that goes, than anyone else. I'm sure he'll be seeing this as a business and bank balance booster too.'

'Hmm, maybe. Jeff, I need to understand who else feels the same way as me though. Can I count on you?'

'Of course you can John, you should know that. I can list half-a-dozen others who are definitely thinking our way too,' he said. 'And a few that aren't,' he added, in a lower tone.

That was mostly comforting.

'Thanks Jeff. Let's have a quiet word later or tomorrow, you can fill me in then. I'll chat my way through them tonight and see what vibes I get from them all.'

'I think some of them are annoyed our internal tensions have been aired in public though. Don't think that was a good move, John.'

Coulson pulled his face into a mixture of blankness and surprise.

'What do you mean?'

'The minutes of the last assembly meeting and the rest of the newsletter: you posted it up on the external web-site.'

Coulson's face darkened to a spectacularly mottled shade of crimson, before he spluttered a reply.

'You mean the one detailing the discussions about strategy? I absolutely did not. Why on earth would I do that? Airing our internals in public is the last thing I would do, you know that Jeff! It came to my attention only a day or so ago and I asked Steven Ingleby to remove them. He thought he may have done it himself by mistake. You know I'm no good at the techie stuff, I couldn't post them up even if they had a first-class stamp on them! '

Jeff smiled at his friend's self-deprecation.

'Well they're still there. So he hasn't done. Anyway I see Jack's arrived now,' said Jeff.

John took a deep breath and looked casually around, spotting Sorensen stood talking to two other members at the edge of their gathering. He looked directly at John, as if he was waiting to be noticed and nodded politely.

The evening passed pleasurably enough, Sorensen made only social conversation with John and in reality most people were pleased to see each other and looking forward to some time for relaxation. At the end of dinner Steven Ingleby, as secretary, announced details of the short golf round planned for early the following morning. Many of the group were players and those that weren't would probably just have a lie in bed until the conference started: witchcraft had no need to be a chore.

John sank a final gulp of beer and said a few good nights: it was getting late and he wanted to be in good form for the next day. He made his way out of the bar and started up the staircase. He felt full of food and slightly drunk, which helped to subdue much of the tension he had felt earlier in the day.

As he turned the elbow of the stairs he became aware of someone behind him.

A voice caressed him from the right - the man fast becoming his nemesis came into view, eyes soft and speaking as if practising the art of seduction. He was about the same height as Coulson: their eyes locked together.

'So. When shall we meet tomorrow John?'

John was unsure how to reply. He ran his tongue around his lips nervously. What came out of his mouth was, 'Maybe a few minutes after breakfast... I'd like to get on with the golf.'

That works, he thought quickly, at least that way there's an excusable back-stop to the conversation.

'OK. Suits me. Let's take some coffee out onto the veranda at the back eh? Hopefully we can find a quiet spot. See you then... and sleep well John,' replied Sorensen. His words lost some of their enchanting qualities as he finished the sentence. Far from being seduced, John now felt the tone change. He nodded - and went on his way to his bedroom, leaving Sorensen gazing up after him until he disappeared from view.

He locked his bedroom door as securely as it would allow and sat on his bed. For heaven's sake this was *not* life or death, it was just an organisation he loved leading, was it worth the worry and hassle of a public battle over its future? He thought it was, but only to a point. He decided he wouldn't push himself beyond that point. Pulling out his e-book reader, he got through a few pages despite some difficulty in concentrating, before he gave up and tried to sleep.

He couldn't.

After what felt like thirty minutes, he switched the bedside light on and pulled out his laptop. Time for a look at his home webcam. All looked quiet, except the fox was back and sitting on his driveway. He watched the creature preen its red fur for a moment or two, then scrolled back through the last few hours at high speed.

Something around 10:45 caught his eye. A figure walking up his driveway. Coulson caught his breath and slowed the video down. He cursed the lack of clarity on the picture: he had invested in infra-red technology for night scanning but the definition wasn't great and without any kind of lighting from the front it was very hard to make out the facial features.

It was clearly a man though. He watched the figure looking at his garage windows, shining a torch around and having a good look round before disappearing down the drive again.

Thoughts of Alan Butler and the conversation with the investigating officer flew into his mind. It could conceivably be him: and from the poor quality video he couldn't rule it out.

Suddenly all he could think of was returning home and watching his video feed live, in case he could dial the police in silence and catch the intruder: assuming the man had any malicious intent and was actually going to return.

Feeling even more under threat from an increasing number of angles, he raided the room's mini-bar and threw two small bottles of Scotch and three beers down his throat. His racing mind slowed to a jog, then a walk and he eventually succumbed to the inevitable heavy slumber.

24

Sorensen went back down the stairs to the bar. There were still plenty of delegates in there socialising, catching up on personal lives and generally getting louder by the hour, driven by the continued consumption of alcohol. The telling of dubious jokes had started; it was that time of the evening.

He scanned the room for his three targets for the rest of the evening. Ingleby, Mclean, and Durston. All good men. All current clients of the software company he worked for.

He walked over to Steven Ingleby, stopping a few yards short of where he was chatting animatedly to a couple of his colleagues. He waited until he could catch his eye and then nodded softly in the direction of the hallway that led out from the bar to the reception area. Ingleby acknowledged the request with the merest flicker of his eye-lids and then followed Sorensen to the empty hallway.

'Good to catch up with everyone Steven, isn't it?'

'Yep, absolutely. In fact I've been hoping to catch up with you about that matter we spoke about last week.'

There was an expectant air in his voice and in his raised eyebrows. Sorensen smiled, recognising the start of a negotiation.

'Me too Steven, me too. In fact it's good news: I can get you twenty-five per cent discount on the next software licence renewal in August. That's the absolute most I can do. How does that sound?'

He knew very well that would be an attractive offer. Ingleby would gain a lot of personal kudos for getting such a hefty cut to the price. And there was nothing Steven had to do for it. *Except help him when the time came.* Ingleby wondered how many other people Sorensen was bribing for their support. Such was life.

'OK that's really helpful, Jack. I'll take that away and come back to you next week. But thanks for the offer!'

Typical negotiating tactic: Sorensen knew Ingleby would be over the moon with this. It was just a formality. He had started the waltz, it just needed the final curtsy now.

'No problem Steven. We need to help each other don't we? Scotland's a small world.'

Ingleby nodded curtly and shot a knowing glance his way.

Jack held out his hand. Ingleby hesitated, just for a fraction of a second, then shook it firmly. He knew he was betraying his old friend. Sometimes, though, you had to put yourself and your family first he thought. Maybe it was time for a change anyway.

He led Sorensen back into the bar where they separated without a further word. Steven really didn't want to extend the sense of betrayal any further by chatting to him in view of the rest of the assembly.

That suited Sorensen too. He picked out his second target for the evening and strode forward with purpose.

*

Coulson awoke, again, at around 7 a.m. He felt drained, with a head that felt like it was being vibrated by a small electric motor. He rolled over and squeezed all the pillows he could manage under his head, and attempted to rest for a little longer.

He managed fifteen minutes then rolled out of bed and headed for the shower room. He let the hot water drench him for a while, hoping it would re-invigorate him. He would be firm with Sorensen, whatever he said, but given he was starting the day off feeling pretty tired he was probably not in the mood to negotiate or play politics.

He sat down in front of the dressing mirror and laid out in front of him the four items he would need later in the day: a leather-bound grimoire containing scripts and chants, a double-bladed athame: which looked like a ceremonial dagger, a silver chalice and a wooden pentacle, the five-pointed star whose points represent earth, air, fire, water and spirit. He looked at them thoughtfully, then polished the metal items with a shoe shine sponge he found in the hotel room, before sighing deeply then bundling them up in the velvet bag ready for the evening.

He dressed casually and wandered down to the breakfast hall. A few of the group were clustered together on a couple of tables and he sat down with them. He noticed Sorensen hadn't surfaced yet: no doubt some of them had stayed up late drinking. At least he could have some breakfast without the tension being ramped up straight away.

He ate well. His body needed the protein and carbs to offset the dregs of the effects of the alcohol. After shovelling the hot food down, he made his excuses and took a mug of coffee outside and sat at one of the metal tables on the veranda. He had a wonderful view of the sunlit countryside around the castle, spray painted here and there with a light early morning mist in the dips and hollows.

Sorensen subsequently appeared so quickly that John felt he must have been watching for his arrival.

He sat down next to John with a matching coffee mug and admired the view with him.

'Good choice of location, John. Is the treasurer pleased too?'

'Heh, yes it's lovely isn't it? We got a good deal, though it's the most expensive one we've done. We can all afford a bit more these days can't we though?'

'Yes, I guess so. It's good to push the boat out every now and then.'

This was polite. Coulson was waiting for it to turn pointy. He didn't have to wait long.

Sorensen turned and looked directly at him, with purpose etched on his face.

'Look John, I just want you to move over. I don't want this to be anything personal, it's just a question of where we lead the assembly over the next few years. We both have its best interests at heart, as I'm sure you know. Can we do this sensibly?' he said.

He was sounding the reasonable man. Or was he just spinning it that way to seduce him into a logical conversation: fair play the British way? He was beginning to feel himself torn a little, swaying towards Sorensen somehow. Maybe because he was tired or because it seemed more reasonable this morning or he was beginning to get weary of the prospect of on-going conflict. Whatever the reason, he felt he was being persuaded.

He remembered Sorensen was the sales director for a major computer software company, skilled in selling products, probably ideas and proposals too. Certainly not something he was particularly adept at himself. That made him sense a disadvantage. He took a sip of his coffee and tried to consider his response calmly, whilst Sorensen ran through his ideas for the assembly once more.

'And of course a number of the group now support me, John. We don't want to tear the assembly apart over this; if you stand down the members can have a free vote on a successor,' he continued.

'Do you really believe you have enough, Jack?' Coulson replied. Coulson's face betrayed his nervousness as he ran his tongue over his lips for the second time during the conversation.

'To be honest, I'm not sure. But some of our members are just being loyal to you: they're a pretty conservative bunch at the end of the day so aren't actively looking for change. Nonetheless, I think I would have a majority in a free vote, once they've had the opportunity for more open debate about it, yes.'

Again, the softer tone.

'Look, I'll at least talk to people over the next twenty-four hours, Jack, and give it a bit more consideration than I have been doing. Just let's drop it for now and we'll talk again before we leave,' he said, surprising himself with the concession.

Sorensen nodded gently and rose to leave. 'Let's make sure we do then,' he said slowly.

Another subtle change of emphasis. Turning back towards threat.

He left.

John leant wearily back into his chair and wondered how he was going to get through the day and into tomorrow.

If he could have seen forward in time a little, he would have realised he didn't need to worry about tomorrow. Today would be his last twenty-four hours.

25

The formal day started at 11 a.m.

They had been housed in the Great Hall, a huge space vaulted with stone pillars. Though a pleasant day, the granite walls of the castle were cool, so a fire had been lit in the massive open fireplace at one end of the hall. The atmosphere and setting surrounded the gathering with a sense of calm grandeur.

There was much business to get through, including formally welcoming new people into the group and vetting other prospective new member applications. It was a busy day, punctuated by an extended lunch that started to show dangerous signs of pushing afternoon into evening.

Ingleby managed to draw everyone back into the hall for the final session, which he surprisingly somehow still brought to a close at 5 p.m.

'Time for a rest, all. We'll meet outside on the front veranda at 6:30, so let's get changed, have some time out and look forward to this evening's fun.'

Coulson stole a glance over at Sorensen. He was talking to McLean. He wondered about what. He pulled his thoughts back to the evening and stood up to leave.

John thanked Ingleby for his efforts during the day and made straight to his room to gather his thoughts. He suspected it might be a testing evening.

*

All the members met outside on the veranda promptly, as planned. It seemed everyone was keen to get together and no-one wanted to miss any part of the proceedings. The veranda was roofed with a breezy yellow and white striped canopy and looked out from the back of the house over the surrounding woodlands.

With the lengthening shadows of evening just starting to show, it was a particularly stunning setting. They were met with a rather luxurious buffet laid out on tables dressed with white linen, dotted around a flagged square bordered by ornate carved stone rails. They helped themselves to food and drinks and filtered down onto the huge granite steps and onto the lush back lawn.

Since it was the longest possible summer's evening, the plan was to have the ritual ceremonies, including the chants, in a wooded glade at the periphery of the castle's estate. It would be a great setting to relax and drink in afterwards too.

Frustrated by trying to hold a glass with a plate of food and devour both at the same time, most sat down on the dry grass and spread their bounty around them.

'Perfect John, great location... and what a lovely evening for it!' came a voice from over his shoulder.

It was the kind of comment he'd been hearing all day. He was buoyed by all the pleasantries around him.

After the shadows had lengthened and everyone had eaten their fill, they started to group together and set off down the gentle grassy slopes to a collection of clumps of silver birch trees, which quickly increased in density for a couple of hundred yards, before they entered the glade in the centre.

John walked down with Jeff and some of his closer friends. Sorensen walked a little way behind them, with what Coulson presumed were a few of his own new found allies. John's discussions throughout the day with the assembly members had not gone quite as well as he'd expected. There were one or two more clear supporters of Sorensen than he'd imagined and some guarded responses from others: which he interpreted as being in Sorensen's camp but too polite, politic or just plain afraid to say so. He was beginning to feel any vote might actually be a close run contest.

The air hung heavy with the smells of summer: fresh cut grass from the lawns upwind, wild hyacinth and phlox from the woods. The sun had started to disappear behind the castle turrets though the light was still strong. John called everyone into the rough circle of the glade as they approached it.

The assembly spread its way around the edges of the open space, about thirty metres across. They had dressed in traditional robes: a practice they only adopted when they were able to be private. There had been a few other guests at the castle, but the evening food and drink had been in a screened area at their request.

John had insisted they wore white rather than black, to signify they were white witches. And no total hoods: that could cause all sorts of issues if a photo got leaked. The last thing they needed were claims they were a phoenix KKK group. Just half-hoods, like a raincoat.

John composed himself and waited for them all to settle down. Sorensen positioned himself directly across the glade, facing him squarely. He seemed to make a show of pulling his robe hood up around his head and let it droop forward a little, creating a shadow across his face. It looked deliberate to John and it unnerved him, but he needed to keep his calm for the sake of the rest of the group. They naturally looked towards him to start the proceedings and a hush soon fell across the glade. He took a deep breath and began.

The gathering had become completely silent.

'Greetings one and all. Wonderful to see you all here of course. Tonight, we're welcoming two new members who are joining us at Litha for the first time. So please all give a warm welcome to Alex and Susan.'

He held his outstretched palm towards each of the two in turn and beckoned them to join him. They had both been replacements for assembly members who had for one reason or other decided to pass on the mantle in their own covens. He embraced them each in turn as the gathering applauded generously.

They walked slowly back to the circle whilst John began a low hum, which turned him into the Pied Piper for a few moments, as one by one the others joined in. One of the group started to patter his hands softly over a small drum.

John pulled his athame carefully out of his robe: he had been too eager pulling it out once before and had scored his skin badly. Its twin edges were razor sharp: not absolutely necessary but it felt right to have them that way.

He started to walk slowly around the glade perimeter in the traditional *deosil* direction, slicing the air with his blade as he went, defining the magic circle. Two members followed him lighting candles at the four cardinal points as he carried on to complete three revolutions of the circle.

The next step was to call two of the four quarters, by drawing a pentagram in the air at north and south points with the blade.

He then returned to his place in the circle and asked Sorensen, as the second most experienced member of the assembly, to call the remaining two quarters.

Sorensen was quick to carry out his task. Now it was time for John to consult the grimoire and start the midsummer rituals they had developed over their time together. He always looked forward to this, it was what made witchcraft special: it had a wonderful calming, spiritual effect on him and for a while he could forget the world of criminality and human frailty.

They started to sing the circle chant.

We are a circle, within a circle
with no beginning and never ending...

Wine was poured into a number of chalices. They continued chanting and singing to build the magical aura, some of the group injecting power and rhythm into the rising energy, beating wooden drums fitted with animal skins.

Dusk was settling around them and their images were losing the crystal clarity of summer daylight. The fading light, fluttering candles and white robes twisted together to create an ethereal atmosphere. The chanting that layered gently over the top of this scene lent it an extra magical air.

There were some specific activities to be undertaken, generally to aid individuals they knew who had particular difficulty in their lives. One of the female assembly members, Sheila Strawson, had been having problems with an ex-lover who had been stalking her. She had made a small poppet of a man, stuffed with straw: the kind of thing that might be considered a voodoo doll.

She held the poppet up and started to insert a mixture of healing herbs and some thorns that physically pricked the doll, inside the cloth jacket she had made for it. It was then bound by a piece of cord made from nettle bark. On Sheila's nod, the group started to chant a purging song, calling upon the spirits of justice and protection to help her.

Lighting a taper from one of the circle candles, she proceeded to hold it under the poppet until it was ablaze and dropped it into an empty chalice, leaving it to turn to a small pile of grey ash. She picked the chalice up and covered it with a lid: she would take the ashes home and scatter them around her house and any other places which she frequently visited.

John knew how supported Sheila would now feel, seeing that the whole assembly had responded to her request for help and focused their spiritual energies on her predicament. In truth, it was hard to know whether this, or any other, ritual really affected the outcome, but it certainly helped the victim feel they weren't alone. He knew this was just like any other belief structure or religion: the human spirit is frail and needs the support of those around them.

After some focus on individuals not present, whom they knew to be needing help, they returned to concentrate on another member of the assembled, as their final act.

Steven Ingleby, for all of his energetic organisation throughout the event, had a serious problem in his life. He was addicted to cocaine. His employment had come under threat, as a result. There had been times over the last few months when it was unclear whether he would be able to carry out his work for the assembly - a short period in a rehab clinic had stemmed the tide somewhat, but it was clear he needed continuing support from his friends and family. In a way, the assembly could be both of those.

'Steven, please come and stand with me.'

John wanted him to feel close, a sense of brotherly solidarity. It was a difficult issue for Steven, John and the all the members. They supported him in his battle, unflinchingly, but Steven had been very sensitive about the whole topic and initially took some persuading to let the group openly help him.

He turned to Steven. 'Ready?' he said, quietly, sympathetically.

Steven nodded quickly.

John handed him the poppet the group had prepared. It had seemed too much to ask to expect him to create this particular version himself.

It was filled with cocaine. Well, it was stuffed with capoc sprinkled with the white powder at least. Filling it with the real thing would have been just a bit too expensive.

Ingleby accepted it and strode somewhat self-consciously to the centre of the glade and sat down on the dry grass. He pulled out a taper from his robe and lit it with a Zippo. John noticed the lighter and struggled to remember seeing him smoke a cigarette over the last two days. He supposed Steven had ditched *all* of his props.

Holding the smoking taper under the poppet's feet, he looked up and around at the circle of friends. They softly mouthed a chant of purification as the poppet first smouldered then leapt into blazing life, quickly disintegrating into blackened cloth. He was holding it over an urn and he caught the ashes. Again, they would be sprinkled around his home, as a deterrent to the thought of further entanglement with the drug. Maybe it would help.

Steven walked back to his spot in the circle and nodded meekly to everyone.

With the formal part of the evening done, John led the ritual to release the magic circle, carving symbols into the air with his athame and repeating the closure chant as he walked around the four points again.

The group then lit a fire they had built with branches and small dead trees from around the glade, consecrated the wine and started to drink copiously. The warm summer's air, the relaxing effect of the wine and the magical, fraternal setting took their inevitable effect. A babble of conversation and laughter took hold of the group, some taking to dancing around the fire in the way that most non-witches believed they always behaved.

John chatted further with many of the group, sitting within warming range of the crackling firewood. It was an intensely convivial experience but his mind kept wandering to the question Sorensen had posed him.

Sorensen rose, somewhat unsteadily, with a cup of wine in his hand and started an impromptu speech, thanking everyone for coming, making special mentions of those who had organised part of the day.

'Of course, none of this would have been possible without the leadership of our head of assembly. We've had a very successful year, what a stunning venue and what a great day. No way we can follow this next year, no matter who organises it! Please raise your glasses to John Coulson!'

The toast was enthusiastically supported.

John however, was left stone cold by the sheer impudence. It wasn't Sorensen's place to speak: by doing so he had started the process of usurping him, taking his place by stealth. The vote of appreciation was no more than an attempt to appear nonconfrontational and inclusive: the age old political falsehood. The subtle hint about next year's organiser wouldn't be lost on them either, even if it only registered subconsciously with some of them.

Nonetheless, sitting down with his back propped against a tree trunk, the warmth of the fire and alcohol took the edge off his anger and he slowly but surely mellowed back into a state of sleepy comfort, aided by gentle chatter with his colleagues and friends.

Steven came to sit by him for a while.

'Thanks for suggesting doing that for me John.'

'Sure... of course. We're here to help each other my friend. We're a strong circle.'

Steven looked him in the eyes and raised an eyebrow.

'You think? Not sure the circle is completely unbroken to be honest.'

Coulson raised an eyebrow back. 'Is everyone involved in the tension?'

'Well, seems most. It's been a great day, like Jack said, but it's feeling more than just a question of who should lead us. It's more about our whole future direction and a bit personal too: feels like you're being labelled the old guard to me.'

John nodded.

'You can count on me though.' He patted John's shoulder warmly and stood up.

'Enjoy the fire anyway John, I'm off to bed.'

Coulson smiled thinly and waved a lazy handed goodnight.

As the fire dwindled, a number of the gathering started to drift off through the trees guarding the glade - some to the hotel, some perhaps to find some space for private pleasure. Almost without warning, John realised he was virtually alone, as Jeff McLean said a goodnight and walked off with two of the others. He looked around the clearing to see Sorensen approach him, together with who John presumed was one of Sorensen's supporters. Jack's face was smudged with shadows from the fire as he walked around the blaze and came very close to John, alone.

'John, it's nearly time,' said Jack.

'For what?'

'For a conclusion.'

Sorensen moved back slightly and stared hard into John's face. He stepped further backwards, turned to his companion and motioned for them to leave John alone.

A moment later, John could no longer hear their footsteps in the woods as they melted away into the trees. He let his head fall back against the tree trunk and exhaled. He felt annoyed this damned issue was marring his enjoyment. Maybe he would just give it up, it really wasn't worth the stress.

He stayed alone, motionless a while and watched the flames dwindle into blackened logs sprinkled with red hot dust. The air had been cooling around his back but the fire was still comforting on his face and after another goblet of wine his head started to nod, as slumber beckoned.

He slid down against the tree trunk, struggling to stop his eyes closing heavily. He pushed them open a little. Beyond the glow of the fire a pale object slid in front of the trees, making no sound. Then an eerie, soft horn-like hoot and it was gone. He realised old hush wing had flown by. Not many barn owls up here he supposed.

Finally, he slipped into a doze, mouth agape, features phantasmically lit by the fire.

The glade became very silent, other than the faint crackling of the dying fire.

Some time later, he awoke with a start and jerked his head upwards, drowsy with sleep. He felt the side of his neck being pricked, he thought by a biting midge, except it started to sting with the electric impact of a stabbing bee. He slapped at his neck in a vain attempt to flatten the impudent insect.

His neck felt warm and sticky as his hand fell down into his lap, where it streaked his robe with a black-red substance. His mind struggled to wake properly and process the information quickly enough.

As his eyes crawled open, the world became a blurred mixture of glowing fire embers and dancing tree trunks.

Amongst all of that a black shape.

A silhouette of someone standing in front of him. He thought he could make out a small knife hanging loosely from their hand. He started to recall the name of Jack Sorensen, but he couldn't quite get it into the front of his mind. His blood pressure had already dropped sufficiently low for him to experience a wave of faintness and nausea, blanketing his brain with fog and indecision. The time of inaction was just a little too long. Long enough to let his life blood run away from him unfettered, through a neat score in his jugular vein.

26

The flight had been punctual and the hotel taxi was waiting for Calum at Verona airport. The trip to Garda town would be a short one and soon he was gazing out over the lake as the car sped northward.

As they slipped past Lazise and its old Venetian Customs House, once home to the Italian Fascist Party, he pondered a little on the area's history. The Roman poet Catullus had lived at the southern edge of the lake: he remembered this mostly since he had been forced to study the poet as part of his grammar school Latin course. It was hard to imagine the ancient Romans other than in battle uniforms and at war: holiday locations seemed at odds with his classroom-inspired history of the Roman Empire.

The early evening sun was glistening across the smooth, languid waters and he sighed with relaxation as the warmth of the air penetrated his bones. He had been looking forward to this break for a while. He couldn't stop thoughts about the Muir twins' case entering his mind though and he tried to concentrate on some of the missing pieces of logic that he knew were there but not yet clear to him. He still couldn't place the name of John Coulson, despite seemingly recognising it during his first meeting with Glenda: and he sensed there was something further missing from his understanding of the players in this case. He knew his mind would keep throwing these fragments into play while he tried to relax here, but he was determined not to let them take over completely.

As the car turned off the lake highway and meandered towards the Hotel Del Lago, he became aware his sense of relaxation was becoming tinged with a nervous anticipation: he knew precisely why.

There was a new face at reception in the small family-run hotel and no-one else to be seen. Perhaps she had moved on: it was a quiet place for a bright spirit. He took his suitcase up to the room himself, went down to the bar and ordered some coffee. After waiting five minutes for his americano, he found himself presented with a Macallan single malt whisky: he smiled wryly to himself and thought he clearly needed to improve his Italian-Scots pronunciation. After a suitably diplomatic pause and a few sips of the whisky, he reworded his request and ordered a white coffee, which went nicely with his scotch. Some things were meant to be.

There were still a few guests lounging around the small pool, enjoying the less fierce warmth of the late sunshine. Refreshed by the alcohol and caffeine, Calum donned his swim shorts and threw himself up and down the small swimming pool until he was pleasantly tired and hungry.

He ordered grilled aubergines with Parmesan and spaghetti aglio e olio, in the hotel dining room overlooking the pool. At least he was safe from pork pies here, he thought to himself as he wandered back upstairs, fortified with a nice large glass of Soave. It wasn't long before he drifted into a deep sleep.

*

He was awoken the next morning by the sound of a powerboat on the lake. It was past 8 a.m. He sat up, shook off his sleep haze and peered out over his balcony at the water. He breathed deeply and felt supremely relaxed. A quick breakfast and then he planned to get out on the lake a bit further north and do some windsurfing. This was going to be fun - and more so if Rosina showed up somewhere during the week. He pushed the last thought out of his mind, had some rolls, fruit and coffee and set off for Malcesine, his favourite windsurf rental spot. If he got a move on he could catch the tail end of the morning *peler* wind.

On the way out through reception he was handed a message. He decided to save it for the journey and marched on down to the station where he waited the obligatory fifteen minutes for the bus to arrive late. Nothing changes here, he thought.

Heaving his windsurf gear into the overhead rack he took a seat and unfolded the message. He'd been hoping for the last half an hour it was from Rosina... and it appeared someone in the hotel had tipped her off about his arrival. She was clearly in town still:

Caro Calum, I know you came! You want some dinner tonight? Call me! Ciao... Rosina xxx

There was only one answer to that question but it still might be a bad idea he thought, as he folded the note back up with a smile and looked forward to the inevitable consequences.

Rosina was just fun. The trouble was she was also incredibly consuming of his time, energy, money and just about everything else after all of that list had been depleted. To hell with it, he thought and started to call the mobile number she'd left on the note.

There was no need for polite conversation, no barrier created by the fact they hadn't seen each other for over a year and only sparsely communicated in that time. Dinner was arranged: whether it would happen as planned was another matter altogether.

He turned his thoughts to the lake and the wind. He hired some equipment and launched himself out on the lake, enjoying a moderate breeze which soon took him a mile from shore.

The wind soothed the sun's scorching heat as he gazed across to Limone and its ancient lemon terraces. He'd read somewhere that the inhabitants carried a special protein in their bloodstream which reduced their risk of heart disease, accounting for an astounding proportion of centenarians in the town. Some people were just downright lucky, he thought, as he took in the dramatic mountain scenery which engulfed the settlement right on the lake's shore.

He surfed for a couple of hours, had a late lunch and then headed back to Garda on the bus: he had an evening to look forward to.

She arrived at his hotel around 8 p.m. to be greeted with a profusion of kisses and greetings from the few hotel staff around reception. He smiled as he watched her arrival from the bar, which afforded him a slightly surreptitious view of the entrance lobby.

The receptionist motioned his hand towards the bar and she turned towards him with eyes full of excitement.

She sashayed into the bar, looking every inch the classic stereotype of a smouldering, sensual Italian woman. She sat down on the sofa next to him and kissed him on the cheek.

'Did you come to windsurf or see me?' she asked mischievously.

'Probably both. Though I expect I'll have to choose now.'

Calum couldn't wipe the smile off his face: she always made him feel like this. Excited, welcomed, completely without rules.

Half an hour later, Rosina's silk blouse floated out with a lakeside breeze via the open doors onto his balcony. Her hot, golden skin wrapped around him in a dreamy evening of passion.

She padded lazily out onto the balcony later, to smoke a cigarette. She picked up her blouse, throwing it around her shoulders and drawing heavily on her nicotine fix. Calum walked out behind her and slipped his hand around her waist. They stared together at the moon and the glistening waters underneath it

'I hope I'm covering your modesty Mr. Neuman.'

'You're a great cover,' was the cheesy reply.

'So what's going on in Scotland? Whose unfaithful husband are you being paid to investigate now?'

'Ha! Well for once I'm not doing that. Actually, I've a rather unusual case on the go at the moment. It's confidential of course, but I'm trying to find some twin boys who are at risk. An interesting woman commissioned me to do it, as well.'

She detected a glimmer of interest in the woman in his voice. Rosina wasn't the sort of woman to be ruffled by that.

She turned to him, without losing contact with his body.

'I'm an interesting woman too. Maybe you'd like to find my twins. Is that good English?'

'Good enough for a Scotsman,' he replied as he pulled her back into the room.

Calum didn't get much more wind-surfing done during the rest of the week but the bill for speedboat rental and room service was almost as large as the grin on his face.

*

A few days later, the weather was especially hot and Calum walked down to the lake front with Rosina, to find a shady table and some scraps of breeze slipping feebly off the water.

He ordered some spritzers mixed with the local grog and a large salad. They settled down to enjoy the view and the wonderful doze of a summer lunchtime heat haze. She picked at some green leaves and sipped the ice cold drink before turning to Calum, face askew.

'Did you expect to find me here this time?' she said softly, with a hint of hope in her voice.

Calum wasn't sure how to answer. He knew he could easily get it wrong whichever direction he threw the answer. He might spoil the fun for good with the choice of a few badly interpreted words. Rosa wasn't normally one to get heavy but maybe time was changing things.

'I wasn't sure. Really glad I did though.'

He threw her what he felt was his most charming smile.

'That's nice. Is that why you came to Garda again so soon?'

OK. This conversation was looking like going down the typical path for a relationship that might be approaching a crossroads.

He hesitated, probably too long for Rosa's comfort, as he struggled to find the right answer.

His mobile phone saved his dilemma with a shrill call to attention.

Cassie's name flashed up on the screen. He might normally have let it go to voice messaging but right now it suited him to answer the call.

'Hi.'

'Hello Calum. Ellie is bad again. She's been hospitalised this morning. Thought you'd want to know.'

'Yes, of course I do. How bad exactly?'

He was suddenly guarded with his words. Rosa knew he had an ex called Cassie, but nothing about Ellie. He had felt too embarrassed over the years about leaving her with her mother, to admit it to any other woman he had known since.

'Well, she's getting the usual treatment: IV antibiotics, physio, some oxygen too. You can come and see her if you want.'

'Ahh well, I'm not in Scotland, I'm on holiday in Italy for a few days, so it's a bit tricky really. I'll keep in touch, let me know if it gets worse. I'll come back early if you think I should: should I come now?'

'OK then. No, I think she's stable enough. Stay there and enjoy yourself. Bye then.'

'Say hello from me...' The phone clicked off at the other end before he had the chance to finish his words.

He felt totally inadequate as a result of that conversation as usual, but rather than dwell on that, he had to address the aftermath with Rosa now.

She looked at him expectantly. He wasn't sure whether that was to get an answer to her outstanding question or to know what the phone call was about. He chose the latter.

'Friend of mine is ill, heart attack, his wife called. He's a really good pal. I might go back if he gets worse.'

'Aha. That's sad.'

'Yeah. All of which reminds me to live for the moment. So signorina, how about lounging on a boat over to Limone this afternoon? We can try some seafood in that new restaurant on the lakefront later and maybe risk a twilight sail back?'

It was just enough to turn the conversation. She gave a small smile.

'Sounds lovely. Let's do it.'

She turned away a little. He knew she felt rebuffed. He would have to make it better now. There was plenty of time left for that and lots of ways he could do it...

They finished their lunch and set off for the port area. He couldn't get the image of Ellie in a hospital bed out of his mind yet though: he would somehow call Cassie tonight to check her progress.

The prisoner walked slowly and casually up the path to Neuman's hotel, entering the public bar from where he could observe reception, and ordered a coffee.

This was when he needed to be lucky. He couldn't wait here all afternoon pretending to sip coffee. He could possibly stay for some food if time drifted on: but that would be all he could really manage without arousing suspicions.

The good thing, though, was that he could practice with anyone. So when the first hotel guest approached the reception desk and asked to check in, he pressed CAPTURE on the small device in his pocket and waited. It worked by remotely reading a genuine key card's magnetic stripe details as they were being written, and replicating them onto a copy card inside the receiver. Clever.

A moment or two after the guest had departed, key in hand, he checked the status on the black metallic device's tiny screen. CAPTURED SUCCESSFULLY sounded good to him. However, he wasn't going to go to the trouble of finding out the room number of that guest, to completely try out the process. That was just too risky: he would have to trust in Charlie that "captured successfully" would translate to "works successfully".

He'd taken enough of a risk already anyway. Wandering by the poolside and taking Neuman's key card while he swam, had been a real risk but a necessary one: he'd made it easy by leaving it in full view on a table by his sun lounger. Silly boy. It was a real stroke of luck though, he'd been racking his brains trying to think of a way to steal or get Neuman to lose his key card, in order to trigger him asking for a new one.

Now he just had to hope Neuman would want to get back into his room again soon.

He wasn't to be disappointed. As he was draining the last remnants of the froth on his cappuccino, Neuman appeared in reception, asking for a key for the one he seemed to have misplaced.

Whilst the receptionist busied herself with the technology, Neuman swung a casual glance around reception, sweeping towards his spot in the bar and halting his gaze at the prisoner for a brief moment.

'Here it is Mr, Neuman. Room 201.'

The receptionist interrupted anything that was forming in his mind and he took the key she was offering to him.

As Neuman entered the lift, the prisoner checked the device in his pocket.

Another capture, another success.

He threw the old key away, assuming it wouldn't work now.

28

By means not entirely clear to him, Calum managed to bring out the best in Rosa for the next couple of days. A succession of dozy lunches, sensual afternoons and balmy evenings blurred past him.

Twice he had called Cassie. Twice she had said Ellie was improving slightly. Twice he felt incredibly relieved: because she was ok and because he could carry on with his fun. He avoided analysing his character based on those observations.

However his sense of a perfectly irresponsible holiday was darkly interrupted a day or so later.

It had been the perfect Garda summer afternoon. Twenty-seven degrees and a deep blue sky that reached down and brushed the gentle ripples of the lake on all sides. He was idling away the afternoon by the hotel pool with Rosina.

His mobile chirped, irritating the serenity of the moment.

He recognised the call tone as the one he'd reserved for Jenna, so decided he had better answer it: she wouldn't ring him on holiday without a good reason.

'Hi Jenn.'

'Hello Calum. Sorry to call you on your holidays, but I have some news I thought you might like to hear sooner rather than later.'

'Uhuh?'

'John Coulson is dead. It's being treated as murder.'

Calum felt shocked to the core and sensed his mouth drop open and dry up in an instant. He swallowed hard.

'When: and where did it happen? And how did you hear about it?'

'Well I'd been following up something I found out a couple of days ago on Facebook when I was chatting to Gordon Muir. I'd rung James Beerly since he's probably the most amenable police officer we keep contact with. I told him a little about the case, not much, just enough to make the request seem reasonable. He did help me then and I thought no more of it.

Then he called me this morning to tell me he'd just heard that John Coulson had been murdered. He had been at a midsummer assembly of his witches' organisation apparently. He thought it would help us to know, as it might hinder our attempts to find the children.'

He blew out his cheeks and exhaled quickly.

'So where and when?'

'I think he said a couple of days back. Up on Skye, a castle not far from Carbost... Glenston?'

'Glenston? That's practically just up the road from us! That seems a hell of a coincidence.'

'Yeh I thought so too. But probably that's *all* it is.'

'Well I'm going to need to tell Glenda. And I think I need to come back early and help you with the work on the boys. It won't look very good if I stay here on holiday after this has happened. Damn. Well I think you know what I need Jenn: just tell me the earliest flight I can get. Any more news on the boys?'

'It's slow going to be honest. I'm walking a fine line between casually befriending them and pushing it too hard so they either get suspicious about my motives, or simply ignore me because I'm boring them. Being female helps but even that has its limitations.'

'No idea how being a female Jenna helps,' he couldn't help teasing despite the shock of the news, immediately knowing he would regret it.

Jenna paused. He imagined she was struggling to hold her tongue. She finally replied.

'Of course, I expect they'll have been told about their father's death. Not surprising they've gone quiet maybe?'

'Ok. Text me when you have the flight times I'll get ready now. No time to get you a present from my holidays now.' Sometimes Calum really rode his luck with Jenna.

He turned to Rosina and broke the news which she had half pieced together from his end of the call anyway.

'I need to get packed straight away, I expect Jenna will find me a flight tonight. Sorry, it's been great Rosa, maybe I can come back later in the summer to finish the holiday. I'll pay the bill. You can stay in the room and eat the dinner tonight if you want as I expect I'll have to pay for tonight at least.'

'Ok, Mr. Bond, I know you have these secret things to do, including me. But please come back again and bring me a pork pie next time, I want to try these English things you love so much.'

She mock pouted at him. Calum thought he might have even seen a little sadness twisted into the cheerful sarcasm. He resolved to make sure he really did return, sooner rather than later. He thought he would still leave the pork pies at home though.

PART III

ENCHANTMENT

29

Alan Butler had now been surveying his victim's location for a couple of days.

The small hotel he was staying in nearby wasn't exactly homely but it was anonymous, cheap and sufficient for a few days. It was tucked away in a quiet village, only a mile from where he would strike. The weather had been kind to him and had allowed him to watch his target late into the evening.

He'd observed there were a few practical difficulties around entering Neuman's hotel at night but he had devised a plan to work around them. He'd spent a little while disguising his appearance before he arrived, in order to deceive hotel staff and any CCTV cameras. Some extra stubble growth, hair dyed from mouse-brown to black and a clip-on earring that left no permanent holes all worked well with a soft tweed cap: he looked quite the arty farty he decided. It also left him feeling a little silly: this was the stuff of Hollywood, not his own life.

He'd also entered the establishment a couple of times after capturing the key card details and talked to the receptionist casually about a possible booking, to further refine his tactics.

Having worked out a plan, the issue of which day to execute it was the one remaining question. It struck him that he didn't know exactly when his subject would leave - and the longer he thought about doing this, the more nervous he became. It had been a great break to discover where his victim would be staying, away from the workplace, but he didn't know what his plans were after arriving there. He realised he would have to act soon, and that translated to today or tomorrow.

His instinct was telling him today, but the years he had waited were mitigating against rushing: he felt he needed to make sure nothing was left to chance. He had to believe he would have only one chance, even if that might not turn out to be true.

He decided to trust his inner guide. That gave him just a few hours to make his final preparations. He returned to his hotel, locked himself in the bedroom and sat on the bed, gathering his composure. He needed to be very calm. He'd managed to obtain a supply of Sotalol - he took one and swilled it down with a glass of water. At least his heart rate should stay a bit more subdued and even.

He would wait until around 11 p.m. before walking up to the location. He gathered his kit together in a soft black cotton bag: hand-gun, silencer, spare cartridge, duplicate hotel key card and then zipped them into the inside of a lightweight jacket.

Picking up the gun had gone to plan: it was a Glock, not a gun he was familiar with. It was a long time since he'd learnt to shoot rifles and pistols in his Army cadet days. Once he knew he had a Glock he delved into a user manual on the net and carefully checked out the mechanics. He'd found the opportunity to try out a few loose shots in some nearby woods, to ensure he would make no mistakes with its operation. Accuracy wasn't likely to be a problem, given the range he intended to be at when he struck.

He waited in his room, sipping mineral water, as the zenith of his aspirations over the last decade rapidly approached.

The hours nonetheless passed slowly and despite the effect of the beta-blocker, he started to feel almost faint with nerves. It was still early but he decided to leave and spend a little more time watching the area around his destination before making his final move.

He checked the foyer area of his hotel from up on the first floor landing: there was no-one in reception as was often the case. He might still be seen when leaving but it wouldn't be abnormal to go out in the evening for a late drink and anyway, his current disguise should take care of any *immediate* consequences of the aftermath.

He strode quietly away from his hotel, trying to keep his pace natural, not rushed. He was soon in a patch of thin woods which encased the country road he walked alongside. It was quiet with very little traffic and he heard the hoot of an owl spread its eerie echo under the moonlight.

The lights of Neuman's hotel, which was situated just outside the small town it served, appeared through the trees in the distance. He took a path up away from the road, so he could make his final approach to the building with the benefit of height. As he closed in on the rambling old hotel, he settled down in the dry grass and watched the comings and goings around the front entrance for a little while.

There was very little activity now and the time was approaching. He had a duplicated card that should work in Neuman's lock. All he had to do was walk into the hotel, up to the room and trigger the magnetic door lock. Then he could kill.

He urinated behind a tree. His nervousness had caused his bladder to panic. They didn't do this in the movies.

When he looked back at the hotel, a sole female receptionist was in view in the lobby. He took a deep breath, exhaled and set off for the front door. As he began to stride up the long concreted path past the swimming pool, he was suddenly blinded by a powerful light that lit up the whole front area of the hotel.

He froze momentarily, before recognising it as a motion sensor switch and taking a deep breath to calm himself, carried on up the path. He walked through the lobby to the lift, pressing the call button. No-one challenged him. He'd made sure his face had been seen wandering through reception a few times over the past day or so, during the daytime. He had figured it would ensure he seemed familiar to the reception staff, allowing him to enter later at night without challenge. It seemed he had figured correctly.

The lift took him to the second floor. There was no-one in the corridor. He moved quietly to room 201 and stopped outside the door, looking both ways before pulling out the key card he hoped would unlock the door. Charlie Marsh had taken two thousand pounds from him for the technology that created it, so there would be trouble if it didn't.

It was 12:45 a.m. and he could hear no sounds from inside the room nor see any light around the door edges or spy-hole. He pressed the duplicate card into the key card reader on the door and, holding the door's handle, activated it. He heard a small metallic click and twisted the knob to push the door open slightly. He felt a little buzz of elation.

It was pitch black inside the room. He listened intently and heard nothing except some faint shallow breathing. He slipped into the room's darkness and closed the door carefully.

At first he could see absolutely nothing. He stood perfectly still and listened with all of his skin. The sleeper's rhythmic breathing was all that was audible, in stark, vivid waves.

As his eyes grew accustomed to the blackness he could make out the bed outline and a slight hump down one side, a dark blur against a grey pillow.

He slid the card into his jeans pocket, then carefully slipped his hand inside his jacket and retrieved the Glock .45. He'd attached the silencer and set the safety off in the corridor, so as to make no sound inside the room. It felt heavy in his hand.

This was it. The sweetest of moments. Time to finally take his revenge. He raised the gun slightly and took aim at the head sleeping on its soft pillow.

Feeling a sudden sense of righteousness and calm, he squeezed the trigger slowly.

The barrel emitted a sharp crack, muted by the silencer. He squeezed again. Then twice more, lower down the body. He listened, as his heart rate soared again.

The sleeper's breathing was suddenly gone, carried away on a sea of pain and lead.

He stood immobile. In his mind images appeared, like a strobe effect, captured as they were lit by the brief flashes of the gun.

There was something wrong.

He tried to recover the images again and concentrate on the detail.

Suddenly, his gun arm dropped in involuntary shock. He had seen a woman's head and long hair on the pillow.

He felt slightly dizzy as his blood pressure went through the roof. He'd heard no-one else in the room: he was sure there was no-one else there. He listened again. His heart was drumming loudly in his ears but there was no sound of breathing in the room.

He moved backwards towards the door frame, felt along the wall with his other hand, searching for the main light switch.

His fingers touched a raised aluminium square and he pressed the first switch he found: the bathroom light came on, right next to him.

It was enough. The light slanted across the bedroom and onto his victim. He reeled backwards against the door, from the sight of blood and splintered white bone fragments on the pillow and the view of a woman's face

Grey brain matter was oozing down the side of the crumpled head, from a large hole: both head shots had hit around the same point. His senses were overwhelmed, and the feeling fled to his stomach. He rushed across the bathroom to the sink and vomited violently.

His vision blurred momentarily and he swayed a little. He sat down on the toilet seat, eyes shut against the blinding whiteness of the bathroom. He wondered where Neuman was, who the woman was: he was sure he had the right room, he'd seen him ask for the key card for this room and heard the receptionist repeat it - maybe he'd swapped rooms for some reason; whatever the reason this was bad, really bad. He realised he had to make sure that if Neuman was here in another room, he found him tonight. He thought carefully, his senses stabilising slightly. This was an upmarket hotel. Reception were likely to instantly recognise a caller based on the room number. He dialled 0.

'Yes Mr. Neuman,' replied the girl at the desk. He muttered 'sorry, didn't mean to dial you,' in the quietest, briefest way he could and replaced the handset on its cradle.

So for some reason Neuman wasn't here and a woman he didn't know had died unnecessarily. He'd seen Neuman with a woman once, when he was watching the hotel entrance. Maybe it was her. No way he'd be able to recognise her now anyway, her face was smashed to pieces. He had to leave fast and rethink his plan. He put the gun back into the bag and stuffed it into his jacket breast, washed off the trails of vomit from around his mouth and left the room. He had the presence of mind to loop a 'do not disturb' sign over the door handle.

He walked down towards reception, feeling sure he would be stopped and questioned. It was foolish he knew, but somehow he felt that killing a person must have left him with a recognisable marker over him, a red *sigil* for anyone in an official position to spot him with.

He walked past the front desk. The receptionist lifted her head and looked at him directly. She smiled – then looked back down at her computer screen, dismissing him without a word.

He walked away from her, barely able to return the smile, his legs feeling unsure of their ability to carry him. A thought seared across his mind: his DNA. He has been sick in the bathroom and he hadn't exactly cleaned it up well. In any case, it was hard to remove it completely if the police techs did a full check. That could be a problem. Could DNA be traced from vomit? He wasn't sure but thought so.

As he walked away from the hotel he started to feel an inexorable desire to run. After fifty yards, he gave in and sprinted up the slope and into the safety of the woods. He dropped down, panting hard, propping himself up against a tree trunk, his fingers curling tensely into the dry leaves carpeting the wood's floor.

He would have to follow his planned exit from the scene and rethink once he was clear of the country. The main thing was to get out of Italy fast. He stood up and looked around for any kind of a marker amongst the trees, so he could see his way back in the darkness.

Despite struggling to keep his panic under control, he soon got his bearings and walked briskly back to his hotel. Should he leave after breakfast as planned? He knew changing plans through panic might cause unexpected consequences. He needed, against all his instincts, to stay calm and rational. It wasn't likely the body would be found until later in the afternoon when the 'do not disturb' sign started to look suspicious. Time enough to leave as planned, no need to get the hotel owner suspicious about an early exit. The police were likely to talk to local hoteliers and a guest leaving unexpectedly at the time of a murder wouldn't need much interpretation. Unlikely to save him from coming under suspicion though.

At least the reception was empty, he scuttled up the single flight of stairs to his room as quietly as he could. No need to advertise his return time unnecessarily. He dropped onto the small bed and rolled over to his rucksack, pulling out a quarter bottle of whisky. His nerves needed it: he drank the bottle in fifteen minutes, driving himself into a heavy-headed drowsiness, falling asleep shortly afterwards, tortured by repeating pictures of the remains of an unknown woman's shattered skull.

When he woke at 3 a.m., to pee the whisky away, he lay awake, unable to sleep, mind still racing through the flick-book images of last night and with his pillow soaked with sweat. After hours of endless tossing and turning, he pulled himself up out of bed and stared out of a gap in the curtains at an emerging Italian summer's day. If only his guts felt as sunny and optimistic.

30

It was a blustery, wet morning and sea spray was lightly flecking the air along the harbour road as Calum walked up to the front door. Jenna was already there and he could smell coffee. He realised that type of coffee now smelt like home, because Jenna always used it.

'Coffee, sir?' rang out into the corridor as Jenna heard Calum enter. He smiled.

'Yes please. Any Italian?'

He walked into the room and sat down.

Jenna came in with two coffees a couple of minutes later.

'I made you cappuccino, is that Italian enough?'

He smiled at her sarcasm and launched into work mode.

'OK, so we need to work out what Coulson's death means and what we do next. Heard anything more last night Jenn?'

'Only Gregor's fiddle and he was a bit off form,' she replied.

He mock grimaced.

'I'm wondering how and when to tell Glenda and what to do next about finding those boys. I suppose if we're lucky the police might let us have some contact information for them, if they've been able to find them already. Someone will have needed to tell them.'

'Surely we need to let Glenda know straight away?'

Calum twisted his mouth and pressed his lips together. He looked unsure. He was scanning the internet, looking for the latest local news reports on the death.

'Mmm, well I think I'll call James Beerly first and see what he can give away to me. If we're lucky we could give her all the news she needs at once.'

'Good point boss. Well, I suppose you need to have a few good points or else I wouldn't call you boss.'

She never gives up, he thought to himself, maintaining an amiable front.

'Before you ask, the boys have been silent on Facebook for the last two days. But we always have that route if your police contacts don't cooperate.'

'True. By the way, Glenda said something about a wall yesterday. What did she mean?'

'Facebook wall? That's your personal place to post your stuff up. Why?'

'Well it struck me on the way home that was a bit strange: she'd previously said she didn't use it - Facebook I mean - so using that specific term seemed out of place. Maybe she'd just heard someone else use the word.'

Jenna thought about this. 'I'll look deeper for any old activity on their pages then, to see if she had been in touch with them if she's ever had an account herself. She doesn't now, I checked a while ago. I don't understand why she would be employing us if she already has a way of contacting them?'

'No, I know, it simply seems a little odd. Anyway, I'll call James now.'

James Beerly was another of Calum's old university friends, testament to his reputation as a social animal in those days. Somehow, Calum had become more self-contained, as life squeezed his youthful optimism with its disappointments, (mostly female) and hurdles, (the ones he didn't clear, due generally to his declining career aspirations). At least he'd kept his sense of humour pretty much intact.

James had graduated at the same time as Calum and entered the police force directly from university on their fast track graduate programme. He'd made Detective Chief Inspector pretty quickly but in recent years his career had stagnated, more likely due to a lack of political astuteness. For that, Calum respected him somehow.

The conversation wasn't as productive as he would have liked though. James was particularly reticent to talk about the children: in fact he had positively clammed up when Calum had enquired as to their whereabouts and steered the conversation elsewhere. He wouldn't even confirm if they had been contacted. What he did share was that the police had spoken to Susan Richardson, Coulson's common law partner, who had filled them in on the details of the event Coulson was attending on Skye.

Calum had been surprised to hear her mentioned as he'd observed no-one at Coulson's house in Lincolnshire. He asked Jenna to look at the videotapes for the previous two days.

'I'll pop over to Carbost in the meantime. Probably unlikely to help us but since it's so close it's worth an hour or two of my time. I'll be back after lunch.'

Jenna mentally translated "videotapes" into web cam files and resignedly began the laborious process of fast forwarding through hours of recording. About time he bought some kit with a motion sensor trigger.

Calum jumped into his car and began the hour-long drive to Glenston castle, about three miles from the village of Carbost on the west coast of Skye. As he drove he chewed over whether to drop this case and just bill for expenses to date. Becoming entwined with a murder investigation wasn't what he had bargained for when he'd taken on the task. Without Coulson to watch and follow to the boys, it was hard to see where the case went next unless Facebook suddenly came up trumps.

He made a mental note to give this a couple more days at most and then discuss with Glenda the practicalities of continuing.

Twisting his way past the bleak Cuillin mountains, he arrived at the castle with the rain continuing in a steady drizzle, stirred up even more on this exposed coastline by a stiff breeze.

He passed the Talisker distillery on the way through Carbost and considered whether to pick up a nice bottle on the way home.

He stepped out of the car and dashed over to the main gate. As he reached the shelter of the overhanging stone arches which surrounded the entrance steps, he was interrupted. Glenda Muir's number flashed up on his mobile.

He answered. He spotted a waiting text message as he glanced at the screen.

It was as if Glenda had read his mind.

'Calum, it's Glenda Muir.'

'Hi Glenda, how are you? I was about to ring you actually.'

'Oh, well that's a coincidence isn't it? I'm fine. Look I wondered if we could meet up again, get an update and work out what to do going forward. Can you come over soon?'

'Yeah, sure, I'll sort it out when I'm back in the office - just mail me with your free times for the rest of this week and I'll confirm with my diary.'

That suited him just fine, given his current misgivings about continuing the search. Clearly he was now going to have to tell her about John without having fully prepared his words. He wasn't sure what kind of reaction he was going to get – Glenda and John had known each other a long time ago, but they did have children between them. It was hard to predict human reactions to death. He started slowly, cautiously and then dropped the bombshell about the timing and location of his murder.

Her reaction was very muted. There was a short silence. A long sigh and some words of regret. On the whole, she took it very calmly. And, it felt, privately.

The conversation moved on and they agreed to meet in two days' time, assuming his diary allowed it. He felt sure he would drop the case if it hadn't been concluded by then.

He pushed the phone back into his jacket and carried on into the castle. It was rather smaller than one might imagine a castle would be.

He enquired at the front desk as to whether there was still a police presence at the place: the receptionist looked at him suspiciously.

'Well, the crime scene's been roped off and there's still someone on duty in the woods where the murder happened. Are you a reporter?'

He often got asked that.

'No, not exactly, I'm a private investigator.'

He was met with the usual blank looks - in his experience the general public didn't generally know how to deal with that answer, caught between wondering whether he *was* actually something of a policeman or more akin to a legalised peeping tom.

He took advantage of her pause.

'Any special or unusual visitors been looking around the hotel, relations of the deceased perhaps?'

The receptionist didn't think so but agreed to ask the manager and came back with a firm no. Feeling the routine deflation, he was pointed in the direction of the woods where he could see police tape plastered across a number of trees.

'I'm not sure if you're supposed to go over there, but it's up to you I suppose.'

As he came closer to the edge of the woods it was clear that pretty much all of the entrance to the extensive woodland was blocked off from that direction. He didn't feel inclined to walk hundreds of yards further to find the end of the tape and spotted a police constable farther inside the woods, sitting on a collapsible chair and surrounded by the faint chatter of a live walkie-talkie.

There was a creepy feel to the place - the rain cast a blurred shimmer around the trees. Knowing a murder had occurred there added to the dark aura and made him shiver.

He felt his time versus reward ratio had run low, so headed off back to his car. The weather had deteriorated and huge welts of rain, driven by fitful gusts of wind slapped against the car windows.

Remembering there was a text he hadn't read, he clicked the message open.

Same unknown number as before:

Remember me? Getting close…

As if he needed to feel any more threatened.

He snapped the phone shut and gunned the car engine, heading back to Plockton.

On impulse, he stopped off at the Talisker distillery to buy a bottle. It helped console his frustration and a couple of large gulps from the bottle before setting off warmed his spirits a little. Clever that, the distillery is 57 degrees north and they make a bottle of whisky at 57 degrees strength. Distiller's edition they called it. He liked the circle that made.

It was the one pleasant thought, in a soup of increasing gloom. A man had been murdered. The case had gone nowhere. And someone seemed to be *trailing* him.

31

Jenna at least had some positive news when he got back, but she swiftly followed it up with two more worrisome pieces of information.

She had found some images on the web-cam of a woman, probably in her thirties, entering John Coulson's house with a key, so she was presumably the live-in girlfriend whom James had mentioned. No sign of the boys though.

'Time-stamped the day after midsummer. The police arrived later on and stayed an hour or so from what I can make out.'

'What you'd expect. Looks like she'd taken the opportunity to go away whilst he was in Skye. I wonder if she's a suspect?'

'We should ask her you know - about the boys I mean,' said Jenna. 'Glenda said nothing about involving her did she? Now that John is dead there may be no need to keep it from her?'

'Yes, I guess that's true. Glenda called me while I was out. I had to tell her about John. I'm seeing her later this week, so if we have no news by then I'll ask her if she wants to do that as a last resort. Otherwise we'll drop this whole thing now Jenna. See if you can whip up any response on Facebook by then or else we're out of it. I don't have a good feeling about continuing now Coulson is dead. You said you had something else to tell me too?'

He sat back expectantly, hoping the rest of the news wasn't bad. He had a nasty feeling in his gut, especially since that second anonymous text.

'Err, yes well I forgot to mention - there was someone trying to get hold of you on the day you left for Garda. A man, he said it was urgent he talked to you but wouldn't say why. I gave him your mobile and hotel numbers. Did he get in touch? He told me his name was John Servant. Also, I had a call while you were just out on Skye, from someone who I think is in the Italian police. He wants you to call him back urgently. Here's the number. He said he would call again if you hadn't rung him back by this evening. I was going to call to tell you if you weren't back soon.'

Calum stood up and started to pace around the room. Jenna looked askew at him - this wasn't normal behaviour from her laid back boss.

'Did this John Servant leave a number? He hasn't called me as far as I know.'

'Nope, said he would be travelling and hard to contact, so he'd call you. He made an appointment too.'

'Ok. Well, we'll see if he gets in touch then. And it was definitely a policeman from Italy?'

Jenna noticed Calum's voice was breaking slightly. He seemed distressed somehow.

'I think that's what he said, but his English was really heavily accented so it was a bit hard to be sure. I hope I got the number down right, I asked him to repeat it three times.'

He imagined that conversation: Jenna was very persistent.

Given the threat to call him later and disturb his evening, he dialled the number straight away, despite an overwhelming desire to avoid anything not straightforward for the rest of the day. The single ring foreign call tone made him instantly nervous for some reason.

'Pronto? Chi parla?'

'Sono Calum Neuman,' Calum replied, hoping the exchange wouldn't continue much further in Italian.

'Ah Mr. Neuman, thank you for ringing. My name is Inspector Rezzago from the Verona police. I have some bad news for you and I need to ask you a few questions, sir.'

Calum tensed. He leaned forward onto his desk and propped his free arm up under his forehead. He muttered 'ok,' quickly.

'I'm afraid a young lady was found dead in your hotel room this afternoon. Her name was Rosina Marcelli. I believe you knew the lady sir?'

Calum suddenly felt his breath being sucked out through his windpipe. He struggled to answer straight away.

'How? What happened?' was all he could manage in a hoarse, forced whisper.

'She was shot sir. In your room. We know that you had left the country early in the evening and Miss Marcelli was seen later in the hotel, alive. We also estimate the time of death to be later, so you are not a suspect sir. But we need to know more about your relationship with Miss Marcelli and the events before you left the hotel.'

'Sure. I mean yes. Of course.'

The questions poured out, searching for and documenting the detailed information he knew from experience any thorough policeman would require. The officer spent a fair amount of time probing whether he or she had any enemies who may have done this: Calum suspected that one of his theories might be that Rosina had been murdered by mistake, in lieu of himself - just something the detective said. Maybe it was just his simple English and he'd read it wrongly.

He shuddered, repeatedly. He was trembling slightly with the effects of adrenaline now and he was struggling to answer clearly.

Jenna watched and listened from the other side of the room, in growing unease, as she began to get a gist of the seriousness of what Calum was being told. Rosina was a name she didn't recognise though.

After twenty minutes of questioning, Calum nodded and hung up. He looked across at Jenna.

He shook his head and rubbed his cheeks hard with both hands, unable to form a meaningful sentence. He stared at his hands and realised he couldn't stop them trembling.

He felt totally shocked and completely out of his depth. He was a private investigator, not a member of the homicide squad. Two murders in a few days, and one a close friend, was not what he expected from his work. More than that, he had no clue as to why these murderers had occurred. No idea at all. He was beginning to feel more than overwhelmed too. He was starting to feel very frightened.

He shook his head again, trying to clear the fog around it and looked up briefly at Jenna then dropped his gaze again.

'That sounded bad. Who's Rosina? Someone you know?'

He looked at her and wondered how much he wanted to tell her. She was young and he was totally horrified by the news. He didn't know if he could burden her with all the detail - but the strain of what he had just been told made him want to share the grief.

'A friend... an old friend. We... well, met up while I was in Garda. She's been murdered... in my room... after I left. The police wanted to ask me questions.'

Jenna spread a hand over her widening mouth.

'My God, Calum. Do they know who did it? Was she a bad person?' She clenched her fist and bit her lip at the same time. 'I'm sorry. I meant was there anyone who had a reason?'

He shook his head slightly.

'No, not that I know of. She was a sweet, fun woman. You know, I don't think anyone, apart from the hotel staff, would have known she was in my room either. It's not as if she was there all the time or anything.'

Jenna saw his face start to crumple. She went to the cupboard in the kitchen and returned with a glass of whisky, handing it to him.

She squeezed his shoulder gently.

'Drink it Calum. You must be really shocked. Will the police want to talk to you again?'

'Maybe. They said they may come and talk to me in person depending on the rest of their investigations. Jesus, first Coulson, then this... what's going on Jen, eh?'

Jenna thought she really didn't know and squeezed his shoulder again, harder this time.

32

In the gloomy grey of a rainy mid-evening in Inverness, Glenda Muir started her beloved tea ritual. If she was truthful to herself, she would agree that it wasn't so much the actual ritual she loved. That had become mindless automatic routine, spilling over into tedium when she was in an impatient mood: which was often. It was more that she was in love with the feeling it created inside her: some sense of calmness, a connection with history and actually some good tea out of the process. It also reminded her of her parents and a childhood in Asia, long gone but fondly remembered.

Remembrance tainted with a rotten heart though. *They never did support me when I really needed it.*

As she looked out of her kitchen window onto the monochrome stone houses and rooftops around her neighbourhood, she bemoaned the lack of colour in the vista.

She took her first sip, swallowed and sighed. The past few days had taken their toll. The end of term was always a busy time, finishing exam marking, tidying up loose ends, preparing material for the new term so she could enjoy the summer break without interruptions. There were always departing students to talk to and farewell parties to attend: it was a good life. She wondered how long it would last.

She turned her thoughts to the visit from Calum Neuman. He seemed to have done as much as she could have expected. What was difficult now, was to work out how to steer him forward from this point. She had wondered whether to take control of that situation when he'd come to see her a week or so ago, but she'd decided she needed more time to think about her approach. It needed careful consideration and she also needed to think about how she would deal with the issue of her sons pretty soon.

She surprised herself by also wondering how to work another thread into this complexity. She had become a little more attracted to the somewhat indefinable Mr. Neuman at their last meeting and she had definitely felt some measure of response from him too. It would be good to have some fun along the way, though the seriousness of what she had to do with the boys weighed heavily in her thoughts over such relative frivolity. Nonetheless, maybe it had been that constant yearning for romance that had stopped her moving him on when he last visited.

After some hesitation, she concluded she would ask Calum to come and see her again. They should discuss future plans and she would ensure he was put on the right route thereafter. After having some fun with him first.

She finished her cooling tea in a few swift gulps and hammered the mug decisively onto the wooden table top. That was what she would do.

She called Calum immediately and arranged for him to come to see her later in the week. He'd been about to call her it seemed: he had some shocking news for her.

She was surprised he had come to learn of John Coulson's demise so quickly, at least it proved her instincts for his contact network had not been misplaced. He'd asked her what path she wanted to take with tracing the children now; he'd already asked the police to assist with whatever information they had and were willing to share.

She'd shut the conversation down, she didn't want to talk about it there and then. The implications of John's death were suddenly pressing on her chest and she started to feel a shortness of breath. She persuaded Calum the next discussion would be better done face to face, once she had taken some time to absorb the news.

Again, her instinct in choosing him had proved right: he was pretty easily influenced. On the other hand, for much more long-standing reasons, he was really the only one she wanted to choose. Killing two birds with one stone came to mind.

*

Calum sat on the early morning train to Inverness, glad he wasn't driving the route. He could spend time thinking clearly. Much of that thinking today had been imagining how Rosa had died. His mind had winced as he constructed images of how it might have happened.

He pushed those pictures away and tried to concentrate on the case. During the first hour of the journey, he'd tried to think through something he had been aware was missing from the jigsaw around the investigation: but couldn't see the shape of.

Now, having fortified his mental capacity with the inevitable tea and bacon rolls, he knew what one particular missing piece looked like. Unfortunately it didn't appear to be in any way useful. John Coulson's name had been faintly bothering him for a while. Maybe it was the thought of Inverness that had triggered the sudden enlightenment, since there was a connection with the town and Coulson which he now remembered. He thumped lightly on the table - he felt deflated it offered little help.

So, Coulson had assisted on a police case in Inverness many years ago, early in his career. The psychologist had only taken a bit part as far as he was concerned, he'd helped profile a stalker who had turned into a murderer. Calum had been involved early on by one of the stalker's targets, she had commissioned him privately to help identify the man, after the police had initially shown lukewarm interest. It had been one of his first cases.

Although that had led nowhere, later on the police become more aggressive in their pursuit of the case. As the stalker moved onto other victims, Calum had stayed in touch with the investigating officers, having helped them with what he had originally gleaned. The murderer had turned out to be a psychopath. He couldn't remember his name, but he resolved to check the details once he was back in the office, to confirm it was indeed Coulson who'd been involved.

In any case, it was unlikely to help him now and he couldn't recall meeting or communicating with Coulson in any way at that time. Another red herring probably put to bed.

He drank the cooling remains of his paper cup of tea and turned his thoughts to the day ahead and Glenda Muir. He would definitely be out of this by the end of the week. Jenna hadn't made any more progress on Facebook. He had no more leads. Glenda could surely now ask the police about the children, assuming they had no reason to prevent communications to the boys. Nonetheless he had a contrary feeling around this being the last time he would meet Glenda. There was a little spark of personal interest which he admitted to himself: a feeling adorned with mental images of an attractive, intelligent, free-spirited woman who appeared unattached.

He remembered Paul Proudson's description of her being a pretty intense affair. He could well imagine that, from the little he'd experienced of her. It didn't dissuade him from continuing to develop a fantasy about what might happen today. Then he thought of Rosa and suddenly he wasn't sure that was quite the right feeling to have so soon.

The train guard disturbed his thoughts, when he asked him to buy a ticket. He shook his head to clear his mind and paid the fare. The train was almost in Inverness. He sat up straight, stretched and started to feel optimistic.

By way of exercise he took a short stroll along the river, which was at its summer low: clear and sluggish, before continuing to Glenda's house. The appointment was at 10 a.m.

As he approached the house, he felt sure he saw the same flicker in the upstairs curtains he'd imagined on a previous visit.

He hoped it was a sign she was impatient or excited about his arrival. He told himself to stop fantasising and strode up to the front door. He raised his hand to the bell and swayed it back again as the door opened abruptly.

'I saw you coming up the road,' she said, by way of explanation.

He was taken aback by her appearance. A silk kimono - bare legs and neck. This was a seduction staring him in the face unless he was very much mistaken. She smiled at his reaction and explained again:

'Sorry, I've not been up too long. I've not had time to dress properly. Come in.'

She took half a step backwards, turning slightly towards the hallway as she motioned for him to come in. She left little space for him to enter, so it was impossible for him to avoid brushing his hand against her as he stepped over the threshold. He flicked the slightest of sideways glances as he moved forwards. She was staring at him, looking for his reaction, sensing the electricity generated by skin against skin.

He swallowed hard and suddenly felt a little awkward.

'Let's sit in the front room.'

He followed her silently into the study, mesmerised by the sway of her lean hips.

She sat - no - slid onto the leather chair, sliding the silk up her thigh a little as she settled into a sprawling provocation. A clock ticked quietly in the background. He felt himself becoming entranced.

'A question from me. What's in your surname? Doesn't sound very Scottish, does it?'

Calum wondered how much personal information he wanted to share with his client: then relented.

'Hmm, well there's a story there,' replied Calum. 'Four generations ago, my father's side of the family migrated from Germany. They were Jews, farmers I believe. The name was originally Neumann with two 'n's. However at the start of the

Second World War, the name was considered pretty embarrassing for a family living in Britain: so it was changed to drop one of the 'n's. That's it, you know my family history now.' He winked tentatively as he finished the sentence.

'Interesting. You should investigate the family tree if you haven't already. You may have some rich relatives in Lower Saxony or somewhere. Anyway, you wanted to see me, so what shall we start with?'

Calum gave a hesitant and nervous chuckle.

'Well, I think we've come to a crossroads. John is dead. Our alternative routes to contacting the boys through Facebook appear to have gone cold. On the other hand, the police investigating John's murder must by now have become aware of the whereabouts of children at the very least. More likely they will have spoken to them as part of the investigation. I think we're wasting your time and money pursuing this case now, I think you should contact the police directly to get to the children: you do have some sort of reason to speak to them being their mother and John's ex-lover don't you?'

'You're right, I agree. Let's do that.'

She stared at him.

He was stunned by the ease with which she'd been persuaded. But pleased. For some reason, he'd anticipated a resistance to his suggestion, even though it made perfect sense. Sometimes apparently locked doors could be opened with the merest of touches. Not for the first time, he was struck by the speed and strength of her will.

'You said we, not I - what did you mean?'

'Err when?'

'Just now, when you said "we're wasting your time...".'

'Oh, I guess I just say that most of the time. I have an assistant, Jenna, so I think of us as a firm, rather than a solo operation.'

'Ah, I see.' She looked impassive, but recoiled internally with a vengeance. She cursed herself for overlooking this: now she would have to make further plans beyond today's. She shelved the thought and brought herself back to the scene unfolding in front of her.

'Crossroads in more than one way, Calum.'

'How do you mean?'

'Well, I've been thinking it would be a shame if you gave the case up... I wouldn't get to see you any more would I?'

Calum knew where this was leading and smiled gently. He started to feel aroused and was aware his eyes were locked onto Glenda's body rather than her face now.

'So... a decision Calum. You need to decide if you want to undress me.' She leant a little further back on the chair, allowing her left leg to swing lazily sideways and outward. One of her breasts slipped casually out of the front of the silk robe.

Calum felt instantly giddy, his arteries filling with a blood rush pumped by lust.

33

Jenna, meanwhile, was wondering whether there was any point in continuing her pursuit of the twins via Facebook. After all, Calum had insisted the case would shut one way or the other this week: there were also one or two new client queries needing attention, on which Calum had asked her to do some initial research.

She checked her own account. Gregor had posted some pictures of the last music night. They looked like the pictures from pretty much every session in recent months. A couple of her friends had been out in Inverness and had some nice food by the looks of the assorted shots of laden plates. Nothing much of interest really. But rather than flip back into work mode, she couldn't resist switching to the false account she'd set up.

There was nothing new from the boys. In fact it struck her that it was odd that there had been such a complete lack of activity over the last week or so, especially from older teenagers who tended to be addicted to their daily doses of Facebook - maybe boys were less gregarious in that medium than the girls she knew. She looked back over the history of their conversations, which had been few and brief.

As she read the messages, she felt, as she had throughout, that they hadn't really connected with her. It had been half-hearted, friendly; but ultimately non-engaging. She'd even copied some pictures from a very attractive girl friend's photo albums and posted them as new profile and cover photos on her home page, letting it look as if they were of herself. She wondered why two boys of seventeen weren't just a little more interested in a pretty girl who was trying to get to know them.

Maybe that was sexist, maybe teenage boys weren't as hooked on their female counterparts as she'd always assumed. She knew Gregor would be though and that made her smile.

She read on, further backwards in time, almost to the beginning.

There was a phrase that caught her eye. She'd felt it was out of place when she'd originally seen it but had passed it by with little further thought. Now she looked at it again and wondered what had made her stop to look at it.

She had been asking Ben what he was doing at the weekend. He had talked about going hill walking and then had said he might go out to a disco on Saturday evening with some friends. The conversation had led nowhere in particular, it had just been another attempt by Jenna to build a friendship and possibly have him drop some important detail along the way. It was the use of the word 'disco' that had bothered her.

She was interrupted by the ring of the office telephone.

It was James Beerly.

'Hi, is Calum around?'

'No James, he's meeting Glenda Muir in Inverness today. Can I help or leave him a message?'

'Well, it was just to pass on some information really, you may as well give him it yourself Jenna. It was just about the children of John Coulson that you mentioned.'

Jenna pricked up her ears sharply.

'We've spoken to John's partner. She says she has no knowledge of his children. In fact she didn't know he had any. Actually, we had already spoken to her when we spoke to Calum last - when he mentioned children it took us aback here so we went and double-checked with her. No record either that we can find, though I guess we could look harder. How sure are you about their identities?'

She thought about this a little, before answering.

'Well, Calum has seen a photo of when they were around a year old. I've had some pretty superficial conversations about music with them on Facebook, but that's it. The rest is Glenda Muir's original instruction on the case and what she told Calum about them.'

'Ok. Well we'd like to talk to them about their father's murder. There seems little point asking Glenda if she was searching for them anyway, so we'll start elsewhere for now. Can you email me their names and Facebook names if they're different please? Ask Calum to get in touch if you turn up anything else Jenna: we'll do the same for you eh?'

'Sure. I'll email you now and pass the message on.'

She put the phone down, sent James an email, and entered a tunnel of deep thought.

So the children were virtually untraceable apart from Facebook - and Coulson's partner didn't even know of their existence. They hadn't really engaged with her online - and they had used a word that sounded very 70s - somehow not quite right.

She thought back to the start of this case and when Calum first met Glenda. He had said something about remembering her from his past, although he hadn't made much of it at the time.

Jenna decided to call him - maybe he could press Glenda further for some detail she had overlooked: even if they decided to close the case they could still pass on any new information to James. Calum was always keen to do that, to keep the relationship with James active, since there were many times they could be of use to each other.

She looked at her watch. He might not have arrived at Glenda's house yet: she dialled his mobile number. It diverted straight to voice mail. Switched off presumably. She left him a message asking him to ring her before he left the house if he picked it up early enough. She closed the call and hoped he might pick it up somehow.

Now it was wait and see, except she wondered more about the boys' use of Facebook and Glenda herself. The fact the police couldn't find any evidence of the twins was a worry. She needed to talk it through with Calum, if only to settle her nerves. Maybe she could research a little more about Glenda while she waited for Calum to return. It couldn't do any harm and there might be something waiting there to be found out, that could help. She made a note to ask Calum to get details from Glenda as to where the boys' births had been registered.

She flipped open her laptop lid again and, armed with a fresh cup of coffee, she set to work.

34

Butler was furious.

He'd abandoned his plans to move to a safe haven directly from Italy. He had to get out of the country straight away and then try for Calum a second time. The only obvious choice now was to return to England and wait for him to finish his holiday. He bought the first ticket back to England the next morning. Gatwick - it would have to do - he'd get a train back up to Manchester.

He worried intensely about his return to the U.K. He expected the Italian police to apprehend him at every possible point along his journey to the airport, through passport control, security and immigration procedures in Gatwick and anywhere on the train journey north. All pointless concern, as it turned out. The journey would have been quite pleasant if it hadn't been for his nerves being continually shredded.

Now he was finally back in his flat, he'd been working feverishly on a plan to complete the task he'd so monumentally messed up on the first attempt.

He had kept a wary eye on any news of the police investigation into the woman's murder: but there'd been nothing so far on English-speaking news websites - though he'd managed to find some references to it on Italian sites, by changing his search criteria and using the web translation button.

He was able to make out that the police wanted to question an Englishman who had stayed at a nearby hotel and left immediately after the murder. Nonetheless, thanks to Charlie

Marsh, he'd travelled on a false passport, ordered his travel through a high street travel agent from behind a heavily disguised visage and paid in cash everywhere. He felt he'd done all he could to make it very unlikely he'd be traced.

The last twenty-four hours had witnessed a drop off in further news articles. He thought how fickle the press and their public were: the next story was always the most important one. At least it made him feel a little calmer, even though he knew the Italian police would still be working feverishly behind the scenes - it was very early days, after all.

He pulled up again the small website Calum used to advertise his services. It still amazed him how much use of the internet had exploded since he'd been in prison. He opened a map of Plockton and the surrounding area. This time he wouldn't stay in the area, but well away from his intended strike site. Another false name and more cash payments should ensure anonymity for his travel arrangements.

He bought a small second-hand car for cash: a Ford Fiesta, in silver, a colour that seemed to cover every third car in the country. He needed to maximise the blandness of his overall profile. Striking again so soon was a big risk, there would almost certainly be a recognition that it was related to the Italian mistake, assuming the police exchanged a least a minimum of information. He wasn't sure about that, but he was planning for the worst case scenario.

This time he would make no mistake. He'd thought that hearing about Neuman's Italian trip had been a stroke of luck, an opportunity for him to commit the act in an unexpected place, minimising the chances of him being traced - but that was history now. He would be absolutely sure he had the right man: the stupid private investigator who had stumbled across a clue fundamental in getting him sentenced. He wasn't sure how he had let it all end with an attempted murder conviction. Towards the end of his time as a free man he had felt anything but free, instead driven on by some insatiable addiction that had totally consumed him. His guts tightened. This, though, *would* be beautiful revenge.

Judging from the views afforded by the Plockton public webcam, the spot up in the pine forest by the television mast on the Duncraig crags was perfect: remote but accessible, commanding a clear view of all of Plockton harbour and any boat or surfboard that might enter or leave it.

It was the surfboards stored by the harbour side that he was potentially most interested in. He remembered that, as a witness, Calum Neuman had apologised to the court one afternoon for being delayed at a windsurfing event. He'd wondered whether it was something, with the passage of time, in which he might still participate. From what he'd seen of Calum's leisure time recently, by following him onto a bus to Malcesine one morning in Italy, he knew it might be. Surely he would take advantage of breezy summer nights here in northern Scotland, where in June and July the sun hardly set. In any case, his rifle would reach right across to the harbour, but a shot or two whilst on the water would be a bit easier as his target would be more discrete.

He clicked on the webcam and surveyed the scene again. He decided his lair would be directly above the ancient castle at Duncraig. He had been able to make a lot of his preparations through the use of this camera, various web literature and maps. Once, he had even thought he had seen Neuman walking down the main street, but the resolution was a little too low to be really sure.

At least, this far north, the quality and length of the daylight should be good most days. He planned to visit the spot each evening from now on, and wait until what counted as dusk here. Sooner or later, he would have his man. He wondered whether to taunt him with another text... then decided against it. He needed to stick to the plot.

He packed up the rifle he'd procured, through Marsh again, into a grey holdall, together with enough clothes for a few days. He started the long drive north. With adrenaline starting to rise, he felt the urge to call a friend. He wondered if she would pick up.

35

That was his trigger point. Calum launched himself toward her. In the smoothest of movements, she caught both of his forearms and held them just in front of her face. She felt strong, vibrant.

'I want to play a little game with you first. Are you willing?'
Of course he was, he said under his breath.

'I need you to be willing,' she repeated, as she twisted her mouth into a wry smile. Suddenly her face had become intensely sensual, alive with the warmth of her grin.

He was slipping into this. It was a one-way street now. She stood up.

'Lie on the floor Calum. Watch me.'

It was a command rather than an invitation. He did as he was asked, wondering what delight she had in mind for him.

She moved a little farther away, facing him, and made her eyelashes flicker rapidly. She suddenly opened her silk gown to him. She slid it off her arms and held it in front of herself, swinging it gently like a pendulum.

Calum was transfixed. Her eyelashes were still shimmering with movement. Her naked body swung in time with the robe. She smiled and asked him to watch the robe, not her body. She was teasing. She started to speak to him about what was going to happen - what she was going to do to him.

'You *will* like it Calum. I'm going to stroke every single part of you. You *will* let me won't you?'

He felt excited and dizzy with desire. The air had become electric with stored sexual energy. He began to feel time slow down, as if the only thing that existed in the whole universe was the two of them - in that place - at that time. Then she told him he would forget all about this visit and pursuing the case after today. He agreed with her. He had to agree with her, there seemed no other possibility.

She held her hand out to him and pulled him upwards from the floor. Then she let go and skipped out of the room and up the open wooden staircase to her bedroom. After a second he followed and caught up with her just as she fell backwards onto the silk bed cover, grabbing the flesh of her inner thighs and wrenching them apart.

An hour later, they lay curled together, cosily tired with spent lust.

Calum stroked the back of her neck, watching his fingertips brush the tiny hairs there.

'Not normally part of the service, but no charge this time eh?' he gently joked.

'Ah well, I prefer this to a discount,' was the reply, as she rolled over to face him and took his face in her hands.

He was very warm and a bead of sweat slipped languidly off his brow and dripped onto his shoulder.

She held his gaze, with a deepness that pinned him to the pillow. He found it uncomfortably intense but somehow he just couldn't look away.

'So... much as I might like to repeat this... we won't. Remember what you agreed. Forget this and any notion of pursuing the quest I set you the moment you leave this house.'

He nodded slowly. But his mind wasn't functioning in the normal way, his answers felt like they were pre-programmed.

She smiled at his acquiescence before rolling on top of him and making him forget everything else.

*

A little later, Glenda got up and made them some lunch. Chicken sandwiches and jasmine tea. He ate the food ravenously; sex was a great appetiser. The tea he was less keen about and he started to wish he hadn't expressed a preference for it on his first visit.

'Well drink up. Sorry but I've a late afternoon seminar to prepare for. I hadn't exactly planned to be doing what we just did. I need to get moving Calum, sorry.'

He got up and dressed, happy for a reason to leave the rest of the tea. She pushed him gently out of the front door and reminded him he would forget her after he left the house: the case was closed now. He smiled and mouthed 'ok'.

As he walked away from the house onto the main road, he began to wonder where he was, and why.

He knew where he was physically, of course... but the *why* part of the question was proving difficult to resolve. He headed off up to the train station with a black hole in his mind that he was struggling to see into and somehow reluctant to enter.

Glenda watched him trudge away, feeling very smug about using her professional skills on yet another man.

She whispered under her breath to herself.

'They're all the same. The same weaknesses, the same problems inside their trousers, the same *fucking* stupidity. Too easy.'

36

Jenna looked at her watch again: still no call back from Calum. She was getting impatient and edgy.

She'd made a list of avenues that she might explore to understand more about Glenda: Calum's friend who had mentioned he had a relationship with her, her university colleagues, students, the maternity unit where she had given birth, where she had registered the kids. Some seemed more viable or useful than others at first sight; but she'd try all she could think of until she got a lead.

Only the first one appeared easy. She started to think of more unusual ways to gather information: breaking into Glenda's house passed through her thoughts briefly - it was attractive, probably because it excited her, more than through any real likelihood of a successful return. Nonetheless, it kept circling back into her consciousness.

She played with the ideas and doodled little geometric patterns around the list with her ballpoint pen. Finally she gave up on it and moved her attention on to the new client work.

The rest of the day passed slowly until Calum arrived back later in the afternoon. He looked tired as he slumped down into his chair, a 5'o'clock shadow around his chin. He rubbed his eyes and yawned.

'You look cream crackered Calum. Did it go well? Any news?'

'Yeah I feel tired. Anyway, the case is closed. That's it, all over. We can move on to some new work now.'

'Did you get my phone message?'

'Err, no. Sorry, I left my phone switched off, I had a snooze on the train on the way back. What did you want?'

Jenna looked hard at him. Sleeping on the train in the daytime wasn't like Calum at all.

'James called. He found no trace of the twins. John Coulson's partner didn't even know he had any kids. I wanted you to ask her more about them, maybe get details of where their births had been registered.'

'Well that's odd for sure. But I'm not sure knowing about the local registration office would help us. In any case, we're done with this. Glenda has closed it. I've told her she can talk to the police about the boys and passed her James' details. We need to move on now.'

Jenna fell back into her chair, disappointed and bemused. She didn't like leaving loose ends but Calum paid the wages and bills so if the client wasn't paying any more, there was little she could argue with. More than that, Calum suddenly seemed disinterested, his attitude more black and white than normal. He usually tended to share her own desire to get to the bottom of things. She'd thought it was one of the main reasons they worked together well.

The phone rang. Calum answered it. It was a new client. Her opportunity to answer Calum back was lost for now and would be diluted for later. She threw him a resigned look and returned to her screen, with a nagging thread of doubt weaving around inside her.

Her phone chirped with a text. Gregor. Reminding her about the gig tomorrow night. Lots of new songs he said, so be sure to be there. She smiled. She'd be there for sure - it was bound to be fun, it always was when Gregor, music and alcohol overlapped. Her mood lifted a little and she peered across at Calum, still in conversation with his new client. He could be a pain sometimes. Good job she *liked* him, she thought, not for the first time.

37

The following day, with Calum out meeting new clients, Jenna pressed on quickly with her 'official' schedule of work, so that she could find time later to pursue her doubts about dropping the Muir case. She knew there was no point pushing Calum on it right now, she needed something specific otherwise he would simply say he wasn't getting paid for continuing to flog a dead horse - a dead horse that had worryingly seemed to gather other bad news.

There was something else though: Calum seemed unusually firm about the case. He didn't talk about it at all after his declaration it was closed. It was almost as if he had erased it from his memory.

She logged on to Facebook and checked for messages or other activity from the twins. Nothing again. She sent them both a message, suggesting there might be a gig for a band they liked, which she could get tickets for - would they like to go with her if she could? It was a pretty brazen move.

On the other hand, it seemed she had nothing to lose right now. Apart from her job. Maybe a part of her wouldn't be too disappointed by that, maybe it would force her to that crossroads decision that she kept poking gently and backing away from.

The question of the twins' actual existence was nagging away at her too. She hadn't done that kind of check before so Googled it, to work out how to go about it. The process was different in Scotland, compared to England or Wales. She assumed they would have been registered in Scotland and tried a search for their names at ScotlandsPeople.gov.uk. It produced an unexpected result. There was a Ben Muir birth registered that year. No Gordon Muir.

She considered the possibilities. Gordon's birth hadn't been registered for some reason - Gordon didn't exist and Ben did - they had been registered in different countries, maybe England - or it wasn't the same Ben Muir... in which case were they both imagined?

She searched the English equivalent and got a complete blank.

To find out more about the Ben Muir she had found, it appeared necessary to pay for that data by credit card. That was something she didn't want to do at that moment, so she reluctantly shelved that particular thread and hoped some other line of investigation would help illuminate it later somehow.

She went back to her assigned work.

It was just ten minutes before she was going to leave the office when she was alerted by the soft chime of a new Facebook message. She clicked onto it: from Gordon. He had de-friended her. There was a short note that said he didn't want to go to the gig and furthermore thought it was strange she had asked him since they had never met. The whole tone of the thing looked pretty final. He was right about her brazen approach though, wasn't he?

She blew out her cheeks and let out a sigh of resignation; she'd blown it, but maybe that was the seal on the case she needed. She thought about replying - then decided against it.

Then another chime announced a fresh message. This time from Ben. Now her senses went into overdrive: Ben had also de-friended her and with a very similar message. In fact, when she looked at it closely, there were only three words different between the two messages. It looked like the first message had been cut and pasted to the second one and changed slightly to disguise its source, but it wasn't a very convincing attempt in her opinion. It looked like the replies had both come from the same person.

Maybe she was imagining this. Maybe they had just conferred and decided as one that they wanted to drop this annoying girl who had been softly pestering them over a few weeks. Somehow her intuition told her otherwise.

She had begun to think there was someone else behind all of this. The use of the word disco, this concurrent cessation of friendship with her, Calum's sudden blankness on the whole affair after visiting Glenda. She increasingly felt that there was more to Glenda than met the eye. Conversely, she had no hard information that pointed her anywhere in that direction at all.

Maybe then, she needed to get it.

The only source that sprang to mind was Glenda's house. She knew from Calum that Glenda lived alone. She asked herself if she could be brave enough to contemplate trying to snoop around Glenda's house without Calum's approval. She decided she was: in fact she already knew that she was, the real issue was whether it was just too risky. Actually, she wasn't entirely sure what the nature of the risk was: of being caught for breaking and entering - or of something more threatening.

The biggest problem was when. She could hardly take the day off to do it. So it would have to be this weekend: she was going to have to make some sort of excuse to Gregor since they would normally be together for some part of both days at the weekend.

She decided quickly to plan for Saturday - she reasoned that Glenda was possibly more likely to be at home on Sundays and the train service was much less frequent then too. She surprised herself at the speed of her decision and chose to tell Gregor this evening during the music session at the inn. Then she suddenly became very nervous about what she was about to do.

She realised what would make her less nervous, was if she could find a way to be sure Glenda wasn't in the house. Time for a brain squeeze. She shut her eyes and squeezed it hard.

Suddenly it shot out like over-pressed toothpaste. She'd text her with a request to meet in Inverness. Not herself. The text would come from her son. Whatever the truth about the twins, surely she would be sufficiently interested to leave her house for an hour.

*

The fiddles were running at a hot pace when she entered the inn. Gregor was playing a mandolin, lodged amongst the small group of musicians sat in the corner of the main bar, squashed around a table liberally stocked with pints of beer. The place was awash with summer tourists and she struggled to get through to the bar to order herself a drink.

She watched the group play, as she had so many evenings over the last two years since she'd come to know Gregor. As the songs flowed one after the other and time passed, the effect of alcohol on the audience and the group deepened and soon the whole room was tapping and swaying to the incessant drive of their jigs and reels. After one of her favourites, 'The Butterfly', they broke off for a beer break. This was when she'd planned to talk to him about Saturday.

He picked his pint up and walked over to her with a smile on his face and a gleam in his eye, high on his drug of live music.

'Hi my gorgeous.' He stroked her face with his free hand and offered her a swig of his beer. She shook her head with a smile and clinked her wine glass against his.

'Nasty stuff, made from grapes. Never seen any of those growing around Scotland. How was life in the Calumdrome today then?'

'Fine. He's on some new case, early days, so quiet for me. Pretty boring really. So boring I thought I might liven up the week with a shopping trip on Saturday, get some new clothes maybe.'

'Doh, I thought we'd go out on the boat on Saturday afternoon? Ah well I guess it can wait until Sunday, the weather's forecast to hold up till next week. Maybe I'll come with you then,

I need some new jeans and I've been thinking about changing my mobile phone to something a bit sexier. Inverness?'

This was entirely unexpected. Gregor hated shopping. He must be absolutely and desperately in need of new jeans she thought, as she stole a quick glance down to the pair he was wearing. She tried to fend him off casually.

'Oh, I thought I might meet a friend there, you know, some girly time. You'd get bored.'

'No I wouldn't, I can come with you, we could shop a bit together and then you can meet your friend, we can have lunch together later?'

This was getting difficult. Gregor was too good at spotting when she was lying. If she brazened this out, he would know there was something wrong - worse, he would be suspicious, through a misguided sense of blind jealousy. It was the only thing she didn't quite like about him.

'Look, it's more complicated than that. Come outside after the final set and I'll tell you then.'

Gregor looked askance at her and sipped his beer again.

'Ok,' he said, with the easy grace that defined him.

For the next thirty minutes or so, Jenna racked her brains to think of a way out of her predicament, until her thoughts bled dry. It would be really hard to find a reason to exclude him that he didn't find the cracks in - either logically or simply in the way she told it. On the other hand, if she told him the truth, she really wasn't sure how he would react. She wasn't even confident he wouldn't blow her cover out of indignation or plain nerves.

The reels reeled on and as the lead fiddle announced the last song, she started to feel nervous, knowing Gregor would stride over to her without any delay. He wasn't one to tarry when there was intrigue to be had.

As the last notes faded into the hubbub of the crowd, Gregor stood up and looked across the room for her. She motioned to him to follow her out of the back room door.

Once outside in the pleasantly still air, she took his arm and pressed herself a little closer to him. A couple of persistent summer midges buzzed around his face and she blew them away.

'Ok, so the reason I didn't want you to come is because I'm going to snoop around a house and may even slip inside it if I can. It's to do with the last case I worked on.'

She had stuck her neck out by being totally honest. Now she tensed up, as she waited to see if it would be snapped off.

Gregor's face twisted with consternation. 'What on earth for, Jenn? You'd be breaking the law! What's so important that you need to do that - and why isn't Calum doing it?'

'I know it's a bit mad but I've a hunch about the woman who asked Calum to take on the case in the first place. Something feels wrong and Calum came back from meeting her with his mind completely shut off from pursuing it any more. That's why it's me and not Calum. If I find nothing, then I guess that's it, but I want to have one more go.'

She continued to explain a little about the case and the Facebook oddities. As soon as she mentioned the murder of John Coulson, Gregor started to bristle with negativity.

'No way you should you be getting involved in this Jenn, no way. I won't come to Inverness with you, not even to go off shopping while you do this. You're on your own. I think you're mad!'

So that was that then, she thought. 'Look Gregor, that's ok. It's up to me, but promise me you'll say nothing to anyone at all about this?'

Gregor hesitated, then fell down the path he always followed when Jenna asked him to be on her side.

'Well, you'd better tell me what's happened when you get back. If you get back without being arrested. I don't want you in danger, Jenn.'

That was more like it. She kissed him on the cheek and hugged him tightly, exhaling all the air she hadn't hardly dare breathe out for the last sixty seconds.

38

Jenna set out on the first train to Inverness on Saturday morning. The weather had taken a turn for the worse and light rain streaked the window next to her seat, cutting furrows through the thin coating of grime on the glass.

She felt jittery, nervous about what she was about to do. She had Glenda's address from the file and had read over the notes a few times. She had no real sense of what she expected to find, other than a piece of the jigsaw that fitted better. If it was a jigsaw Calum had thought completed, well, there were still some bumps punctuating the smoothness of the picture, leaving it looking somewhat unsatisfactory in her view.

She'd texted Glenda late the previous night, from an old phone with a few credits left on it. She could throw it away if it got tricky as she hadn't transferred the old number when she bought her smartphone. No reply yet though.

She decided if she hadn't got any answer by the time she arrived at the house, she would take a cursory look around the outside from a safe distance, to see if she could establish if Glenda was home or not - then return if necessary every hour or two until she had run out of time. Standing near the house all day until something happened, or it became obvious there was no-one at home, seemed rather dangerous.

Gregor entered her thoughts again. Perhaps his attitude to this, even allowing for his loyalty in keeping it quiet, was why one day she would leave Plockton. This was exciting and yet Gregor wasn't interested. Music, the sea and his friends were his life and she wondered whether they would ultimately prove to be more important than her.

The train driver was a little slow with the brakes and the sudden jolt at the next halt interrupted her train of thought.

'Ticket please, young lady,' boomed into her ears at the same time, from behind her shoulder. She rummaged in the pocket of her black padded jacket and produced a rectangle of card for the train guard.

'Hmm nice try but I'm not an usherette,' he quipped, handing her back an old cinema ticket. She chuckled at her own distractedness and groped around again in her pocket until she found the train ticket.

'Sorry, I'm a bit sleepy,' she protested, receiving a resigned sigh from the guard.

She leant back into her seat cushion and continued staring out of the window at the highland scenery. At this point in the journey it was almost steppe-like, open flats of scrub scarred by small rivulets. The train crossed a flat wooden bridge over one of the trickles of water and wove its way onward, across to the eastern mountains.

She thought how different it would be when she left the Highlands: and it was at that point that she knew she would indeed do that. The time was coming closer when she would spread her wings and start to explore a more far-flung horizon.

An hour later and she was in Inverness, walking from the station through the city centre, towards Old Edinburgh Road.

It was still raining, which happily allowed her to have an umbrella over her head without looking odd. It helped obscure her face from the view of anyone inside Glenda's house as she approached it, at least from the upstairs floor and she angled it towards the house to maximise the cover.

She glanced at her phone - her text message still hadn't been replied to.

As she walked past the front windows, from the other side of the street she noticed a small car parked on the stone flagged driveway and a light on in one of the ground floor rooms.

The knowledge that someone, presumably Glenda, was at home was encouraging in one sense, since it was unambiguous, but clearly she now had to wait for another pass or two and hope that Glenda had some chores or entertainment that took her out of the house at some point during the day. Or that the text bait worked.

She found a small cafe a little further down the street and had a cup of tea. No sugar. Gregor always said she was sweet enough without it. Twee, for sure, but it was still nice to hear him say it somehow. She grabbed the newspaper which was folded up in the rack by the door and proceeded to read it, column by column, cover to cover.

After an hour had passed and she felt she had received more than sufficient hospitality for the price of a cup of tea, she set off back down the street, still clutching her umbrella tightly and slowing her pace as she approached the house again.

The small car had gone. There was no longer a light switched on in the front room. Maybe the text had worked, even though she'd received no reply yet. Her heart leapt and to prevent herself chickening out of the next step, she crossed the road immediately, swung up hard against the row of conifers lining the drive and walked up the side of Glenda's driveway.

As she stole into the back yard, it became clear that it was reassuringly private. Well screened from the neighbours' gardens by a seven foot high wooden-lap fence all round a concreted yard, that was bare except for a few potted plants in one corner, arranged casually around a garden table and two chairs. Not a green-fingered gardener then, she thought.

She looked up - the kitchen on the ground floor had a small window left open but she noticed her position was visible from an upstairs window of one of the neighbours. She needed to calculate fast.

The fact that Glenda had taken the car was reassuring, it probably meant at least a shopping trip or a visit to friend's rather than out buying a newspaper, but there was no guarantee about that or the length of time she'd be out of the house. She'd still had no reply to the text, but the longer she waited, the more likely it was she would be caught before she had looked around fully. Standing outside the house just increased the possibility that a neighbour would spot her. She moved quickly towards the kitchen and inspected the main casement below the open awning window.

It was a standard arrangement with latches on both the side and bottom of the casement. However, neither of them appeared to have a lock on them, they were the original Victorian fittings by the look of them.

She hauled herself up onto the window ledge so that she was half-crouched on it and reached down through the open awning to the latches. She opened the side one with ease, then stretched down further towards the bottom one. She didn't have long arms so it was difficult, her jacket caught on the rough timber surround and ripped slightly, making her curse to herself. With a final push of her upper torso though, she managed to hook her middle finger around the painted metal strut and pull it free.

She was inside in a flash and quietly pulled the window shut behind her.

She stood perfectly still and listened. Only the tick of what sounded like a grandfather clock coming from the hallway, beyond the kitchen door, broke the silence. She need to move quickly and look for the study that Calum had described. The bedroom was also on her mind to explore early.

She moved forward and became aware of a faint glow in the built-in cooker. On closer inspection she saw that the grill was switched on. Did that mean there was someone in the house or had Glenda gone out expecting to return in a few minutes? In any case, she reasoned she didn't want it to catch fire whilst she was in the house, so she very carefully switched it off, muffling the click of the switch by holding both hands over the dial as she twisted it.

She made her way through into the hallway and spotted the study door open. She stepped quietly over the threshold.

39

Glenda had spent most of the morning preparing herself for the task looming ahead of her.

Her thoughts were laced with speculation over the reason behind the text she had found on her phone first thing that morning. It could hardly be from her son. So who was it? And why masquerade as her son to actually meet her?

It was more than suspicious and although the suggested meeting time at Inverness station was conveniently and strangely just before her planned train out of the same station, she wouldn't stand at the ticket office at 10:30. Instead she would watch from somewhere hidden, for as long as she could before the train left, to see if she could work out who was behind this. She decided to text back an acceptance just before 10:30. It might be better to keep whoever it was on tenterhooks, unsure if she would show.

With a small rucksack slung loosely over her shoulder, she locked the front door behind her, pausing to drive her VW Golf into the dilapidated brick and timber garage attached to the side of her house. She set out on the walk to Inverness station, with the spring in her step muted by the thoughts of what she had to achieve. If only Calum Neuman had worked alone this would have already been over. Now though, she was going to have to risk exposure of her true motives and freedom one more time.

Walking under the grey stony skies, passing grey stone houses made gloomy by the soaking of rain, the vista matched her sombre mood. Finally, the man who had imprisoned her heart for so many years was dead. He would not outlive her now, he wouldn't be able to enjoy another woman for a single moment longer. Why should he feel that he could do that, after he had let her down, when he had ruined a perfect love? He had deserved her retribution. No longer would she agonise over the thought of his body entwined with some other bitch. She wished she'd stayed to suck his blood into her mouth and spit it back over him.

With an umbrella above her head and her mind full of advance previews of an impending assassination, she arrived at Inverness station. She debated whether to have something to eat with her second-rate cup of tea - she had only had a slice of toast for breakfast. With that thought, her mind suddenly fizzed with alarm.

She had left the electric grill on: or had she? Yes, she was absolutely sure it wasn't the usual absent-minded uncertainty about leaving the lights on, when you were on the way to the airport for a holiday flight, which always proved to be unfounded. She was absolutely sure she had left it switched on. She cursed herself fiercely under her breath.

She realised there was no time to walk back home and check, so she reluctantly hailed a taxi from the station rank and asked the cabbie to do a quick round trip to Old Edinburgh Road, with a wait of a minute or two at the property. Given it was a circular trip back to the station the driver was naturally delighted and accepted her invitation to put his right foot down hard.

'Always like being asked to do that - almost beats "follow that car!"'

'Glad I could please you. I'll find something for you to follow next time.'

The frostiness in her voice shut him up for the rest of the mad dash to her house.

She remembered she was going to reply to the text invitation so hastily typed out *Ok. See you shortly.*

Within a minute or so, she jumped out of the cab and ran up the path to her front porch, fumbling with her keys as she approached it.

Once through the door she made a bee-line for the kitchen and found she had been mistaken after all. The grill was definitely switched off. But she noticed it was still warmer than she might have expected, which was odd, though in her current haste it made no real impression on her thoughts.

She was glad she'd made the trip back though - there was a small window open in the kitchen and she softly thanked providence for being there to close it, especially as she would be away overnight.

She closed it firmly and turned around to leave the house.

40

Jenna searched swiftly through the contents of the shelves around the study. There were dozens of books in here and she reasoned she wouldn't have time to look through them all, so picked out a few from the higher shelves and those that weren't covered by any amount of dust. She found nothing out of the ordinary, a few book marks with odd scribbles on them, none that made any sense to her.

She turned her attention to the writing desk. The top drawer was full of various stationery, paper clips, ink, staples, ball pen refills and the like. A second drawer was stacked with printer paper and a third one with old postcards. She picked these up and looked through them. She recognised none of the names. None had the surname Muir either, apart from those with Glenda's name on.

She rifled her way through the vertical letter slots in the top part of the bureau: amongst the bills and various business correspondence was a white envelope. She slid her hand inside and pulled out a photo of two children: boys, about the same age – around a year old maybe. Calum had mentioned Glenda had one photo of the twins as small children: maybe this was it. Nothing written on the flip-side. She hesitated a moment and then put it back in its place, realising a single copy might be missed fairly quickly.

She looked around the room. There was nothing else obviously worth searching, so she made her way back into the hallway. The wooden staircase led up from the left hand side and to the right was an old painted door, bolted at the top. The cellar, presumably.

She slid the bolt open and twisted the knob of the wooden handle. There was a light switch inside, on the wall at the top of the stair well. She pressed it.

It seemed to click twice, even though the light came on and stayed on.

Then she heard some more clicks, which were asynchronous to any of her own movements.

She suddenly became aware the sounds were behind her and that someone was coming through the front door. She slipped down onto the second step of the cellar stairs and pulled the door behind her quickly, her heart racing. She flipped the light off and leant against the wall to steady herself and tried to remain perfectly still. The step creaked as she moved into position and she instantly froze into a posture resembling a deranged scarecrow, desperate to avoid any further noise.

She heard some footsteps go right past the door she was standing so close to, through the hallway and into the kitchen. A small pause, then an exhalation of breath and a softly spoken 'fuck'. She waited, glued to the spot.

Her right hand, which was slipped inside her pocket, suddenly tingled with a vibration which nearly stopped her heart beating. A text message. Luckily the phone was on silent but the buzzing was still audible. She didn't think it could be heard through the door though.

After a moment or two, the footsteps retraced their path past her again and out through the front door, slamming it shut with some force.

She held her breath for almost another full minute until releasing it with relief. She wondered if the grill had been the reason for the visit. The visitor, which she presumed to be Glenda, had gone straight out again: that was probably signalling a fair amount of time for her to continue snooping around. She checked her phone for the text. Confirmed. So she had some time, but had better move quickly.

She made the best of it. After another minute of hesitation to ensure Glenda wasn't gong to return for some other reason, she decided she was safe. Starting in the cellar, she undertook a thorough search of all the rooms downstairs and then went up the creaking wooden staircase, to what she presumed to be the main bedroom. It was a darkly decorated room containing a large wrought iron bedstead adorned with pure white lacy bed linen, topped with a luxurious looking silk throw.

The built-in wardrobes concealed a number of over-stuffed shelves and drawers which she set about with gusto. Again, it was wasted effort, as were the bedside table drawers. She looked around the bed and then under it. There she found a small leather case, which looked like it had been manufactured well before the age of plastics.

She pulled it out, taking care not to do anything to it that could be noticed. She pushed the locking tab - it was either very stiff or locked. She sat and thought back to her search of the rest of the house, remembered a key in the bedside table and went to retrieve it. She pushed it into the keyhole. Bingo. That was *very* lucky. It fitted the lock and she slowly lifted the lid of the case.

It contained a large selection of photographs and newspaper cuttings. After a minute or so searching through them she soon established there was a link between each scrap in the case. They were all of or concerning one man: taken, cut or copied at varying ages. She knew him, she had seen pictures of him whilst doing the initial research for Calum. It was John Coulson.

There were dozens of them. Many photos of him as a young man, probably his student days by the look of the backgrounds. Then more sporadic photos of him in professional looking settings - most, if not all, of the later ones were screen dumps of internet pages. All jumbled up with a number of articles on his involvement in police cases, with his name highlighted in yellow marker wherever it appeared.

She realised she had seen no other photos or references to John anywhere else in the house. This stash was intended to be kept away from prying eyes and somehow signified a deeper, different relationship between Glenda and John Coulson than Calum and herself had perhaps understood.

John Coulson was also dead. Her spine tingled with a shiver and she suddenly wanted to get out of the house.

Jenna stuffed the case back under the bed, having replaced the contents as close to how she had found them as she could remember. As she pulled away from under the mattress, she noticed a slight gap between the mattress and the base of the bed: as if something was lodged under the mattress, close to the edge. She lifted the mattress a little to look: it was heavy though: 3 or 4 bottles of pills, one of which had caused the gap near the edge of the mattress, a red silk bag which was empty - and a pistol. She took a deep breath when she saw the weapon, then let the mattress flop back down; it was too heavy for her to hold up any longer. Her mind raced. Coulson hadn't been shot, had he? No, something else she thought. Strangled? She wasn't sure. Now she was well and truly spooked. She stood up and left the bedroom immediately, with an urgency driven by a rising sense of panic.

As she went back out through the kitchen, she noticed that the small window was closed. Glenda must have shut it. That was a problem, since she couldn't shut the large window as well as the awning above it completely. She climbed out through the main window, shut it successfully via the awning and then pushed the small window shut as best she could. It looked closed from the outside but from the inside the latch was not quite hooked home. She just hoped Glenda wouldn't notice or would pass it off as of no importance.

Scanning the street around her before she moved onto the path, she put her head down and walked hurriedly back to Inverness station. Remembering where Glenda probably now was, she took some side streets parallel to the main road until she got very close to the terminal.

Pulling the hood of her jacket down so it slewed across part of her face, she walked into the foyer, scanning as she went with her peripheral vision.

No sign of Glenda. She wondered what she would think of the no show. What the hell - no way she could tie her to it. She headed for her platform early and waited.

She was glad to reach the comforting security of the train, sitting lost in thought on the journey home about the significance of what she'd found. She'd broken one of her own rules, about public drinking, and bought a can of beer on the station platform before alighting the train. Feeling a need to calm her nerves, she cracked open the can seal and took a few deep draughts.

So Glenda had a thing about John Coulson. Not just the normal thing: a very big thing. Maybe a twisted one, at least a fixation or obsession. Moreover, she kept returning to the fact that John Coulson was dead.

*

Glenda had rushed back out of the house and into the waiting taxi.

The driver thought about asking her if she had got what she wanted, then decided against it. Best get on with getting her back to the station, judging by her mood.

She paid him with a sweep of her hand and a drop of a ten pound note which he missed, then recovered.

'Keep the change. Thanks.'

She scurried into the station entrance and walked around the opposite side from the ticket counters. No-one obviously idling there. She checked her watch - almost 10:30.

She took up a position from where she could watch the ticketing area from a distance and waited, reading the newspaper she'd stuffed into her bag. How she was supposed to recognise whoever had actually texted her though, was difficult to know. Could it have been Calum? She was hard pressed to think of anyone else with the right information and motivation just now. But she thought she had taken care of him.

Forty minutes passed uneventfully. She checked her phone: no more texts. This was as long as she could leave it. She needed to catch her train now. She walked briefly around the foyer one last time, with no result, then headed off to her platform.

She settled into her window seat and rang Mackie's taxis in Plockton, to book her ride from the station.

As she sat deep in thought in her seat, wondering whether to text back again and demand an explanation for the no show, she couldn't have known Jenna was seated in the next carriage.

41

The rain had hardly abated when the train drew into Plockton station. Glenda thought it useful - at least she could have a large cagoule hood over her head and maybe even wrap a thin scarf around her lower face. The one thing she needed to be careful of was bumping into Calum if he was in the village today. She thought it very unlikely that anyone else would recognise her, despite the close relationships of families around the sparsely populated Highlands. They lived on opposite coasts after all.

She hopped out of the carriage and turned smartly towards the platform exit, scanning ahead for a sign of her taxi.

There it was: a white saloon. She nodded a greeting to the driver and jumped into the back seat.

'Afternoon madam. Good job you booked me with all this rain then?'

'Indeed.'

The car windows had misted up with the cool rain outside and the driver's body warmth inside the parked car. Glenda rubbed the back of her hand over the glass, so she could see out. They started to turn right out of the car park and onto the road leading down to the loch and the village centre.

Suddenly Glenda caught her breath. Amongst the three or four people who had got off the train with her and who were now all making their way on foot down to the village, there was a young girl. A girl that reminded her of an image on a piece of paper she had in her bag. She started to fumble for it as she turned her head to keep the girl in view for as long as possible.

'Holiday or work?'

'Neither,' she snapped back.

The driver became the second owner of a taxi that day to decide Glenda wasn't worth the effort of conversation.

She asked to be dropped off on the loch front and bought a sandwich and drink in the village store. She positioned herself on a bench at the far end of Upper Harbour Road, huddled under an umbrella, and lit a cigarette. From there she could watch the whole harbour front relatively unobtrusively. Her thoughts drifted - the brief bit of surveillance of the proposed meeting at Inverness station had drawn a blank; no explanations for that strange episode came into her mind at all, except for completely wild ones.

She would watch the street for a while then take a look at Neuman's registered office. It was unlikely they would be working on a Saturday she thought, but the possibility needed to be excluded. She looked at the flimsy paper photograph of Jenna Strick she'd printed off from a web-site that Calum's investigation business maintained. She remonstrated with herself again for not spotting Jenna's presence on the site, when she'd originally taken a brief look around it before deciding to engage Calum.

At least she now had a way of recognising Jenna. The picture was very clear and Glenda felt sure that she would be certain it was Jenna if she saw her. She was now more certain that the girl outside the station had been her, even seen through the wet car window: so there was probably a good chance she would spot her sometime that day. It didn't occur to her to wonder where Jenna had been that morning. Her mind was firmly in forward gear.

After a miserable hour waiting in the rain, during which not many souls passed up the street, she consoled herself with the beef and mustard sandwich and another cigarette, washed it down with some Irn Bru and made her way to Neuman's office, which she'd researched on a street map the day before.

As expected the door was locked and no lights were noticeable inside. A quick peek through the side window showed what was apparently the office space, to be deserted.

The next step would be the three village hostelries. She planned to hover around all three during the afternoon and into the evening. So a second lunch in one and an evening meal in another with a drink or two in the third, would do to start. Plockton was a small, self-contained, place. If Jenna was here, she felt sure she would find her in a day or two.

A dreary afternoon ensued and it crawled inexorably into evening. The pub she found herself in for her evening meal livened up considerably with the arrival of some local folk musicians, which lifted her mood a little. Nonetheless at 10 p.m. she decided to leave for the night and come back the following day. With the last train long since gone, she called Mackie's again for a taxi and booked into an anonymous looking bed and breakfast place she had spotted near Strathcarron station. She checked in under a false name and paid cash.

Having eaten and drunk all day, in the interest of behaving as a normal patron at the pubs she'd been surveying, she simply needed a good night's sleep now. Surprisingly, she managed just that.

The following morning was accompanied by bright sunshine and a brisk wind. Glenda's bedroom curtains fluttered gaily as if delighted by the nature of the day. She awoke late, squinting her eyes in the sunlit room and rolling over to sleep some more. There wasn't much point in hanging around Plockton too early on a Sunday, she would only draw attention to herself and the pubs weren't open until lunchtime. The sun was good news though, she could wear dark glasses today to disguise herself without looking too conspicuous.

*

By the time she'd made it across to Plockton, it was late lunch time and with the breeze up, Calum Neuman had decided he would take a sail out on his windsurfer. It was a great day for it. He'd spotted Gregor getting a board ready too and asked him to do some racing to add spice to the afternoon. Gregor was always up for that.

'OK, out to the island and back first!' he yelled across the gap between them.

They pushed off together from the pebble shore, both pulling back hard and pumping their sails to get maximum acceleration.

The breeze was onshore and they both had to be careful to avoid each other as they tacked across to the small island halfway out into the loch. As they rounded it Calum was slightly in front and pressed home his advantage in the following wind to land first back at shore.

'1-0,' he exclaimed breathlessly.

'Ok, big guy, but now to Craggan isle - you won't win this one old man,' Gregor shot back.

They turned around and pushed off again, under the watchful eye of Glenda who had arrived in the village half an hour earlier and had been surveying the harbour from the same bench she had sat on in the teeming rain yesterday. She hadn't recognised Calum in his wet suit at first but once he had turned in the wind to face inland she knew him at once. At least she now knew where he was, despite wishing he was elsewhere, so that she could walk more freely around the village for a while.

As the two men left the water again, she noticed a young woman approach the loch-side. She sat up straight and scrutinised her more closely. She pulled the photo of Jenna out of her pocket again and compared the two.

It was her. She was a young and pretty girl. It seemed a shame but she had her in her sights now and tensed herself up to be ready to follow her wherever she went next. It struck her how easy it was to take someone else's life if you were determined enough. The difficult bit was to not get caught.

What happened next remained a blurred memory well after that day, for most of the actors in the scene.

Jenna shouted out across the water to the two windsurfers, it sounded like some kind of hello. Calum and the other surfer both turned to see who was shouting at them. Calum turned a bit too sharply it seemed and overbalanced on his board, slipping off it like a stone into the loch waters. As he slid a loud crack resounded around the harbour.

The surfers and Jenna looked up in surprise, together with a couple of other people on the harbour front. Then there was another crack and this time Calum jumped, bobbing around at the side of his surfboard. He shouted out to the other man and dived under the water. Another two sharp cracks and the area around the boards was lanced with flashing arcs of spray. The mixture of locals and tourists around the harbour front scattered like pheasants at an autumn shooting party, all mad flapping and tail feathers.

Glenda realised in amazement that someone was shooting at them. She crouched slightly herself, wondering what was going to happen next. Jenna started screaming and ran off out of sight somewhere, and then the shooting stopped. The second man had got out of the water and dived behind a rowing boat moored to the harbour side. Calum still hadn't appeared from under the water. She wasn't sure if he'd been hit or was just lying low for as long as his breath would last.

She had that question answered ten seconds later as Calum surfaced noisily, feverishly dragging himself out of the water on the harbour side right next to the boat the other man was lying behind. He joined him behind the makeshift shelter, as what turned out to be the final shot rang out, apparently doing no damage other than some splintering of the boat's planking.

Suddenly the air was punctuated by echoing shouts, people close to the harbour front were communicating with the two men lying behind the boat, persuading them to lie still until the police arrived.

Glenda knew immediately her opportunity had disappeared. She pressed her lips together in a bitter smile. An imminent police presence in the village was now guaranteed to make it much more risky to continue with her plans. She concluded it was better to retreat and live to fight another day. She shuffled away from her seat, up and out of the harbour, trudging nervously back to the train station via the brae over the village to catch the next train home. Her heart had sunk - she realised she knew who had been doing the shooting.

She had encouraged him though, hadn't she, so what was she to expect? She should have told him she had dealt with Calum, but he hadn't been easy to contact. He was a fool at times really, as well as a classic psychopath. She'd always felt he wasn't balanced like other people, even right back in the beginning.

As she sat in her second-class seat and sipped more poorly-made tea, she felt shaken badly off balance by what had happened in the harbour. Despite that, she thought there might be another way to get to Jenna. It might be risky given she'd effectively cut Calum out of continuing the investigation. Anything Jenna said to him about pursuing previous paths of investigation was likely to be met with a negative response from him. But it was only a small risk and one, she calculated, worth taking.

42

Alan Butler pulled his rifle apart and threw it into the holdall on the forest floor. He ripped off the cheap camouflage gear he was wearing and stashed that into the bag too. Neuman had been unbelievably lucky to avoid those shots and now he simply couldn't afford to stay there and hope that he and his friend might reappear from behind the boat any time soon. He had to run and run fast.

He raced down through the trees to the end of the track where he'd semi-concealed his car behind a clump of bushes, slung his bag into the boot and launched the car down the track towards the metalled road with an explosion of leaves and forest soil from under his rear tyres.

He knew he would have to drive long and hard now, he needed to be well away from this place before the police got to the site and started to comb the area for possible source points for the shots. He'd try to get to Glasgow before holing up somewhere in the anonymity of a big city.

He watched the first shot again in his mind in slow motion. He'd tracked the two windsurfers for a while before taking a shot, Neuman was coming directly towards him, pretty slowly and there wasn't much vertical movement from the surfboard, yet as he pulled the trigger and squeezed it past the point of no return, Neuman just suddenly turned and instantly disappeared from his viewfinder. It was unbelievable bad luck. To deepen his anguish, his second shot had been poor and missed altogether: his lack of practice over the years had counted for more than he'd expected.

He gripped the steering wheel as if he meant to squeeze every ounce of moisture out of the leather cover, partly through a need to keep the car on the downhill track but mostly through sheer anger. He swore over and over again, staring fixedly ahead while the scenery poured past him.

Sweat dribbled down the side of his temples and into the corner of his eyes where the salt started to sting. He wiped it away with a cursory brush of his shirt cuff. The track was bumpy and the speed he was driving didn't help the nauseous feeling starting to swell and gurgle inside his stomach.

He swerved round a right hand bend, throwing his wheels onto the edge of the track where the tyres lost traction momentarily, spraying loose dirt and vegetation into the trees, the car swaying on the verge of spinning. He straightened up and surged down a straight section to where the track joined the metalled road into Duirinish at a very acute angle.

He barely had time to look right over his shoulder as he joined the country road. The split second spent looking virtually backwards, though, was enough to remove any reaction time for the beast on the road ahead of him. It was ten yards away, straddling both sides of the narrow road and unavoidable. He had just begun to push his right foot onto the brake before the pedal tore backwards into his shin, propelled by fifteen hundred pounds of longhorn highland cattle.

He screamed violently as the pedal ripped backwards and the steering wheel hit his chest, padded by the exploding front airbag. He was momentarily aware of a terrible pain in his legs and a white powder haze swirling softly around his field of vision, before he lapsed into the haven of unconsciousness.

The cow screamed too and rolled over with the impact, allowing the car to finally lurch into its bulk and crush its ribs, tearing open its stomach. A flood of blood and partially-decomposed grass slid across the tarmac as the animal screamed one final time and thrashed its head down onto the road, knocking itself dead.

PART IV

DECEPTION

43

Glenda trudged up her front path and unlocked the front door, dropping her rucksack into the hallway and making a beeline for the kitchen. She needed proper tea, nothing else would do right now. A cigarette to accompany it was a close second.

As she entered the kitchen and filled the kettle with water, she noticed one of the small top windows was flapping in the breeze a little. It wasn't fully shut. Something clicked in her mind as she realised it was the window she'd closed when she had rushed back to switch off the grill the previous day. Then she remembered the grill was still unusually warm when she'd checked it. All at once she knew there had been someone in her house.

She made the tea and wandered carefully around the house with the cup of hot liquid in her hand, looking for any other signs of disturbance and ready to throw the cup at anything. She had picked up a carving knife in the other hand, just in case.

She couldn't find any other giveaways of anything odd, so finished the tea and got undressed. After a quick shower she made a fresh brew of Oolong to take to bed with her.

Settling somewhat nervously into bed with her laptop nestled onto the duvet on her thighs and a cigarette between her lips, she caught up with her emails. Nothing there to keep her awake. She started to think how exactly she might lay a trap in Facebook for Jenna Strick.

It was a shame she'd been so brusque in cutting off communications from Gordon's and Ben's accounts, but maybe there was a way to repair the electronic relationships and lure

Jenna into a convenient situation. She hadn't known who Jenna was at first, having a Facebook conversation with her had just helped the pages look a bit more realistic to a reader like Calum, so she'd gone along with it.

She picked up the separate laptop she had bought to use for the boys' Facebook accounts. It was second-hand and she thought it couldn't be easily traced. Setting up dummy accounts had seemed a good thing to do, to help create a credible story around the boys: Calum had taken the bait eventually it seemed, though she suspected Jenna had actually done the leg work. She smiled to herself at Calum's probable deception over his Facebook expertise: he was just trying to impress her. That made her feel a little crooked warmth inside.

After a number of attempts to get the wording right, she finally leant back for one final read of the private message she'd written to Jenna. It looked good and the wording and language were right for boys of their age. She pressed return and switched off the laptop, hoping there would be a reply by the morning.

It was time for her nightly dalliance with her love. Feeling under the bed with one hand, she pulled the old case out and opened the lock with the small key from her bedside table. Ironically, she thought that maybe she was going a little mad, fondly lusting after someone who was now a dead man.

Almost immediately she recognised there was something not quite right. The picture on top was in its normal place. But around the edges of it, she could see a different set of images to those she had come to know so well through her daily leaf through most of them.

One of the newspaper cuttings was out of chronological order and had become visible from the top, where it hadn't been so before.

She leant back onto the propped-up pillows. Now she was concerned. Together with the marks of some kind of entry into her house, this told her someone had been snooping around. She could only think of two possibilities: the police and Jenna Strick.

Calum was under her spell and the police ought to have a warrant. Jenna's persistence so far in the Facebook conversations had preyed on her mind over the last few days. Her thoughts hardened into an even firmer resolution to ensure the Jenna risk was eliminated as soon as possible. The police, if it had been them, would be far more difficult to deal with: but it didn't seem likely they would have broken in, found what they had and not been waiting for her when she returned home.

Her mind raced with thoughts and worry, making it hard for her to think of sleep. There was usually a sure fire way to help her do that, so she started to pull out each article or photo from the case and stare at it, dreaming her dreams of what she'd wanted, needed, but never got. She tenderly stroked one of her favourite photographs, imagining it being reciprocated, the curls of her hair pulled aside from her face by his fingertips. She closed her eyes and let the pleasure drift over her. She lay still for a while, her head starting to sink away into sleep, only for it to be brought back up to the surface by images of the open window.

This time it wasn't going to work. It seemed a sleepless night had beckoned her into its endless ache.

Seven miserable hours later she hauled herself out of bed and switched on her boys' laptop. There was no answer yet: it was too early to expect one; she turned it off again and went into the kitchen to begin the tea ritual.

She pulled out some bread and toasted it, spreading it thickly with kaya jam, an old favourite she'd picked up a liking for during time with her family in Singapore. The sweet coconut spread mingled with the cool butter inside the hot toast and made her relax a little. Now she had to wait. It was intensely irritating but she just had to wait.

44

It seemed an absolute eternity before four armed policemen arrived in Plockton and shepherded Calum and Gregor away from their makeshift shelter towards the safety of the nearest building, which happened to be one of the inns. They hunched their shoulders down and ran into the building under the protection of bullet-proof riot shields. The landlord produced two large brandies for the pair of them and then downed one himself for good measure.

Jenna was waiting inside, along with one or two of the regulars who had been trapped in the pub when the shooting started. She threw herself at Gregor as he came into view and hugged him tightly. At that moment she realised, even though her head was telling her she should leave Plockton soon for the wider world, her heart told her right then that it wasn't going to happen for a while yet.

'So who would be shooting at you two?' shouted the barman across the room. They both looked up at him with glazed stares and shrugged, remaining seated on two wooden chairs and sipping their brandies without uttering a word between them.

Jenna considered the question though – she'd been speculating on it herself since the shooting had happened. She couldn't help but think that somehow Glenda Muir might be involved. She had nothing concrete to substantiate that feeling, but Glenda was out of her house on Saturday and came back to check the grill. She had probably gone away somewhere. Was it to Plockton? And there was that woman in the taxi yesterday who had been staring at her. Something had worried her about that. It had been hard to make out her face clearly through the rain-smeared window; but had it been her?

She knew that wasn't a strong enough piece of information to base anything on, but it somehow spooked her. She also knew that she ought to tell Calum what she'd been up to in Inverness and what she'd found. He needed to make his own judgement on recent events. It was Calum who had been shot at after all - at least that was what she presumed, though it was entirely possible that Gregor had been the target. That thought really made her shiver.

'Hug me more, I'm still shaking,' Gregor said.

Calum looked on, pale as a sheet. 'Can you hug me too?' he said, in the general direction of the two of them. That utterance triggered a couple of the local village ladies, who up to that point had been feeling no more than helpless bystanders, to promptly sit down next to Calum and squeeze him hard from both sides.

One of the police officers was clearly in charge of the four of them and started to summarise the situation to all of the current inhabitants of the pub. He was a burly man in his forties, unshaven and looking more than a little bewildered. Calum thought he looked like he hadn't been expecting to be on duty today.

'Ok folks. We are currently keeping everyone here until we can be sure we are not going to get any more shots fired at anyone. So please bear with us until we can give you folks the all clear on that. We've blocked off the routes into and out of the village for the moment, to control the risk. I need to talk to one or two people now to gather some more information.'

With that, he walked over to Gregor and Calum and sat down with them. He asked those sat close around them to move to the other side of the bar. Then the questions began.

'DI Johnston. I believe you were the two men shot at originally? I need to ask you exactly what happened. Firstly, did you see which direction the shots came from?'

'Well not exactly,' ventured Gregor. 'But the shots that hit the boat seemed to be coming from across the harbour rather than from the village. I expect you can tell from the bullet holes in the boat?'

'Aye we'll get someone out there to take a quick look and see what ammunition we can find. We've asked for support to scour the area so we'll start over the far side of the harbour anyway. Is there anyone you think could have wanted to do this?'

Calum and Gregor shook their heads and said no in absolutely perfect unison. They looked almost comical to Jenna. She coughed a half laugh, borne out of intense nervousness.

They all remained in an almost dreamlike state of shock, for a further two hours or so, before the police gave them permission to go home, along with the other members of the public who had been in the inn. Gregor went with Jenna to her flat and Calum to his own place.

He hadn't been there long when his mother rang, enquiring anxiously as to his safety. Even though it was well meant, Calum felt irritated after the initial exchange as she insisted he go round to her house for a while. For some reason his assertion that he was fine on his own, was treated with as much disdain as a small boy refusing to put on a raincoat when venturing out to school on a cold grey morning. In the end she couldn't be resisted, so he picked up his jacket angrily and walked up to the other end of the village where she lived in a small terraced house.

At least he would have done were it not for the five people, three microphones and a portable, shoulder-held video camera, all looking and pointing directly into his face as he stepped out on the pavement.

Cuillin FM, BBC Radio Scotland, West Highland Free Press and the Ross-shire Journal had been the first of the media to the scene. It always amazed Calum how quickly they found out, or how speedily the police gave their press contacts the nod. Then again, there were plenty of busybody types who would alert the press too, for the sake of feeling fleetingly important.

'Calum Neuman? John Hancock, BBC Radio Scotland, I'd like to ask you few questions about the incident this afternoon. Is that ok? Do you know why you were targeted for this shooting?'

Calum tensed himself, tried not to react to the provocative and assumptive questions that flowed one after the other from all of the reporters in front of him. His brain was telling him to say no comment and for once it managed to override his natural reaction to kick out.

He rubbed his chin and lowered his head slightly. 'Sorry everyone, no comment right now. Please leave me for the moment, I'm not exactly in the right state to talk about it, I'm sure you understand. Now... if you'll all excuse me?'

That was much easier to say than to get done. For such a small group of people they made it quite difficult for him to leave his front door and eventually he had to physically push one of the bunch aside to make a way through them. Gently, of course. They followed him for a few steps until he turned round to confront them.

'Ok, that's it. No further please. I'm going to my mother's home and do not want her subjected to any of this. Please go away and I'll talk to you all tomorrow.'

He knew he might regret that promise but it had the desired effect, after one or two muttered grumbles from the BBC team and a suggestion of a 9 a.m. session the next day. He turned purposefully on his heel and strode away to his mother's house, as the reporters watched carefully as to where he was disappearing, for future reference.

His mother opened the door as he approached, obviously waiting for him from behind the curtains. She ushered him in and hugged him briefly.

'How about a nice cup of tea?'

'Some whisky would be better please Mum.'

She pulled an impatient face at him.

Here we go again he thought. His mother had been this way with him ever since his father had drunk himself into an early grave at the age of fifty-eight. Understandable he supposed, but he wasn't an alcoholic and had no intention of becoming one. He felt trapped by his knowledge of his mother's experience of countless nights with a comatose drunk, curtailing his own freedom to have a drink when he felt like one.

'Well, I suppose in the circumstances it's reasonable,' she grumbled, as she went across the room to the small wooden bureau upon which was displayed a solitary bottle of whisky. He had always thought it strange she had kept any alcohol in the house since his father's death. Maybe that one bottle was a kind of mobile tombstone, a reminder to all of the dangers within.

She poured him less than a pub measure and handed it to him with a resigned look.

'What did the police say? What happened? Mrs Jackson from next door told me she'd heard shooting but I didn't hear it myself.'

For the next thirty minutes he answered her questions, trying to remain calm and not get irritated, though it was difficult. He was released from his interrogation by the ring of his mobile phone.

It was DI Johnston, whose muffled voice could be heard set against a police siren and car engines.

'We've found a man who we think may have been the one shooting at you. He's been in a car accident and looks barely alive but he has a rifle with him. I'll send a car down to you, can you come up and see if you recognise him please?'

Ten minutes later a car arrived and whisked him off up towards the Duncraig crags. The sunlight was starting to fade and the tall tree line cast thick blurred shadows across the narrow road as they sped around the harbour edges and up into the woods around the crags.

The car swung hard round a left hand bend into a cauldron of lights, police officers and crime scene tape barriers.

Calum was directed out of the car towards the centre of the incredibly bright searchlights and to what his eyes were slowly adapting to tell him was a wrecked silver saloon.

'It's a pretty nasty scene, I hope you don't mind,' said a firm, clear voice that ambushed him as he arrived at the saloon. DI Johnston appeared alongside him.

'He's in the ambulance, they're about to set off. Come with me quickly.'

The ambulance filtered into Calum's vision like a ghostly apparition, on the far side of the glare of the lights. The rear loading doors were still open and a paramedic was attending to the occupant of the slide-in stretcher with an oxygen mask.

'Do you recognise him? From the ID on him it seems his name is Alan Butler.'

Calum hesitated. The name was familiar but he didn't recognise the man.

'Well no, his face doesn't look familiar. But his name does ring a bell.'

'You know him?'

'I'm not sure, it just seems familiar but I don't know why at the moment. I'll have a think and let you know if I get any inspiration.'

Johnston appeared a little crestfallen. 'Ok well here's my number, call me when you remember.' He pressed his calling card into Calum's left hand.

'I need to travel with this gentleman to the hospital. We'll talk later.'

It was a command rather than a request.

With that he leapt up into the ambulance and shut the door. It disappeared swiftly down the hill. Calum was left holding the card in one hand and his chin in the other, scratching it slowly in deep thought. He couldn't retrieve the detail around the name of Alan Butler from his memory, but he knew it somehow: he'd do a search of his old files immediately.

He was offered a police lift back to the village and asked to be dropped off at his office.

45

Calum had entered his office wondering if he'd left the lights on after the previous occasion he'd been there. It turned out Jenna was in the building too. Surprising at this time of the evening.

'Hard man eh? Shot at in the morning and still in the office on Sunday evening?' Jenna teased Calum, wanting to rise above the events of the day for more reasons than one.

'Just call me Arnie! I guess I could say the same about you... how's Gregor?'

'Shaken obviously, a bit stirred too. He's starting to ask who the target was. He's gone home and I said I wouldn't be long here. What happened up there?'

'Well it seems they have found the guy who shot at us, he's in a bad way, looks to have hit a cow with his car. They're taking him to hospital, but I wanted to research his name... it seemed familiar. Alan Butler.'

'Never heard of him. Anyway I've done what I need to do, I'll see you later.'

Jenna packed up her papers, switched off the laptop in double quick time and disappeared swiftly. She didn't want any questions from Calum at this point. That was overriding her natural curiosity to stay and find out whether Calum did indeed know the attacker. Calum started to wonder why she had been in the office on Sunday but, equally, didn't ask before she left. He was too impatient to start his own investigation into Alan Butler. He half thought this was something he could ask Ellie to search for and just tell him what she found but quickly dismissed that - he wanted a quick answer and she may turn up some details that were inappropriate for her. That was a *really* silly idea.

It didn't take long for his efforts to bear fruit.

Searching his computer's hard drive for the name threw up a few references, all pointing to a case early on in his investigating career. He'd assisted in an issue which had eventually been handed over to the police force. There had been an element of criminality which he wasn't able to pursue comfortably and which his client realised needed the full attention of the police.

His internal light-bulb went on with a vengeance and simultaneously illuminated the solutions to two unanswered questions.

He had remembered a few days ago that John Coulson was mutually involved with a case some years back and he had meant to fully check it out - but had never got around to it - he'd totally lost interest in the Muir assignment now. The information staring at him from the computer screen confirmed that Coulson had indeed been associated with a case he'd worked on: and also that the suspect in the case was none other than Alan Butler. A psychopathic stalker, later turned would-be murderer.

The horror of the implication dawned on him, slowly at first, then with a rush that pushed his heartbeat downward into his stomach.

He probably *had* been the sniper's target.

He made a call to James Beery to check Butler's release date. Even though it was a Sunday evening, James was able to help him out and confirmed Butler's release had been less than two weeks back.

He wondered how many more shocks he was going to get. Two people murdered and an attempt on his own life, even if unrelated, were unsettling his grasp on the certainty of a life tomorrow. On the other hand, it seemed there *were* some definite connections. He became convinced it was all more than just coincidence.

He called DI Johnston with the news.

The detective was quick to fuse all the recent events together.

'Ok, so we have a psychopath who has you and John Coulson in his sights for revenge immediately he leaves jail. Coulson dies, you were lucky to escape the shooting and I suspect we'll find the death of the lady in Garda that you told me about, was somehow related. We'll check Butler's movements but I'm pretty confident we'll find traces of him in Italy, unless he's been particularly clever in covering his tracks.'

'I suppose it makes sense. I don't understand why Rosa was part of this but I guess she could have been a piece in his revenge scenario. Strange he didn't try to kill me too in Italy if that were the case? Unless he thought he *was* killing me that night?'

'Hmm, well we'll possibly never work that out unless Butler recovers and decides to co-operate, but if we can trace him to Italy in that period of time, I'd say we know it was him. Proving it might be another matter, of course.'

'Any news on his condition?'

'Not too good, but I understand he'll live. When he's in a fit state, we can interview him. He might decide to come clean: those who have planned and taken revenge often do, in my experience. It's a big relief for them when they finally nail a person who's been in their sights for a long time: if Coulson *was*. They often need to share it, even sometimes with the police. I'll be in touch when we've more news.'

Calum put the phone receiver down and heaved a huge sigh. It was comforting that the police were so clear in their interpretation of the dreadful events of the past couple of weeks. He'd noticed he had struggled to think clearly about Coulson and his two boys recently; for some reason whenever his mind alighted on that subject, it felt like he had walked into an opposing magnetic field which pushed his mind backwards. He put it down to weariness and shock and also started to worry whether he was approaching the age when his mental agility was starting to diminish.

What was really taking centre stage in his mind was shock at how vindictive some people could be. A criminal with a conviction decides to take revenge on those that helped cement the case that proved he actually *was* evil. He wondered what justification Butler had created for himself, to justify his actions. That kind of nagging need to return some hurt was alien to Calum's psyche.

The events of the day and the receding effects of constant adrenaline pumping around his arteries had started to take their toll and he suddenly felt very weary. He walked down the street to his home, hardly registering the police cars parked at either end of Harbour Street and slept soundly for ten hours.

*

Jenna, on the other hand, had been suffering a rather more tortured attempt at sleeping.

As if it wasn't enough to be wrestling with the question of what to do with the knowledge of Glenda's secret stash of John Coulson memorabilia, she now had another challenge. Gordon had sent her a Facebook message suggesting she join him and some friends for a drink on Tuesday night. This, after a request to end their message chats only a few days previously. He apologised for the de-friending, saying it had been finger trouble on his keyboard and meant for someone else. That sounded false, given Ben had de-friended her around the same time. What was even odder was that he'd suggested meeting up in Portree, on the Isle of Skye. That seemed eerily close to Plockton.

On both counts, she had to decide whether or not to share this information with Calum. The same Calum who had been shot at, so wasn't going to be at his affable best.

If she didn't tell him, then she would risk his wrath later on. But if she did report this all back to him, given his current mood over the case, there was every chance she would be told to drop it. Logically, that was probably the right thing to do but she smelt a rat amongst these latest events and it wasn't in her nature to drop an interesting lead against her instinct. Gregor often described her as his Rottweiler, which she thought a bit unfair as she was pretty relaxed about most things.

Nonetheless, there was a warning signal flashing at the back of her mind. It felt completely wrong that Gordon had now invited her, but there was pressure to accept, given it was she that had tried to start the friendship. It also felt slightly dangerous and somehow that was attracting her. She observed the conflict in her mind with a coolness somewhat beyond her age.

She'd stayed over with Gregor; he needed the comfort of someone to hug through the night, which she understood completely. But her mental battle with herself had kept her far from sleep. That, and the heat of his body combined with his nocturnal thrashings, conspired to leave her exhausted. By the time the first few shreds of violet light had crept under the blanket of night and gently lifted it towards dawn, she was craving some more sleep.

She poured herself quietly out from under the duvet and walked wearily down the stairs to make herself some coffee. She cradled the mug in both hands, staring out through the back window at the soft folds of velvet sky that signalled a fresh new day.

She had made a decision. She would meet Gordon and explore Glenda's past relationship with Coulson somehow.

Furthermore, she would keep all of this from Calum for a little while longer.

46

Gregor stumbled downstairs around 10 a.m., dishevelled, unshaven and looking distinctly un-refreshed. Jenna smiled at him and ran her hands through his hair and around his neck.

'Coffee my love?' she mocked him softly.

Gregor grunted a muffled 'Mmmmm,' and sat down at the kitchen table, awaiting service.

She stayed with him all morning, talking about the events of the previous day and trying, in doing so, to pull his spirit back up into its usual zone. After making him some lunch, she excused herself, saying she needed to catch up with Calum and headed off to the office. Whilst she didn't think she would be expected at work this morning after yesterday's traumas, it *was* Monday after all.

She found Calum in the office, sitting at his desk. Not surprising to her: he was a pretty level-headed person and wasn't likely to suffer *much* emotional damage whatever life dealt him.

'How's Greg?' he asked.

'He's got man shock. I expect the police will want to speak to him today. I think he's dreading going round the questioning loop again with them.'

His eyes widened in genuine shock at her apparent flippancy.

'Man shock! He's been shot at for heaven's sake. What did you give him for that, two Paracetamol?

Anyway. Actually he wasn't shot at, so I doubt he'll get much more questioning. I worked out who Alan Butler is and it seems it was me he was after, not Gregor. I'm surprised they haven't told Greg already. I got told this morning Butler is likely to pull through ok, so no doubt the police will be questioning him as soon as they can.'

Jenna leant against the door frame and stared at him intently.

'But why was it you he was trying to shoot?'

'Well, putting two and two together, I'd say it was because I helped early on in a police case that resulted in convicting and imprisoning him. It looks like pure revenge. I checked the files last night after you'd gone. Given John Coulson also worked on that case, I'd say Butler's a prime suspect for his murder too.'

'John Coulson worked on it too? You didn't tell me that! When did you realise that?'

Jenna checked herself. She'd probably been too aggressive in her question and tried to calm herself.

'I don't tell you everything Jenna. It occurred to me a few days back that I might have known Coulson from somewhere, but to be honest I didn't think it was relevant, just a coincidence.'

Jenna grimaced. 'Well at least there's some logical explanation to what happened in the harbour then,' she offered.

He nodded wearily. 'Maybe we can get back now to some normal investigating work eh? A nice case of a cheating wife to spy on or something equally mundane will suit me fine for a month or so now.'

Jenna knew he'd be bored with that within a fortnight but kept silent. She had some sympathy with him but couldn't help feel intrigued with meeting Gordon and finding out more about Glenda Muir.

'I'll go and tell Gregor then... and maybe pop back here later if that's ok with you? I feel pretty tired to be honest, didn't sleep too much.'

'Sure, I think we all need a little time to settle back to normality.'

All of us except you, she thought as she picked up her jacket and left. She had no intention of returning to Gregor's, instead she made her way home and settled down with her personal laptop. She called Gregor first to tell him the news about Alan Butler, then put her mind to work on Glenda.

She started by scribbling down some notes on how she might look further into Glenda's past and character. There was always lots of material on the web if anyone could be persistent enough to work through it, especially around an academic who might have published research papers and the like. There was Paul Proudson, whom Calum had eventually mentioned to her later on in the case, as a former boyfriend, albeit a long time ago. There was Gordon, whom she was now certainly going to agree to meet the following evening, who hadn't seen his mother since he was too young to remember, but may have picked up things from his father.

Beyond that she struggled; any other avenues or contacts would probably only be uncovered by the initial work on the web.

She set about the search task immediately. She made copious notes on every reference she could find, of which there were around 150 on the first pass through. She listed the names of every person who seemed to have had some relationship with her, which were primarily professional, grouping them into categories based on which element of her life they'd touched. She'd published a fair amount of papers on various aspects of hypnosis. It didn't seem worth reading them in detail as they mostly appeared as a foreign language to Jenna, but she scanned them all for any people references or interesting aspects. In the end, it was only people's names that she wrote down, nothing else surfaced that took her attention.

Glenda had obviously had a strong side-line in private hypnotherapy. Jenna joked with herself that she must have hypnotised Calum to drop the case, given his attitude to the assignment after his last interview with her. From the references it appeared that she'd been practising privately from around five years after her graduation.

All mildly interesting but none of it raised any concerns or *helped*. She pulled all the references together again and started to write them into a chronological sequence.

As she did this, one aspect stood out starkly from the paper in front of her. There was a gap in the timeline. A gap of two years or more, about a year after she graduated. There were simply no references at all, although there were pointers to her first post-graduation year, in the employ of the university. Not necessarily unusual. She may have done some travelling before she got stuck into a career. But even so...

She thought back to Calum's first interview with Glenda. She logged onto the office server and pulled the notes up on her laptop.

It wasn't clear from the notes when exactly she had the children or when exactly she had split up with John and bade farewell to the boys, but it looked to be around the start of that blank period. The only obvious way to find out was to ask someone from her university days, but where could she start? There must be a large doubt anyway, as to whether anyone she found would choose to tell her anything personal. She paused and wondered whether Paul Proudson would help her. Worth a try... but first there was the matter of Gordon.

She logged back on to Facebook and dropped him a short reply agreeing to meet up on Tuesday night. About an hour later she'd had a response. He'd suggested meeting at the Zoo bar in Portree at eight – and thought they could get some food there too.

It all seemed too straightforward; clinical almost. There was no real warmth in his messages, just some fairly routine 'hi, how are you's' that left her with no more clue as to his personality. Bizarrely, she realised, it made her more determined to meet him.

She looked up at the clock: it was 6 p.m. She would grab a quick snack and then call Paul, by which time, she assumed, he would be home.

47

It was almost 9 p.m. by the time Jenna called Paul Proudson. She found his number in Calum's contacts in the office email account. He answered the call so quickly she wondered if he had been about to dial someone himself.

Evidently he had been drinking. His slightly elongated vowels and delayed responses betraying his attempted air of sobriety.

'Ah... yes... hi Jenna, Calum has mentioned you once or twice. How are you?'

'Fine, fine. I wanted to pick your brains over some things on the Glenda Muir case. You remember Calum spoke to you about her a while back? Are you ok to speak for a few minutes? Sorry it's a bit late.'

'Fire away, it's a bad night on the television anyway.'

'Well, so, Calum said you once had a relationship with Glenda – he mentioned it after the two of you spoke a little while ago. I've been researching Glenda's past and there seems to be something of a black hole of information about her for a period of about two years at what would have been the end of her degree course. I wondered if you have any thoughts on that?'

She heard a long sigh, which sounded like tiredness, rather than boredom or pain from the question.

'Well, Calum's been spreading my personal life around hasn't he?!'

She smirked to herself.

'Not really, just the odd thing useful to the case... Calum's not a tittle-tattle, you know?'

Loyal girl this one, he thought. Calum did seem to get lucky with things like that. Maybe he was just good at relationships.

'I guess so. Well, as Calum might have told you, I didn't know her for long and to be honest didn't hardly see her again for the whole of my time at university. It was a brief fling, early in my first year there. I vaguely remember someone telling me she had 'gone off the rails' a couple of years later on but I never knew any details. It wouldn't surprise me if she had, she was a bit intense... almost to the point of being a little erratic and even unstable at times. But that's it really.'

'Can you think of anyone, maybe the person who mentioned Glenda's situation to you or someone else, who might be able to cast light on that episode... whatever it was?'

'Let me think,' he said. 'I guess I can probably think of one or two people from around her course or who knew people on that degree stream... '

'Any names I can contact?'

'Well, no. I mean, let me talk to a couple of people to see if I can find a way to contact them. It'll be easier than you calling them cold. They're much more likely to tell me something that's sensitive, if there is anything like that to be told.'

'Oh that's brilliant, Paul. Let me know then. Do you think you can do it this week?'

She could almost hear him smile.

'Sure, sure. You're pushy, but... sure. What are Calum's thoughts on this though?'

She took a deep breath. She needed this bit to go well.

'He doesn't know I'm calling you. Would you mind keeping it quiet for now? It's just that Calum seems to have completely lost interest in the case. To be fair it kind of came to a natural conclusion but there's something odd about the way he's been acting since he last met Glenda - and from what he used to say about her, she sounds a bit unusual to me. Almost weird. I want to do some more digging around before I put it all together for him.'

'What kind of things about Glenda? Tell me, I'm intrigued?'

'Well, nothing I want to talk about yet really. I want to dig some more first. I hope you understand.'

'Ok. Well, Calum's a lucky man to have such a committed assistant. Alright, I'll call you as soon as I can. I'm not sure I really like going behind Calum's back though. So promise me you'll come clean with him, with whatever we find? Miss super sleuth?'

Jenna agreed and blushed as she put the phone down, smiling contentedly to herself.

Her thoughts drifted to tomorrow and she started to ponder on what she might wear for her meeting with Gordon. Nice, attractive. Not too sexy... but maybe a little. That should do it. If it *was* Gordon, she wanted to loosen his tongue...

48

Calum was doing the job he hated most: case close down. When an investigation was effectively done, he made a point of writing up any final observations and tidying the remaining loose ends as quickly as possible. He'd been putting off closing down the Glenda Muir case. He didn't really know why he'd found this one so hard; he usually forced himself to do it the day after he agreed an instruction from his client to finish. As well as being good routine for him not to delay a job he didn't like doing, he needed to get his invoices out promptly.

Nonetheless, for some reason he'd found it very difficult to start this one. His mind sheared away from the prospect every time he tried to entice it to his desk. It wasn't just about starting the job either. It was exceptionally hard to concentrate on doing the various bits and pieces: expense receipts collation, totalling, invoicing, etc. He wondered if it was his recent stressful experiences taking some kind of toll and contemplated taking another holiday soon. The memory of Rosina soon dampened that idea, and brought the same dull, sick feeling back into his stomach that he'd felt when the police had told him of her murder.

He hadn't been in a good mood to start with in any case. The meeting with the press to which he'd reluctantly agreed for 9 a.m., had been a painful experience. It wasn't something he felt at home with. Being a private investigator, for him, meant just that: private. He'd managed to squeeze his way out of it after fifteen minutes of mostly meaningless exchanges, leaving some slightly exasperated hacks behind.

Still, he felt violated and angry. His own private world had started to come under a public microscope.

He rubbed his temples hard and let out a long sigh before dragging his attention back to the screen.

He finished the final invoice and had started to collect all the various electronic notes and documents into one folder marked as *complete*, when he came across a couple of files whose title he didn't recognise. The first one, entitled 'GM notes' appeared to describe various aspects of Glenda Muir's life, ranging from school to her current professional work. The second, which was labelled 'GM chronology', had the same contents as the first at first glance but arranged into a timeline.

He sat back, scratched his stubble with the tips of his fingernails and delved deeper, inspecting the timeline more thoroughly. As he scanned the chronology, he noticed there were some notes around her relationship with John Coulson that had an addendum 'ref: case under bed'.

There was only one person who could have written these files: Jenna. He checked by reading the files' properties: there indeed the author had been auto-recorded as Jenna. The last edit times were showing as yesterday.

'Shit. God damnit. Why's she done this after I told her to stop?' he whispered to himself.

He felt his anger rise quickly and sat with his head in his hands, massaging his temples again in astonishment and disbelief.

There was no reason he could think of for her to have not mentioned these notes to him, especially as the files were edited since the investigation was closed. What was more, the reference to a case under a bed was worrying: what did she mean, whose bed and what was in the case?

Even though it was late, his instinct was to call her straight away. After a little thought, he decided to chew it over for the rest of the evening and talk to her first thing the next morning; it was out of character for Jenna not to keep him up to date with her research - there might be a reason that would make her defensive about why she'd kept it from him. He needed to think carefully about how he would approach her with it. He couldn't work out why she'd left the files in full view on the server. Maybe she'd saved them there by mistake, rather than on her laptop's hard drive. It wouldn't be the first time she hadn't been aware of where she was saving documents on their office network.

Although some undefined pressure in his mind was pulling him away from doing it, he printed off the chronology and took it to bed with him. It was a relaxing place to read and by experience he often found a new perspective on things by reading propped up on his pillows, cosily surrounded by the duvet.

By the time he flicked off the yellowish glow of his bedside light, he had noticed one or two things about Jenna's view of Glenda's life that worried him.

49

Procuring illegal poison at short notice had been a bit of a challenge. Glenda had her professional career to thank for solving that particular problem. Her work in clinical psychology and hypnotherapy had brought her into contact with more than a few characters who lived in society's twilight zones. One or two had become her friends and some her lovers - though she was always very careful she went down that particular route only after their treatment had finished.

Yesterday, she'd managed to lever one of those past relationships to her advantage. A pharmacist with a lust for older women had been putty in her hands, both mentally and, after his present to her, physically. She had left him in bed, with the closed sign on the glass door pane of his shop and some sodium cyanide in her pocket. Stupid man. But weren't they all?

Ever since she'd received a positive response from Jenna Strick, she'd been thinking carefully how best to achieve her aim on Tuesday evening. She hadn't met Jenna so she felt reasonably confident she needn't worry too much about being recognised. If only she could have seduced the bitch. That would have been easier and squared a nice neat circle with Calum. But she'd never had the stomach for intimacy with other women.

She would set off early in the morning. She wanted to visit the bar at lunch time and get a detailed scene in her head, then she could plan carefully for what she'd outlined in her mind. Headscarf and dark glasses seemed a good idea for the rest of the day. As she looked in her rear view mirror, she saw the image of a fifties movie star and imagined herself travelling in an open top sports car on a mountain road somewhere in Italy, with Gregory Peck beside her.

As she sped across the highland plateau, she remembered why she lived in northern Scotland. The bleakness. The dour weather. The resilient people. It was all so exquisitely sombre and depressing. It satisfied her dark soul. So would killing the bitch. Especially after she had seen and read on her Facebook page how close Jenna was to her boyfriend. Sick how some people were so happy.

She pushed a CD firmly into the open drive in the dashboard. Roy Harper was a bit before her time but she'd discovered him via an older lover. The opening chords to Another Day made her smile darkly. This wasn't going to be just another day.

The mountains and lochs flowed past her and it was lunchtime by the time she arrived at the Skye bridge and took the road up towards Portree. The yellow gorse was vibrant along the hillsides and the sun had just started to slice through what had been a cloudy day as she dropped into the town and parked her car a suitable distance from the bar. A pretentious name she thought: Zoo.

She walked into the bar and ordered a mineral water. There was hardly anyone in the place and judging by its decor and the advertisements she'd seen on its website, it was aimed primarily at the evening crowd.

The bar was long, with chromium fittings and up lighters set into glass. The stereotypical cocktail bar. Away from the bar area, tables were placed all the way around a long rectangular room, centred on a small dance floor with a number of tiny booths set off each wall. She hoped Jenna would sit somewhere in a busy spot when she arrived. No obvious CCTV though.

She had seen enough for now. Her main concern was how soon the bar would fill up. She wanted it to be crowded when Jenna was there - given that it was tourist season and bearing in mind that the small town of Portree was hardly a late night hot spot, she thought 8 p.m. might be about right. On the other hand, maybe she could update Jenna with a slightly later time, just to be sure.

Jenna and Gordon had exchanged phone numbers in their last conversation on Facebook. She texted Jenna with a revised start time of 9 p.m. on the cheap phone she'd bought from a market stall and then headed off to the other end of town. She'd already switched her own phone off; she wasn't sure how GPS tracking worked but she wasn't going to take any chances.

She parked the car in a quiet spot overlooking the sea and tried to concentrate on reading a novel to pass the time. Stephen King was her thing. Every few paragraphs she read, though, were interspersed by images of Jenna in the bar, Jenna ordering a drink, Jenna drinking that first order - pictures of herself walking past Jenna with a sinister delivery concealed in her hand - thinking how she would feel walking out of the bar afterwards, struggling to stop herself running away, screaming silently to herself that she was going to get caught.

Real life, though, has a habit of ruining all the dress rehearsals you care to make.

Despite the tiresome activity of her mind, she managed to read some lengthy passages, before closing the book to watch the clock on her dashboard as it spiralled round and round towards evening.

She flipped Roy Harper back on. He'd got as far as Don't You Hate the White Man?

She was resolute now. She sang along, replacing Man with Bitch. It made her feel ready - ready to kill.

She needed to eat first and set off for the fish and chip takeaway she'd spotted a little further back down the road. A good portion of protein wrapped in batter was what her choppy stomach needed right now.

50

Calum awoke the next morning to the strains of classical music on his alarm radio. It was a soothing way to start the day. Much more peaceful than listening to the interminable ramblings of a self-important DJ twittering about something they thought was funny enough to share with the rest of the country. Maybe he was getting old.

He'd been awake during the night, turning over and over in his mind the discoveries of the previous evening. His biggest worry still, was why Jenna had worked on this after being told the case was shut and hadn't told him. The reference to a case under the bed was particularly troubling him - if it was the bed he was hoping it wasn't, then why had she done it and how on earth had she got herself into a position to be able to get under the said bed.

There was also the gap in the time line document he'd found. Perhaps it was a blank because Jenna hadn't been able to research anything to fill it, or because there was a more sinister explanation. He preferred the former answer and thought it the most probable one, but he'd learnt over the years that he needed to keep all options on his mind's table.

After a shower, tea and toast, he strode down the harbour to the office, announcing his arrival as he walked into the hallway. There was no answer. Maybe Jenna would be in a little later, although, he reminded himself, he *had* told her to take some time off. He decided to leave it until 10 a.m. and call her if she hadn't showed up by then.

He heard the post arrive on the doormat and went to collect it. Amongst the typical assortment of junk mail that always disappoints its recipient, eternally hoping for an unexpected tax refund, was a letter from the Cystic Fibrosis Trust. It contained some details of a fundraising event in Edinburgh the following month that he'd volunteered to help with. An occasional offer of his time was the least he could do, given all the help he'd received from the immensely kind people he'd met there during Ellie's life.

He pencilled the details into his diary and wrote a note confirming his involvement. He sometimes wondered if this was love for Ellie by proxy, something to make up for the deficit in attention he actually gave her.

Some days, like today, life felt really tough. Recent events, a reminder of his daughter's condition, doubts about Jenna's openness, all combined to push him towards jumping into what he thought of as his lifeboat mentality. He just wanted to hide and ride in it, shutting off the external world, safe and protected. Sometimes it didn't quite reach that level of calm and hovered between the two extremes, a kind of numb journey through a watery desert, buffeted by a swell that refused to be ignored.

After some coffee, and given her non-appearance, he dialled Jenna's mobile. The call went straight to her voice mail message. She didn't have a land-line so he put on his jacket and walked round to her flat. There was no response to the door bell. He paused and thought for a moment, then walked on to Gregor's place. There was no-one there either. Gregor might be at any one of his many day time jobs, so he walked around the village via the obvious possibilities, before he found him in one of the pubs, getting the bar ready for lunchtime opening.

'Hi Greg, seen Jenna this morning?'

'Nope, not since yesterday morning. She not in work?'

'Well no, but I did tell her to take some time off. You didn't waste time getting back on the bicycle!'

'Too long off it and you forget how to keep your balance,' quipped Gregor.

'Well, call me if you see her?'

'Sure. It's odd, I thought she might have popped round to see me this morning too.'

Calum left Gregor looking slightly puzzled, which was a much more diluted version of what he was feeling himself, and walked back to the office.

*

He had only just crossed the threshold when his mobile lit up with Cassie's name across the screen.

'Hi, what's up?'

'Ellie took a bad turn this morning, the doctors seem worried.'

He heard Cassie catch the last couple of words in her throat and whimper softly.

His heart skipped a beat and he could feel himself starting to think that this was all he needed; he shook his head softly and told himself off for feeling anything like that.

'Oh, oh dear. Shall I come?'

'Yeah. Yes please.'

It sounded like a plea as well as an answer.

He sighed.

'Ok I'd better drive over then... be there as soon as I can. Are you at the hospital now?'

'Yes. Dring ward. It's an ICU. Come straight in.'

He clicked the phone off and turned around, heading for his car. It shouldn't take too long on a summer's day during the middle of the morning.

In fact a couple of cow herds and some slow moving vehicles frustrated his drive and he arrived at the end of lunchtime. He thought about Ellie during every minute of the journey, right up to when he perched the car half over a pavement in the overcrowded hospital car park. He walked straight through to the ward, where he found Cassie sat wearily in a bedside chair, dozing gently.

'Hi. You not get much sleep?'

She looked up with a start, rubbing her pale blue eyes slowly. He'd always loved the colour of her eyes.

'No. I came in really early this morning after the hospital called me. She's been on antibiotics for over 24 hours though, so hopefully she'll improve now. Not had anything to eat either. Sorry, I need to go to the loo, I'll be right back.'

'Sure, take your time, get some breakfast. I'll sit with Ellie.'

She jumped up quickly, startling Calum in the process and causing his daughter to moan softly. He looked over at her.

Ellie's face was pale and sweaty.

It was how she often looked during the bad episodes of her illness. He consoled himself with the thought that she looked no worse than usual, letting out a soft breath of relief. He wondered if it was misplaced, he knew he couldn't tell what was happening inside Ellie's lungs.

He watched her for a while, and then spoke to her softly, whilst Cassie was still out of the room.

'Hi angel. How do you feel? Don't worry if it's too hard.'

'Bit tight, breath... ' she wheezed.

'Bit better than last night though... not as hot... '

'Ah that's good then, the antibiotics must have started to kick in.' He smiled encouragingly at her. At the back of his mind, he had started to think about Jenna and what she was up to. He simply couldn't help his mind straying. He had a bad feeling about this somehow.

'Well, I'll stay a while; see how you go on eh?'

He took her hand and squeezed it affectionately. Ellie reciprocated, weakly.

The door handle behind him clicked and Cassie walked back into the room.

'Sorry about that, just got caught short, must have nodded off for a while and missed my morning toilet slot.'

'Too much information!' declared Calum, who surprised himself with a little laugh.

'Well I gobbled a bacon roll on the way back too, thanks.'

Before he started to struggle with what to say next, a doctor in blue scrubs entered the room.

'Morning, Ellie. Oh I see Mum and Dad are both here. Well, I assume it's Mum and Dad? How are you feeling this morning?'

'A bit better I think.'

He introduced himself as Dr. Jordan to Calum and proceeded to check Ellie's temperature and chest.

'Mmm looks like the drugs are starting to work nicely. We'll give them another 24 hours then hopefully you might be well enough to get up out of bed. Let's not rush it though eh?'

Cassie and Calum both looked at each other and shared a restrained, optimistic smile.

The doctor had disappeared almost before they had returned their gaze to Ellie.

'Thanks,' Calum shouted after him through the door as he stalked down the corridor and turned swiftly into another side room.

'Good news, hey love?'

Ellie smiled and nodded. Cassie moved over to sit on the bed and put her hand on Ellie's forehead, stroking some wisps of hair away.

'She does seem less feverish,' she declared.

'Well, I'll go get a sandwich, haven't had any lunch. Want anything more Cass?'

'Nope. I'm fine thanks, you go and get something.'

He wandered down the corridor, following the signs to the WRVS shop and stood in a short queue while he surveyed the sandwich selection and picked out his choice.

'And a cup of tea please,' he said.

He sat down briefly to take a few sips of the tea. It tasted tainted in the white Styrofoam cup. He wondered if he should stay much longer. He knew there wasn't much he could do and not a lot he could think to say to Cassie - Ellie couldn't speak too much either. Maybe he'd stay an hour then head back.

He shuffled back into the room, sat down on his chair and started to eat his sandwich.

'What is it, Dad?'

Calum looked at her quizzically.

'The sandwich?'

'Hmm you must be slightly better if you're wondering about food. Beef and onion. Want some?'

She shook her head and smiled faintly.

'You got anything more for me to help you with, Dad?'

Her voice kept fading intermittently, like a bad signal on a mobile.

'Err, no not at the moment love. I'll let you know when there is,' Calum replied with an involuntary glance at Cassie. She frowned and was about to say something.

'Well, I'll stay a little longer and maybe go about three. Want to watch some TV?'

She shook her head again, as Cassie look disapprovingly at his suggestion.

The next thirty minutes passed slowly.

Cassie talked about a weekend trip to a theme park they had planned; no doubt to lift Ellie's spirits. Calum told Ellie a little about some of the more interesting cases he'd worked on recently - names withheld and adult detail skipped of course. It was a somewhat tortuous experience and Calum finally broached the possibility of actually leaving. The whole process reminded him of not wanting to be the first person to get up and leave a party.

He kissed Ellie, waved goodbye to both of them and trudged dispiritedly down the corridor. He hadn't gone far before the balance of his attention tilted towards Jenna again.

He walked out into the car park, meeting a cool breeze. It had clouded over and was chilly for mid-summer, even by Highland standards. He unlocked his car door - he was half into his seat when his eye caught sight of the all too familiar piece of sticky plastic covering a parking ticket plastered onto the bottom of his windscreen.

He sighed loud and long, ripping it up and throwing it into the back seat, wondering what kind of excuse might be enough to get it rescinded. He fired up the engine, squeezing the accelerator tightly under his foot out of frustration and began the drive home.

51

After his return from Inverness, Calum spent the remains of the afternoon searching through the rest of Jenna's work on the case. He was still finding it very hard to concentrate for some reason, but his concern for Jenna was somehow helping him win the battle for focus.

There was little more of interest, so he turned his attention to her email account. He was reluctant to open it; even though he had always known that her password was, rather unimaginatively, the name of her boyfriend. He hadn't used that knowledge before today, but instinct told him to log on and read what he could find. He clicked open the inbox and scrolled down through the recent arrivals, her sent mail and some folders she'd created.

It didn't take long to spot something of interest. There was an email in her inbox from Paul Proudson. He noted it and looked through the rest of the folders. That was the only significant email he could find. He opened it.

His blood pressure took a significant jump skyward.

Tried to call you Jenna but no joy. Basically, I've got a bit of insight into the gap in Glenda Muir's CV. One of the guys I knew from her course stream stayed in touch with her for a little while after university. Apparently she had a kind of breakdown or something similar, Robbie (my friend) mentioned morbid jealousy, I'm not sure if that's a condition or just a phrase? Something to do with her relationship with John Coulson breaking down. Sounded pretty serious, I believe she was in an institution for a period of time.

Anyway, that's all I have for now. Call me if you want! Don't forget you promised to tell Calum as soon as I came back to you.

He conceded that he was apparently supposed to be being brought up to date with events shortly, judging by the last sentence, but it looked like it was Paul that was suggesting it, rather than Jenna. He couldn't understand what had got into her.

Despite his anger with Jenna, he nonetheless found himself enticed by the information Paul had dug up. With an intuitive sense that he'd discovered the tip of an iceberg, he searched for the term "morbid jealousy".

This disorder occurs when a person typically makes repeated accusations that their spouse or sexual partner is being unfaithful, based on insignificant, minimal or no evidence, often citing seemingly normal or everyday events or material to back up their claims.

Unlike other delusional disorders, people who suffer from this disorder have a strong association with stalking, sabotage or even violence. It can be found in the context of schizophrenia and delusional disorder, such as bipolar disorder, but is also associated with alcoholism and sexual dysfunction and has been reported after neurological illness.

Men and women differ dramatically when it comes to morbid jealousy. Men who suffer from morbid jealousy are more likely than women to use violence and also are more likely to harm or kill with their hands rather than a blunt object. Women on the other hand, when using violence, tend to use a blunt object or knife... the final resort to stopping infidelity inside of morbid jealousy is to commit partner murder.

So many possible angles on Paul's information sprang from these first few sentences. Too many. His mind raced, though still somehow constrained by a mental pressure to avert his mind from the subject, a pressure which was beginning to irritate him. He forced his mind forward, trying to match the various aspects of the definition with everything else still burgeoning in his head regarding the Muir case and Jenna.

His mind was now tortured by the fact he couldn't contact Jenna. The fact that someone affected by morbid jealously might turn to violence was also worrying him; the obvious assumption might be that Glenda had killed John Coulson. Or was that his over active imagination? This was all based on someone's memory of what had affected her all those years ago. He decided he should call either Glenda or James Beerly to follow this through. Again his mind was, subconsciously, pushed away from Glenda and he chose James. Maybe there was some update on the Coulson murder that might help pull this into perspective.

He closed the email, marked it as unread, and shut down the system. Then he called James, unaware of how this was going to prove to be such a pivotal decision.

'Hi it's James. Leave me a message, I'll get back to you soon. Thanks.'

Damn. He tried his mobile too, only to hear the same message.

Before he had time to think of his next move, James called him back.

'Sorry mate, on the loo.'

'Oh, too much information! Listen James, I wondered if anything more had happened on the Coulson case - just that one or two pieces of information have turned up here which *could* be worrying and I wanted to see if anything matched with what you'd turned up now?'

'Well, no firm suspects still. We know how, where and when. It's the simple who and why that we're still working on.'

'Ok. Maybe it's nothing but Glenda Muir and John Coulson had a relationship which seems to have been associated with a period of mental illness for Glenda. I don't want to set false hares running but, well, just a thought.'

'Send me what you've got Calum. Always worth a look when you get your head into something. I'll follow it up and let you know. By the way, we did eventually establish that Coulson has no children. You know, Jenna was asking about them originally? Not sure where she got that idea from?'

Calum froze and suddenly felt his brain tearing into overdrive. He screwed his face up and scowled at the phone microphone.

'How do you know that for sure?'

'We asked his partner and looked at his medical and tax records and... no sign of kids. Looked pretty clear cut to me Calum.'

That sounded pretty conclusive. He needed to drop this call and think through what it meant.

'Look, Glenda Muir said the whole reason for the case was to find her children for her. Now you're saying they don't exist. Coulson is dead. I need to speak to Glenda and work out what this really means. I suggest you do too - let's compare notes later. I'm beginning to worry about Jenna. She continued to investigate the case unbeknown to me and definitely against my instructions. Now I can't find her. It might be nothing but I need to check out exactly where she is, as a priority. I'll call you later James... and thanks.'

'Sure friend. You've given me some food for thought there, thanks. I think I may need to speak to Miss Muir myself... talk later.'

Calum sat with his head drooped, supported at the temples by two fingers, his elbows dug into the desk top. He was thinking furiously about Jenna's situation and alarm bells were ringing along every synapse in his brain, which was making it difficult to work out which one to listen to first.

One thought did bubble up to the front of his mind though. Not one he felt entirely comfortable with but he hoped the need would justify the means. He pulled out the small address book in which he kept the various IDs and passwords he needed to operate in the internet world. He found the one he wanted and took a deep breath. This might be risky. He wondered if one of Jenna's friends might spot him logging into Facebook or know it wasn't Jenna somehow and tell her. That could cause a real rumpus with Jenna: and he wasn't savvy enough about Facebook mechanics to really know how risky it was.

He'd often noticed her inputting her password and he'd kept a note of it just in case. He decided this *was* that case and he started to scroll through her conversations with Gordon Muir.

He felt almost electrocuted by the final exchanges about meeting in Portree at 8 p.m. He looked at his watch: it was exactly 8 p.m. Right now, his information was that Gordon didn't exist. So who the hell was the Gordon Muir she was talking to on Facebook and now meeting up with? He headed straight out of the door for his car.

52

The daylight was still almost at full brightness at this time of the year in the Highlands and Calum put his foot down as best he could through the narrow roads down to Kyle. He was five minutes from the Skye bridge when he swept round a left hand bend to be faced by the rear end of a multitude of cows, slowly being led up the road, on the way to the milking sheds. He banged the steering wheel in frustration, inadvertently blasting the horn briefly and causing a couple of the cows to shuffle sideways and the herdsman to glower at him as if he had driven over both of them.

He sat back, realising there was nothing he could do except wait for the herd to move onto the track to the farm. He had no idea how far away that was. He blew out a heavy sigh of quasi-relaxation and drummed the fingers of both hands frantically on the steering wheel. Ten minutes later he has was able to press on again, waving a hurried goodbye to the herdsman and crossed the bridge after 8:30, pushing on towards Portree.

When he arrived it was past 9:30. He parked his car erratically on a street close to the bar, half on the pavement and ran the remaining hundred yards to the place. It reminded him he could do with being a bit fitter. He slowed to a halt, took a few deep breaths and entered the bar cautiously. By the time he made it there, there was no sign of Jenna. She'd said on Facebook she would be wearing a yellow hat so that Gordon could easily spot her. He knew the hat well. He thought she wore it to annoy him, it was so damn unlike what *she* expected he would regard as suitable office clothes. In reality he didn't care what she wore. Right now he'd happily buy her ten more hats if he could find her safe and sound. Now, he was really worried.

He walked purposefully over to the bar itself. There was a fair crowd in, but he managed to get the barman's attention quickly.

'Hey, did you see a girl in here earlier, yellow hat, kind of cookie-looking? Maybe with a guy or two?'

'In fact I did man, yeah. She left in a hurry a little while ago, I saw her being sick outside the front door. She must have had more than I thought, but she got helped away by a woman and a guy into a car I think. Just got a glimpse from here, I was busy serving ... '

Calum's mind spun yet again.

'Can you describe them?'

'Who wants to know?'

The old routine barter. He pulled out his wallet and pushed a ten pound note over the bar.

'A colleague. Please?'

'Yeah a young guy, dark hair... and an older woman, long hair, looked blond from here.'

'The woman was tall? In her forties?'

'Aye, I'd say so.'

'Thanks. See which direction the car took or what it looked like?'

'Well off to the right, it was silver I think, couldn't see right well from here and I wasn't really taking notice like I said.'

'Ah fine that's helpful, thanks.'

Knowing he had as much information as he was likely to get from the barman, Calum turned towards the door. Then he remembered something.

'Was there a guy in here with a grey baseball cap, no logo, about eighteen?'

'Umm... lemme think... yeah, he was here earlier. Left a while ago. Sorry, but I need to serve these people now... '

Calum reset his thoughts for what seemed the tenth time that day.

So the twins didn't exist but one of those non-existent boys, or someone matching the description given to Jenna on Facebook, had possibly been here. It sounded like Glenda *and* Gordon had helped Jenna into a car. This was no simple coincidence - especially as he was here around the same time as Jenna. What the hell was going on?

He knew had to talk to Glenda but he'd begun to realise that he would have to be very careful what he said to her. He walked back to the bar, ordered a cola and went into a quiet corner to think quickly about that call. Yet again he felt the sense that he was unable to approach Glenda, but the worry about Jenna was starting to override that now. After ten minutes, he rehearsed his intended words and went outside to make the call.

53

Jenna had woken early. She knew there were quite a few things that could blow her off track from meeting Gordon that evening. For one, Gregor might want to see her later at the pub. Calum would soon start thinking she might be back at work, especially as she had already been back in the office once, even though he'd said she didn't need to rush back. She might also chicken out.

She decided she would stretch out Calum's offer of some leave of absence, take today off and get some retail therapy to calm her nerves. A couple of new tops, some lunch and a catch up with a girl friend would keep her out of harm's way, so she set off for Inverness on the first train, returning in the late afternoon. She took the brae path back to her house to avoid seeing Calum or Gregor or anyone else who might alert them to her whereabouts.

She wandered off the path a little, scrambling down a stony incline into a bowl-shaped area resembling a small amphitheatre. She sat down on one of the banks and peered over the open air church. It had been here since the Free Church movement had started in the mid-1800s, at a time when the church was heavily politicised. Groups of independent-minded people had set up these places so they could worship free of other influences. Now, it was just a grassy depression overlooking the end of the harbour, but she imagined how it would have been filled years ago by local village people, worshipping in the rain on inclement days.

Her mind was starting to focus on the evening ahead. She stared out over the loch to the grey crags beyond. It was a last chance to question whether meeting Gordon was a smart thing to do. She wasn't really too bothered about what Calum or Gregor might think about it. It was her own choice and she was only concerned with assessing the danger to herself. In reality she decided in an instant, but sat still for a few minutes, enjoying the solitude and warming sun before picking herself up off the grass and striding back up the brae.

She tripped along the remaining rough stone pathway down into the village and slunk into her flat, with an intention to get on the road to Portree pretty sharply. At least she had an extra hour now that Gordon had changed the meet time.

Her battered red Fiat was a focus of pride: she'd only been able to buy it by way of a gift of money from her grandmother, after her A level exam results. Most of the money had gone on the insurance, leaving just enough for this ten year old specimen. A quick change and make-up took longer than expected, because she couldn't decide how hard to try with her overall appearance. In the end she wiped off some of the make-up and dressed down a little from the outfit she'd started with. She jumped in the car, gunned the ignition and set off briskly on the road down to Kyle of Lochalsh, towards the Skye bridge.

She struggled to concentrate on the driving, which was a risky situation to be in given the one-track roads down to Kyle. Not every driver drove carefully and on one stretch she had to take a rather bumpy drive along a grass verge when she didn't recognise an oncoming driver's speed early enough. She felt as if she was floating slightly above reality, pushed on by an irresistible force: a bit like the final few hours before her A level exams.

She kept asking herself: why did he want to see her now, what sort of information was he likely to share with her, wittingly or otherwise - and where would that lead with Glenda? She told herself she would find out soon. She also told herself that her mother and most of her friends would not approve of her meeting someone via an internet contact, without some friendly company. It was risky and the tension pressed her foot down even harder on the accelerator.

Soon she was over the bridge and following the road north towards Portree, eventually dropping down into town via the same route that Glenda had taken not so long beforehand. She parked in town just as her mobile flashed up Gregor's name silently on the screen. She picked the call up.

'Hi Greg. How's things?' Before he had time to answer, she thought she would take an offensive approach.

'By the way, wondered what you are doing tomorrow night, there's a film on in Kyle I'd like to see.'

'Err yeah, sure my love, can do.'

'Cool, will sort it out tomorrow then. I can't talk now though, signal is going to fade on the next bit: I'm on the train, I met up with Mica, you remember from school? We met up in Inverness; I'll be late back tonight so call you tomorrow?'

'Yeah sure, OK. Love you.'

She felt smug at the ease with which she had turned what was a probable invitation to the pub tonight, into a different conversation altogether. Sometimes, she knew, she was too sharp for her own good.

She started to click the phone off and spotted there was a missed call from Calum. She picked up his voice message enquiring as to her readiness to return to work. It came across as slightly edgy and that unnerved her; Calum was usually pretty laid back and had offered the time off after all. She sent him a text saying she was feeling better and would be in the office tomorrow. Hopefully that would be enough for now.

It had been a warm day but it was cooling down now. She put on a light cotton jacket from the back seat and then a yellow hat: the one she'd told Gordon to look out for. She looked at her watch; it was 8:35 p.m. A little early, but she wasn't the sort of person to get hung up about being fashionably late and set off for the bar, which was set on a quiet side street just a few minutes away from the seafront. She walked in through the bling-smart glass door and over to the bar.

She looked for Gordon; he'd described himself in some detail and said he would wear a grey coloured baseball cap with no logo, until she arrived, at which point the embarrassment would be shoved firmly back into his pocket. It had made her smile.

He didn't appear to have arrived yet, though it was hard to see for sure as there was a surprisingly good crowd in the place for a Tuesday night. She looked around again: a mixture of tourists, students, locals - but mostly youngish. No, Gordon and a baseball cap with no logo were definitely not present.

Jenna ordered herself a sparkling water and some peanuts and sat at the bar nibbling the nuts until they were all gone. It had just turned 9 p.m. and she was feeling pretty nervous so she ordered a vodka and tonic to smooth the edges of her jitters. She thought she would call Gordon to check on his progress and pulled her mobile out of her jeans pocket. No signal. The walls were probably too thick in this old building, she thought - and the signal strength around large parts of the island wasn't terrific anyway. She walked quickly out to the front door and dialled his number. No reply. She stood there for a moment before sending him a text saying she was in the bar and how long would he be. She waited for a delivery report and walked slowly back to her seat.

9.15 came and went.

She finished the dregs of the sparkling water and raised the vodka and tonic to her lips.

Then her phone chirped again. It was a text. Funny how they could get into the bar but not out. She put the glass down, her lips barely wet with the alcohol and pulled the phone out of her pocket impatiently. In her haste, her right elbow slid on the glassy bar surface and propelled her glass a couple of feet further down the bar and over the edge of the counter. She cursed herself and glanced at the text.

Really sorry Jenna, delayed by one of the guys, will definitely be there by 9:30-ish. Sorry!

Ok. He had better be she thought, pressing her lips together tightly.

She also noticed a new email from Paul Proudson, in her office account. She opened it.

Ok. So Glenda had been in an institution after her break up with Coulson. That was worrying. She wondered how that related to Coulson's death. It sent doubts racing around her head about the meeting with Gordon too... for the simple reason that she didn't understand where Glenda really fitted into this. The whole situation made her increasingly anxious.

And her heart was starting to race; much faster than just feeling nervous should be causing.

She stood up to retrieve her glass. The barman was looking at her as if he suspected drunkenness was the cause of the glass missile a few seconds before. She stared at him and noticed the edges of his face had taken on a soft focus. She moved her attention to the missing glass and leant over the bar to try to locate it. It, too, was looking distinctly jellylike around the edges.

She leant back into an upright position, trying to make sense of what she was seeing and overbalanced backwards slightly. She would have fallen if it were not for a group of local girls stood in a group behind her.

'Hey watch yourself,' one of them spat at her, trying to contain the spillage from the drink in her hand.

The words hardly registered with Jenna, as she found herself suddenly feeling very nauseous. Grabbing her bag she fled straight for the front entrance and was shocked to find herself vomiting a sheet of baked beans and bile over the path outside the door. She stumbled, her body ending up wrapped around the door frame. She became aware of a sharp pain in her gut and her limbs were draining strength at an alarming rate.

She slid towards the floor, desperately trying to hold on to reality in the shape of a door post, breaking nails as she dragged them across the wood and sweating coldly across her forehead.

It was as she slumped against the outside wall adjacent to the door, that she became aware of a woman's voice and a faint shadow being cast over her.

'Stay there, I'll take you to the hospital, I'll just pull the car round.'

'I'm... I'll be ok... who...?' were the last words Jenna uttered before everything started to go dark.

She wasn't really aware of being pulled into a car, or of the woman who had spoken to her being assisted by a passer-by, keen to help in an apparent emergency. There was a smell of plastic all around her face as she drifted into unconsciousness, face pressed into the join of the back seat cushioning. It felt like she was suffocating.

She also didn't know anything about the long car journey to Inverness and the challenge her body presented to the woman in trying to smuggle it down into her cellar.

54

Stupid bitch. How damn clumsy could she have been?

Glenda held her breath for nearly a minute watching Jenna, to see if that first sip had been enough to strangle the life out of her pathetic little body.

She had watched her knock her glass over and lean over the bar until all she could see was blue denims, then rear backwards into a group of girls. There seemed to have been a bit of an altercation and then Jenna had stumbled quickly towards the door.

This wasn't in the plan. She knew she needed to make a snap judgement. If Jenna survived the poison, things could get very messy. She would almost certainly tell the police why she had been there. She had to be sure that Jenna would die. Her heart pounded even faster than its already astronomic rate, as she hurriedly decided she would either have to give her more poison in the car and then dispose of the body, or move her somewhere else to finish the task.

She sprinted to her car and brought it next to the front entrance of the bar. By then Jenna was sitting up against the outside wall, held up only by the friction of her jacket against the rough stone, by the looks of her sideways lean. To try to administer more of the poison would create a huge risk of being seen. No way could she do that now.

Glenda was wary of making herself known to Jenna but knew she had to do that now. She spoke to her, told her it would be all right and that she would take her for treatment at the hospital. She was aware of someone stood behind her, a young man in a black jacket and jogging pants.

'She alright? Too much booze?'

People make judgements too quickly sometimes, she thought.

'Yes I think so. Can you help me with her into the car, young man? I want to get her to hospital quickly without having to wait for an ambulance?'

The man looked at her, thinking about a question, but it didn't make it to his lips before Glenda motioned for him to grab Jenna's legs. He complied - there was something about the way Glenda Muir gave instructions that made it hard to resist.

It was still a struggle to get the girl's body into the back seat. She grunted involuntarily as she fell back across the rear cushioning and Glenda pulled her head up and swivelled her legs round into a vaguely upright position, before strapping a seat belt around her.

'Thanks so much. I need to rush.'

The man stared at her as she jumped into the front seat, banged the door shut and floored the accelerator. A question came tumbling out quietly from between his lips.

'Is she going to be ok?'

Glenda didn't hear him. She was too busy careering down the street, trying not to break the speed limit. She mustn't be stopped by the police now and a speed camera photo of her would be evidence that would be difficult to shake off.

She was soon clear of the town and Skye, then the well-known dangers of the country roads forced her to focus on driving safely, before she calmed down a little. Maybe she would take Jenna home. The worry was whether she would wake before then.

She pulled off the road into a farm track entrance, drove down it fifty yards and got out of the car. She opened the back door and sat next to Jenna. Her chest seemed quite still underneath her thin jacket. Her mouth however, was emanating small wisps of breath, condensing in the cold, clear evening air.

She felt Jenna's wrist and pulse. Her skin was cool and her pulse was steady, though rather fast. Her breathing was shallow. Glenda wasn't quite sure how to interpret all of these signs but her instinct told her that she wasn't going to break through into consciousness imminently. She briefly considered dribbling more poison into her mouth but then realised she didn't have a clue as to where she could hide the body in this area.

Panic started to grip her. Having your drink spiked in a crowded bar would create lots of anonymous suspects. A body just off the main road to Inverness was a different thing altogether. She resolved to press on homeward - she could park her car at the back of her house and move the body inside with little risk of being seen. Then she could consider her next move a little more clinically.

She stepped outside again and rummaged around in her boot, pulling out an old tow rope and a couple of blankets she kept in there for emergencies. She needed to guard against Jenna waking up on the journey, unlikely as it seemed.

Pulling Jenna's heavy, dead weight sideways, she managed to strap her under both rear seat-belts and bind her wrists together with the tow-rope. She wasn't sure it would hold well if she struggled; the rope was thick and hard for her to pull tightly into a knot. It would have to do though. She threw a blanket over Jenna's body, twisting it under her head and one of the seat belts, to make it hard for her to pull it free if she woke. She laid the other blanket over her, spread wide to disguise her body shape.

She leant against the car a while, breathing deeply after the exertions of manipulating an unresponsive body and weighed down by the uncertainty of what she would do once she arrived home. She spared herself a few minutes for a cigarette, blowing the smoke out of her lungs in long blasts, trying to calm herself and to analyse the situation. Pressing on to get home as soon as possible still seemed the best option to her clouded mind.

She lit another cigarette with the butt of the old one.

She sucked a deep draw into her lungs and shut her eyes tightly, holding her breath. As her brain swam with the nicotine and lack of fresh oxygen, a face in a white hood came into view. Her pulse quickened even more and her stomach went into a tight gripping spasm. She saw the flash of the dagger, blurred pictographs along its blade, streaked with the dark red blood of the man she had loved *and* come to hate. Her bile rose and suddenly she lurched forward and vomited into the grass.

She fell against the side of the car for a moment, recovering, feeling the air flood back into her lungs and revive her. Her mind flung her back into the present, and the body on her back seat.

She pulled herself wearily down into the front seat again and re-joined the main road, heading for home.

PART V

DISCLOSURE

55

In fact Calum made two calls. He'd thought it might be more sensible to try Jenna again first. The call went straight to voice-mail though, probably switched off or out of signal range.

He took a deep breath, let his rehearsed words fly through his mind again momentarily and then dialled Glenda.

Same result.

Damn. There was really only one course of action he felt he could and should take now. Somehow he knew Jenna must have been to Glenda's house to find the case she mentioned in the notes he'd discovered. It was the only obvious place to go to now.

He set off on the road down to the mainland bridge and resigned himself to the long drive over to Inverness.

It took him a little over two hours. He started to feel famished and stopped outside the city at a fast food drive-through, to pick up a burger and eat at the wheel. He hadn't eaten since lunchtime. Strange how tension and activity could make you forget your body's normal needs. Then when something broke your focus, just a little and for only a moment or two, it all came flooding into your senses with a vengeance.

Now he needed to do what had been on his mind for the whole journey: tell the police what had happened and what he was up to. Whilst he wanted to find Jenna himself, he'd realised as he drove through the bleak central highland landscape that he could end up in an unexpected predicament at his destination. A confrontation, if it happened, that might turn nastier than he would hope. There was an unpredictability about the whole situation now.

He dialled Beerly again. It was late, but he picked up, thankfully.

He started to gabble nervously.

'James. Listen, it looked like Jenna had been invited to meet one of the boys that you say don't exist. I went to the bar in Portree. She was there according to the barman but was seen drunk, getting into a car helped by a woman, who matches Glenda's description, and a young man. The barman also thinks someone matching the description Gordon Muir gave to Jenna on Facebook was there... he left a bit earlier according to the barman, or at least I think he did. I'm on my way to Glenda's house now. I can't raise Glenda or Jenna on their mobile phones.'

He was now feeling embarrassed to be telling James that things had got this far without a call to the police, and waited for the inevitable.

'Well you know you should have called before it got to this point, if there was anything worrying going on. But I'm not sure this is anything we need to intervene in. Your assistant gets drunk. She drives off somewhere. I'm not sure what grounds there are for the police to get involved?'

He nearly reacted angrily but he needed to keep his police contacts onside. He flicked through the facts again - and thought James might just be being realistically cynical. An experienced policeman doing his job in other words.

'I guess so,' was his reply, accompanied by pursed lips and a scowling face.

'Jenna isn't like this though. She's been investigating Glenda behind my back. It isn't like her to get drunk either. I can't think of a reason to meet Glenda when she was supposed to be meeting the son either. There's no mention of Glenda in the Facebook conversations. It feels wrong James. I'm going over to see Glenda with or without your help. I'll let you know what happens.'

'Fair enough. I'll keep an open mind on it. But for now...'

Calum ground his teeth together tightly in frustration. He hadn't been *that* concerned about the police intervening as such, he'd just felt he should tell them. So much for honesty being the best policy. He looked at his watch. 11.55 p.m. He straightened himself up in the seat and pointed his car towards the city centre.

Twenty minutes later he was parked outside Glenda's house. He noticed there was no car on the drive. He got out of his car cautiously, after first checking there was no possibility of anyone seeing him from a window, then walked briskly down the side of the drive way to a point where he could see most of the rear of the house.

Glenda's car was parked down there, close to a back door which looked like it led into the kitchen. It struck him as odd. Most people park on their drive, they don't drive to the back of the house, mostly because it makes it harder to get the car out onto the road the next day. Human beings usually gravitate towards laziness.

As far as he could make out, there were no lights on anywhere in the house.

After his decision to drive here and confront Glenda, he suddenly found himself seized by indecision. It was very late and he couldn't be sure that Glenda was the woman seen assisting Jenna. What if she had just been driven home by a well meaning passer-by? Not the sort of thing people tended to do for each other, especially an older person for an anonymous, young, drunk female. But maybe he should check somehow first.

He found himself feeling somewhat foolish for not thinking of this earlier.

He slipped back to his car and called Gregor.

A rather sleepy voice answered. 'Yeah?'

'Greg, it's Calum. Sorry to call you so late. But I'm a bit worried about Jenna. I wondered if she was with you. Did you see her tonight?'

'No. I didn't,' was the rather snapped answer. Not like Gregor, Calum thought. He sensed an issue of some sort.

'Were you supposed to?'

'No, not really no.'

He was getting stonewalled for some reason, which just made him more determined to get an answer.

'When did you last speak to her?'

'Err, earlier tonight. Why?'

'Greg, I think you're not telling me something. What was she doing and where was she?'

'Look Calum, I don't know, I don't know where she is. I don't want to talk about it right now ok?'

'Greg, to be blunt, I'm worried she might be in danger. She was seen getting into a car outside a bar in Portree tonight, with a young man and a woman who might be Glenda Muir. She was going to the bar to meet Glenda's son, who I'm being told doesn't exist, though I'm having my doubts about that particular point now. If you know anything, I need you to tell me right now. It could be really important.'

A silence ensued. Calum let it prevail, hoping the void would force Gregor to speak again.

Eventually his patience paid off.

'How do you know she was going to Portree, Calum? Did she tell you? She didn't mention it to me.'

That put him on the back foot a little, he had to decide to be truthful.

'Well, to be honest, because I logged into her Facebook account. She was meeting Gordon Muir at 8'o'clock tonight so I went to the bar to be sure she was ok, since the police have told me this boy doesn't exist. I was too late to see her though, she'd left in a car with the man and woman before I arrived.'

'Ok. All right. *I'd* better tell you the truth then I guess. I went to the bar too.'

Calum gasped at the sheer coincidence.

'I didn't see you there?'

'Well, I was there at 7:45. I waited an hour since she was supposed to be meeting this guy at 8. I rang her earlier and she seemed to pass me off with a flaky answer. I just got suspicious, don't really know why, just my instinct. So I hacked her Facebook account too and found out about the meeting. I always knew her password.'

Gregor gave a nervous laugh as he owned up to his behaviour. They both knew they'd shared a confession they couldn't tell Jenna about.

'And what happened in the bar?'

'Nothing, she didn't turn up. I left after an hour, maybe a bit less, like I said, then came back home. She's not here at her place either. I tried calling her again later and got her voice mail. So this Gordon Muir, you know him then?'

'Yes Gregor, well kind of. But he isn't her lover or anything, you don't have anything to worry about on that score. I'm nervous that it might be more serious than that. Look, call me if you hear from her ok?'

'Sure, sure. Shall I come over?'

'No, I'm in Inverness. I've told the police about the situation. Stay there, watch out for her and I'll call you if I have any news Greg. All right? I need to get moving.'

It took some time to persuade Gregor to stay in Plockton, but in the end he agreed.

Calum turned his thoughts to Glenda.

He looked out through his windscreen at the house. Still no lights on. No-one around the street. This could all play out in a lot of different ways. He wasn't sure he was ready for all possibilities.

Taking a deep breath, he swung the car door open and briskly got out, closing the door gently behind him.

He walked back to the front of the house, rang the doorbell, and waited for a response.

56

The headlights of Glenda's car swung slowly into the driveway and illuminated the side of the house. She drove slowly down the drive to the end where there was just enough room to veer left onto a concrete area behind the back door. As the car stopped, the PIR sensor light triggered and bathed the car in a bright yellow glow. She'd forgotten about that and jumped out of the car quickly, entering the house to switch it off.

Now the area around the car was quite dark. She was sure she wouldn't be seen. More of a worry was whether she could manage to move Jenna's still limp body. She had been worried she would die on the journey.

That concern had created an internal tussle with herself: she wasn't quite sure now why she hadn't just killed her and dumped her on one of the many remote places off the main road. Was it really logical to have brought her back here just to be able to think about the place to leave her dead body? Or was she actually looking for some thrill in watching her die under an electric light?

Yes, she thought that had some attractions. The girl had been too clever and nosey by far - she deserved to provide for someone else's gratification in return.

There was some spare clothes line in the cellar which she fished out of one of the various plastic storage boxes she kept down there. She looked around as she pulled it out of the box and decided to bring Jenna down there. It was invisible from any windows and if Jenna couldn't be kept quiet, there was little chance she would be heard from there. Not that she planned to let her utter anything. That thought triggered her to find some tape and a rag to gag her with.

She jogged back up to the kitchen and checked that none of the neighbours' windows which overlooked her car were lit. She was safe on that count and would have to risk someone sitting in the dark looking out of their window at that moment. She opened the car door, switched off the door opening lights and took a look at her victim. The weak ambient light was enough to see her face was pale and she'd dribbled out of one side of her open mouth.

'Pathetic,' she muttered under her breath.

Pulling her half-upright, she tied some clothes line under Jenna's armpits, to form a yoke of sorts. She could pull this more easily than trying to grasp parts of her clothing or limbs. She also wound some tape around her lower face after struggling to push a small rag into her mouth.

It was quite a struggle, but she managed to drag the body slowly out of the car and up the two steps into the kitchen doorway. As she entered the kitchen the light from the front hallway spilled onto Jenna's face. Her eyes flicked open, instantly wide, an illusion of death. The bumpy traverse along the ground must have pulled her into consciousness. She farted loudly. It made Glenda curl her lips in disgust and she kicked her, rather tentatively, in the groin.

Glenda was already perspiring from the exertion of moving Jenna and now her senses went into overdrive and she started to drip nervous sweat from the tip of her nose, one or two drops splashing onto Jenna's forehead and causing her to blink. She definitely wasn't dead then.

Glenda pulled Jenna across the kitchen linoleum and towards the cellar steps with a renewed vigour. By the time she'd pulled her down into the damp, cold room, allowing her head to bump painfully on the stone steps on the way down, she was wringing wet with sweat. She collapsed backwards onto one of the larger storage boxes and stared at her victim.

'BITCH... BITCH... BITCH.'

It was the only word she could imagine right now. She knew it was this girl who had looked under her bed, who had defiled her temple to John, had screwed up her plan to close the whole episode down cleanly. She was just a bitch. Like all women. She leaned forwards over her, choked up some loose phlegm and spat it over her face.

The only thing she had to decide now was when she would kill her. Five minutes or fifty? How much pleasure could she get from those minutes? The adrenaline was warming her body, and she relaxed a little and started to anticipate making Jenna suffer - watching her face crumple with the pain of cyanide-borne death spasms.

Where would she put her stinking body though? She realised she needed to finish this and move it tonight, whilst it was still dark. Her house was close to the river Ness and that was the obvious solution, but a better one would be further away. The depths of Loch Ness were easily reachable but, she thought, less likely to be searched if she came under suspicion; it was such a large expanse of water. She would drive along the north road on the loch side and find a quiet spot - she knew a few.

She felt in her jacket pocket and her fingers wrapped around the smooth glass vial of pain. Ten minutes. Ten minutes to savour it. She pulled the vial out and placed it in front of Jenna's face.

'Your invitation to dine with the devil.'

Jenna's eyes bulged and instantly swam with tears.

The silly cow. She deserved to die for showing no spirit.

Glenda felt a huge strength rise inside her, it filled her throat and she roared it out at Jenna in a twisted primal growl, an inch from her terrified face, showering Jenna's face with flecks of spittle.

It took some time for the doorbell chimes to penetrate the savage trance she was submerged in. When they did, she became both intensely angry and very agitated. She listened, wondering who it could be at such a late hour. No-one sprang to mind. She decided to ignore it and returned to staring at Jenna's terrified face. Her eyes betrayed some hope at the sound of the door bell. Fuck that!

After nearly a minute, she decided that whoever had called had given up and started towards Jenna. Then the bell rang again, a longer, more persistent push of the button. She cursed and realised she might have to deal with this.

She put the light out in the cellar, causing Jenna to bellow a muffled groan into her gag. She shut the door behind her and walked up the stairs to look carefully out of the landing window, from where she could observe the front path.

Calum! Why would he be here at this time of night? Could he have known Jenna was going to Portree? Even so, why come here? What's more, why hadn't the hypnosis she'd put him through kept him away?

Whatever... in choosing whether or not to open the door, part of her thinking was whether she would be able to influence him again. It had been easy last time.

He looked like he wasn't going to go away. Under a pounding pressure, it felt like she had no choice but to try.

She checked her clothing and pulled the blouse out of her jeans, trying to make it look as if she had just thrown her clothes on, flicked on a bedroom light that could be seen from the front door and then waited a couple of minutes before walking down the stairs to the front hallway.

She opened the door briskly, in a mock temper.

'Calum? What on earth are you doing here? It's very late, I was going to bed.'

'I know, I'm sorry to disturb you. But I have a few questions that wouldn't wait. Do you mind if I come in? It won't take long.'

She scowled at him whilst she was calculating the best way out of the predicament she was in. Maybe it was better to act normal, let him ask whatever was on his mind and then eject him as fast as possible, rather than refuse him and arouse any dormant suspicions.

'You'd better come in then. But only for a few minutes ok? I'm tired.'

Calum nodded and stepped over the threshold, feeling all of his senses rise to full alert.

57

Before he knocked on Glenda's front door, Calum had decided that he would talk to her in the kitchen. His reasoning being that it was the room closest to the car. If Jenna had entered the house it might have been through the kitchen door and she could still be in the kitchen.

He walked down the hallway briskly, giving Glenda no chance to direct him anywhere else by the time she'd closed the front door behind him.

'I thought we would go in the study,' she said, with a tone that scolded him for thinking of going anywhere else.

'I thought you'd make me some tea,' he countered as he swept into the kitchen, switched the light on and sat firmly down on one of the wooden dining chairs.

He looked briefly around. Nothing looked out of place and there was no sign of Jenna.

Glenda was feeling very much on the back foot all of a sudden, which was exasperating. She needed to be in control of this situation and struggled with herself to stay calm. She felt fresh beads of perspiration forming on her right temple.

She sat down opposite Calum and asked him what sort of tea he'd like to drink.

'Any is fine, I know you like making it.'

He smiled. Glenda felt unnerved by his apparent confidence and she sensed he knew he had somehow gained the advantage in the conversation.

She stood up and started her tea ritual, for one last time.

As she stood with her back to him, his eyes swept across her body. His mind felt a recognition, a warmth, something intangible he wanted to remember. But the internal resistance to thinking about Glenda that he'd experienced over the last week or so was still there somehow and he couldn't find a way past it.

He shuddered and shook himself mentally, as if to reboot his head.

'Have you been out tonight?'

Glenda was still facing away from him. The contours of her lips tightened perceptibly as she considered her answer.

'Yes, though not sure what business it is of yours Mr. Neuman. Let's get to the point. Why are you here?'

She whirled around to stare very directly into his eyes. She need to gain the upper hand in this conversation. Now she was looking down at him and had put him on the spot with her question.

'Ok. I *will* come to the point. It's about my assistant, Jenna. She appears to have been out tonight on Skye, to meet your son Gordon. I did ask her not to work the case anymore so I'm not sure why she did this or what the purpose of the meeting was. I found out about it after she left for Skye.

However, I'm worried about her. I went there around the time she was supposed to meet him and she'd left. In a car according to the barman, helped by a woman and a young man. Apparently she was drunk. I assume you've been able to contact Gordon and Ben via the police since John's murder. So I wondered if you could ask Gordon where Jenna is?'

A dozen questions and uncertainties flashed through Glenda's mind as he spoke.

'Well it's late. He will probably have his phone switched off. Why on earth would he be meeting Jenna anyway? And how exactly did she find him?'

'No idea. Especially as he doesn't exist.'

He really wasn't sure about this. It was a risk. A big risk.

He saw Glenda freeze momentarily, then soften considerably.

'What? Calum, I think you've been drinking! Let me get you another, something stronger. Do you like whisky?'

Buys me some more time, he thought.

'Ok. Just a little one, I'm driving.'

She forced a smile at him and pulled out two glasses from a cupboard together with a well-used bottle of single malt. She poured two small measures out and dripped some cold water into them from the tap.

'Cheers.' She looked warmly into his eyes and took a sip of whisky. She swallowed it and gently swayed her head from side to side.

'Mmm, that's good Calum, it's one of my favourites... so, Jenna isn't at home?'

'No. Her boyfriend doesn't know where she is either.'

'Look, I'll try to call Gordon in the morning, I did get his number from the police after John died. It's too late now, remember I haven't seen him for a very long time. Clearly I don't know his character *well*, but I'm sure if they've met then there'll be nothing to worry about.'

So she's lying, Calum thought. James Beerly had made it quite clear Coulson had no kids. And she's not getting mad about Jenna meeting Gordon either. That didn't stack up. He wondered how far the lying would go.

'So he does exist then?'

Glenda looked genuinely exasperated, to Calum. But she spoke to him very calmly, in a pleasant voice.

'Look, I don't know why you're asking me such a silly question but I engaged you in the first place to find them. Why would I have done that if they didn't exist? I mean, why spend all that money on you?'

It was a good question, Calum thought. He also thought he'd love to know the *real* answer.

He too had something tricky to mention though.

'I'm concerned that Jenna continued to investigate you after I had closed the case. I think she may even have found some of your personal things. If she did do that, I'm sorry for it and I'll put an end to it as soon as I find her.'

Glenda was somehow still maintaining a poker face, but the smiles were fading. Her eyelashes started to flicker.

'I see. What do you mean by my "personal things" Calum? My underwear?'

Calum hesitated.

She smiled knowingly at him and narrowed her eyes, making her eyelashes dance faster.

'Would you like to see my underwear, Calum?'

Calum found himself unable to answer. Suddenly, he felt tongue-tied, choked to the point of not being physically able to form a single word. With that constriction came a strange bedfellow: he was feeling himself relax as the same time.

Glenda swayed her head, her long hair shimmering around her. A silken matador's cloak.

His head swayed empathetically with hers, like a snake in time with the pipe of a charmer.

She talked to him in intimate detail about her underwear. Though he heard her, he wouldn't remember the words. Just like he couldn't remember being in her bed the last time they met. She felt confident she'd placed all of his memory of tonight behind a mental screen, a screen he would find very difficult to peer through in the future.

'Heh, look come with me, I have something to show you.'

She rose from her seat and knocked back the rest of the scotch. Calum did the same. She'd calculated fast. *If this didn't work, she would be in serious difficulty.*

58

'Come on handsome, what are you waiting for?'

Glenda motioned for Calum to follow her along the hallway until they reached the door that led down to the cellar. She stopped at the threshold, opened the door then walked down a couple of steps and turned back to look at him.

Calum wondered why she hadn't switched the light on and hesitated at the first step.

She pulled her blouse open, exposing her bare breasts and smiled at him. She took two steps slowly further down until, frustratingly, her face was the only part of her he could still see in the light thrown from the hallway.

'Offer's only open for five minutes.'

He moved down after her, switching the light on with his left hand as he moved down past the switch.

What happened next he wasn't really sure of, but as the light illuminated the steep staircase, he blinked at the bright light bulb hanging just in front of his head, felt a wrench at his ankle and saw the cellar floor rushing towards him from twelve feet away.

Pain surged through his skull as it cracked onto the concrete floor. It bought him to his senses.

His forearm was doubled up under his face and lessened the impact a little. He squinted sideways to see a large pole-shaped object swinging towards him.

He moved his head slightly, just enough to direct the pole to thump very painfully against his ear.

The impact caused him to roll backwards, where he bumped against a wall, leaving him lying on his side looking right across the room. Glenda was arcing a baseball bat towards him again and beyond her he caught a glimpse of a body on the floor.

'BASTARD.'

The bat swung down and smashed against his outstretched arm. The blow was a firm one, it shook him to the core and the vibration made his already battered head wince with a slicing blade of pain. His head slumped down a little.

Glenda glared at him. He watched her withdraw a small glass tube from her pocket.

'You can watch the bitch die first,' she spat, as she held up the vial and pulled off the stopper. She leant over and started to tilt it towards the flared nostrils of the bound form on the floor.

Calum looked at the body, which was wriggling and groaning, six to eight feet away from him. As the head rolled towards him he saw Jenna's terrified face.

The agony in her eyes lent him a surge of strength and he launched himself upwards onto his knees at Glenda, his arm outstretched to try to knock the vial away from her.

His punch was crucially accurate. Glenda wasn't expecting such a lightning upsurge from Calum and his fist thumped into her own, causing her to gasp and the vial to fly backwards in her hand, smashing against her upper row of teeth.

As she gasped she sucked in a slug of the deadly liquid and her lungs vacuumed it into her digestive system. She spat violently at the almond-like aroma that was starting to fill her senses, her saliva flecking Calum's hair as he fell forwards, let down by an ankle full of searing pain that wouldn't allow his upwards thrust to continue.

Glenda dived forwards towards Jenna's face, her mouth wide open and dripping the remains of the cyanide, in a last attempt to force some poison home.

Calum threw out his fist again and banged Glenda's ankle. It was the last ditch tap tackle he'd learnt in his rugby-playing days.

It served him crucially well this time: Glenda tottered over and fell sideways against the opposite wall, only three feet from Jenna, who was desperately turning away from her.

In the end, she didn't need to move. Glenda, in those few short seconds, had involuntarily gulped in enough of the neat poison to suddenly start to convulse, as a slick of pain grew like a typhoon from inside her. She arched her back and gurgled a desolate cry.

For a moment, she was a wolf howling high into the wind. Then she was a concave form, draped between the floor and wall, frothing saliva and dying like a dog.

59

Calum watched Glenda die in terror, the living breath sucked out of her by her own weapon. He was transfixed by her face: its elegant features creased by spasm and shocked by the intensity of the pain. She was soon dead. Her body tilted sideways slightly, as if drunk and urinated a large yellow pool across the floor as she lost control of her vital functions.

As the edge of the spreading liquid veneer crept towards Jenna's body, Calum was snapped away from his trance and shuffled over to help her. He was able to pull the tape away from her face, piece by piece and as he released each fragment, her crying become freer and louder. Finally he pulled the rag from out of her open mouth and let her breathe freely again. She took some deep gulps in amongst the heavy, body-jerking sobs.

'Calum, I'm so sorreeeee...'

'Sssssh, not for now. Are you hurt anywhere?'

'I feel like I've got lots of bruises on my back... and my head... is really hurting. I still feel sick... she was just so mad...'

'I think she maybe *was* mad. I'll ring for help. I can't really stand up, think my ankle's sprained.'

'I think she tried to poison me Calum, just before you came. I think I passed out earlier. I think I must have had my drink spiked or something ...'

He leant back against the wall next to Jenna and dialled James Beerly.

'Calum. We're on our way to you. I assume you're still at Glenda's house?'

'Yeah. Not really in a position to go anywhere else now, either. So how come you're on the way?'

'One of the investigating team interviewed Alan Butler this evening. We'd been waiting for his injuries to improve before we could talk to him properly; this was our first real opportunity. We weren't allowed much time with him but he opened up with little effort from us... he was pretty much caught red-handed anyway. The ballistics guys matched his gun to the bullets found around the harbour. He seemed to have decided the game was up. It appears he had a grudge against you, as you found out yourself... but he says he was inspired to turn it into action by Glenda. As soon as we knew that, we headed off to your location. I didn't call in case it alerted Glenda. What's the position there?'

'Too damn late mate. It's all over. She's dead. You'd better call for an ambulance. Jenna and I are a bit the worse for wear.'

'But you're both all right?'

'I'm not sure. I'll patch up ok I think. But Jenna might have been poisoned. Glenda had something in a tube. We need to get her to hospital fast.'

He glanced towards the smashed glass vial still partly gripped by Glenda's dead hand.

James's voice crackled back from his car hands-free.

'Ok, we'll get whatever that is taken to the hospital with you for analysis. I'll get an ambulance organised. We're only a couple of minutes away. I'm switching the sirens on, you'll hear us now.'

Calum picked up the whine of the roof-mounted sirens immediately. For once, he found them wonderfully comforting and slid back down to the floor in relief.

He waited with Jenna in the cellar. He couldn't have made it up the staircase anyway.

'So what happened at the bar Jenna? Did you see Glenda there?'

'Well no, no-one. I went to meet Gordon there. He was late and then I started to feel really sick. I went outside then it went really hazy. I think I threw up, I seem to remember talking to someone and then I passed out. I came round here. I know I shouldn't have done it Calum. I'm really sorry. I didn't expect all of this.'

She started to cry again, in waves of heavy sobs.

'No, you couldn't have seen this coming.' He didn't feel angry with her now. Just relieved she was alive.

There was a banging at the door... then a splintering of wood as the police kicked the front door open, followed by a thunder-like rumble of rubber boots on floorboards as they searched for him and Jenna.

They were soon surrounded by half a dozen police, all in riot clothing. They were helped upstairs towards the hallway where they waited for the ambulance to arrive, as the police began the painstaking process of forensic examination of Glenda, the cellar and the rest of the house. A technician carefully retrieved the remnants of the glass tube from Glenda's hand and bagged it.

Beerly was with the unit, though it was another officer, DI Johnson, who was asking the questions. Calum presumed that was because he'd been the officer in charge of the shooting attempt on his own life.

'Sorry Calum but I need to ask you a few questions. I think you understand. The young lady too. But we'll do it in the ambulance, we need to get you checked out as a priority.'

Calum nodded. Jenna followed suit, with a dazed wobble of her head.

They started to slowly recount the events of the evening in the few minutes before the ambulance arrived and then DI Johnston and a police constable accompanied them to the hospital.

They crowded into the back of the emergency vehicle. Jenna laid on the bed and Calum sat on the seat at the end, whilst the two policeman half crouched against a small bench along the side of the compartment. The detective continued with his questioning until he decided he had asked enough for the moment. He seemed satisfied for now. Jenna had explained she went to meet Gordon to try to find out more about his mother; Calum seemed to be trying to help Jenna out of a potentially dangerous situation, and they needed to be examined and treated for what appeared to be minor injuries and possibly poisoning.

He escorted them out of the ambulance and into A&E reception. After a brief discussion at the triage desk, they were ushered through to an examination room, where a doctor attended Jenna immediately.

There was one question bugging Calum.

'How did Butler know Glenda?'

'Umm, well, apparently she tried to treat him with some experimental hypnotherapy, some kind of research she did after her university course. He got some extra privileges in jail for agreeing to it. Sounds like she must have been either plotting this for some time or maybe she just got lucky in having someone she could influence to do her will. Either way, it looks like they had a joint interest in getting rid of you. Why Glenda had that motive, we're not clear about though.'

Jenna looked up.

'I think I may know why she *might* be predisposed to something violent or irrational,' she offered, interrupting her doctor's attempt at diagnosis.

The detective looked at her askance.

'Do tell, young lady.'

Calum listened intently too, looking at Jenna's' ashen face and feeling guilty for what had happened to her.

'Well, my research of her past threw up a gap in her CV. I managed to find out she'd been in a psychiatric institution. I think it might have been caused by her break up with John Coulson. She was jealous of him having other relationships I think: in an extreme way.'

'But why try to kill *me*? And you Jenna? To cover up the whole investigation of the twins? Who, by the way, I think *may* not exist. Given what you've said then maybe the twins were all in her head, something she wished she had but didn't? By the way, did you see anyone in a grey baseball cap in the bar?'

Jenna looked at him sharply. 'How come you know anything about a grey baseball cap?'

Calum realised his mistake, but he knew he would have to tell her about searching her files anyway, so what the hell.

'I think you can work that out Jenna. Anyway, did you?'

Even in her exhausted state, she managed a half-hearted scowl.

'No. Not at all. Anyway, maybe we should check out the photograph of the twins. Try to work out who they really are - maybe a friend's or relative's kids?'

'Maybe Jenna, though I think that's for DI Johnston now, not for us.'

Johnston nodded his head sagely and bid his farewell.

'Hope they find nothing too wrong with you both,' he said. 'I'll be back this afternoon once you've had some rest. Until we clear up one or two things, you'll have Constable Blake here to guard your room. We'll send another PC along very shortly as I expect you'll be separated.'

Calum and Jenna looked at each other, not sure whether to sigh with relief or be worried by his remark about needing a guard. "Better safe than sorry", ran through both of their heads, unbeknown to each other.

Jenna moved closer to Calum on the examination bench and nestled her head against his arm. He pulled it up and curled it around her, squeezing her tightly.

Calum began hesitantly.

'Look, I'm sorry for looking at your emails, but I was worried about where you were and couldn't get any answer from your phone. Anyway, seems I was right to worry?'

She thought about being indignant but quickly decided against it.

'I guess so. I'm glad you found me that's for sure.'

She dropped her head a little and her eyes started to moisten. Damn this. No way was she going to cry in front of Calum for a second time today.

'Next time, tell me what you're up to, eh?' he said kindly.

She nodded meekly and cuddled up a little bit more, surreptitiously dabbing at her eyes, as the A&E doctor continued his examination.

60

Calum and Jenna were treated in separate, adjacent rooms in the hospital, where their respective doors were watched over keenly by a constable from the local force.

Calum had his ankle strapped lightly... other than that he had a lot of nasty looking bruises but the doctors assured him he would be fine in a few days, though to expect some stiffness where he'd been hit and fallen. He was waiting to be formally discharged.

Jenna on the other hand, as well as some large contusions on the back of her head from where she'd been dragged down the cellar stairs, was found to have traces of cyanide in her blood. She'd been given an antidote and told she would be kept under close medical observation for 24 hours. Now she could understand why she had been so sick in the bar. It must have been the drink... Glenda must have spiked it before she eventually ended up bundling her into her car. She remembered she'd only taken the tiniest of sips before her phone buzzed and the drink got knocked over. How close a call had *that* been.

She mentioned the dropped glass to the police officer outside her room, who asked HQ to arrange to send someone to the bar, so the floor could be properly cleaned.

'Don't want the owner's dog sniffing the floor and keeling over do we love?' he'd said.

The imagery made Jenna laugh.

'So now you're going to walk around with a scrubbing brush as well as a poop-scoop when you take your own dog for a walk?'

The young constable flushed, realising it was also her pretty face that had caused that reaction.

By early afternoon, Calum was allowed through to talk to her. He sat on her bed, wearing a white medical gown, which he was struggling to keep wrapped properly around himself to preserve his modesty.

'Calum, please, keep it all under cover!' Jenna teased.

So she was recovering fine then, he thought. He was relieved. It took him by surprise just how much. He realised at that moment that Jenna had grown into a whole lot more than just an office assistant and reminded himself, again, to do something about that once they were back home. He really needed to recognise her contribution more, before it was too late.

They talked warmly, their newly enhanced closeness the product of a shared nightmare. They went over the details of how each of them had separately approached the climactic events in Glenda's house, sharing different perspectives of what had unfolded and how they'd felt.

Eventually, Calum broached the subject which had been prickling him.

'So why did you actually continue to investigate Glenda after I closed the case?'

Jenna's face looked like it had been waiting for the question forever and was relieved it had now arrived.

'Well, basically it was because you seemed so suddenly disinterested in it. It was odd. You were odd. You *are* odd at times anyway, but, well it was different to your normal odd.'

Calum didn't quite know how to react. As ever, she could disarm him completely.

'How? In what way?' he said.

'Well, it was almost as if you were under her spell, as if she had convinced you to drop it and you were in complete obeyance.

You know how you normally hang on to things, analyse and think about them after the event? Well it was out of character that you didn't. Just a difference that worried me. I couldn't let it go even if you could.'

There was little he could think to say in response. He didn't want to be the heavy-handed boss, expecting her to follow his instructions robotically. Not today for sure. She'd done the right thing, even if she had put herself, unwittingly, into danger. He admired her persistence and courage - no, he needed to accept she'd not been wrong to carry on investigating Glenda.

He cradled her hand with his own.

'No problem. Sometimes rules are meant to be broken. Well, this one worked out for the best didn't it? The guilty one got caught.'

'And killed,' Jenna reflected soberly.

'I checked out what Paul had said about 'morbid jealousy'. It seems it can lead to some pretty nasty reactions. I'm no expert and I guess it will come out of the police investigation but Glenda looks to have invented the children as something she desperately wanted but never had. I'd guess she'd wanted to have a family with John Coulson.'

Jenna nodded a woman's understanding of the tension that might have created in her.

'She must be under suspicion for Coulson's murder now, but being dead kind of hampers the police's objective there. As for you, well it's clear she wanted you out of the way Jen. I guess your continued contact with Gordon must have freaked her.'

Jenna shrugged that off with a slow roll of her eyebrows.

'Weird. She looked from the outside like a bright and interesting woman with a good career. Why on earth would she let this thing with John and the children take over her life? She must have had plenty of other male friends and opportunities, she was pretty attractive wouldn't you say Calum?'

'Indeed.'

Jenna thought his tone sounded self-conscious.

As he said that word, it stirred up a feeling about Glenda again that he couldn't quite fathom. He was beginning to think that was the best way for it to be.

'There's an old Scots saying: "The lass that has many wooers often wails the wast". I guess it speaks for itself.'

They both reflected on that before Calum stood up, rubbing a sore spot on his back and moved towards the door.

As he approached it, he heard the deep, lazy accent of Gregor's voice somewhere down the corridor. It sounded like he was talking to the nurse at the station inside the ward entrance.

'Look, you need to speak to Gregor now. I can hear him outside. I'm sure they'll allow him in. I know he's been worried about what you were up to in Portree. Don't be too mad about why he became concerned, he was guilty of the same snooping as me. He was just worried.'

He threw her the kind of warm, knowing wink that asks for understanding. She smiled ruefully back in what he read as grudging acceptance.

He left the room and shuffled back into his own, hoping he wouldn't be hearing a lover's tiff through the thin wall once Gregor was ushered in.

61

A few days later, Calum was already immersed back into the depths of his latest assignments - the routine stuff that made him feel comfortable with his life. It descended into drudgery at times but the repetition provided what he wanted from his career: some interest, a continual stream of new people to meet and not too much stress. He was glad that, most of the time, he managed to get that. He often wondered what percentage of people didn't achieve some kind of happy life balance and suspected it was the majority.

The simple routine of the morning wasn't enough to stop his mind from drifting to thoughts of his lunch from around 11 a.m. though, and today was no exception. Around midday he looked out of the window to check the weather, spurned his light jacket and walked out of the office in his shirt sleeves, ambling over towards the loch side. It was a bright, breezy and warm July day. Jenna came with him, for a change. Usually she spent her lunch time away from both him and the office - they seemed to have been closer though since the whole experience of Glenda's death - it was comforting to be in each other's company somehow.

They sat on the sea wall and unwrapped their sandwiches. Calum had bought some cold ginger beer from the village shop before sitting down on the crumbling stonework. He looked at the bottle and chuckled, remembering how his heart had pounded one night in Lincoln. His mind drifted onto the prospect of a succulent pork pie too.

'What?'

'Nothing. Just thinking about something funny.'

'Gonna tell me?'

'Nope. Not now. It's kind of embarrassing.'

'Go on then!'

He knew she wouldn't give up. He relented and told her the story of the exploding ginger beer.

She giggled and looked at him affectionately.

This time of year was just wonderful on the west coast of Scotland. There were a few casual sailors out in the harbour and a couple of windsurfers tacking out towards Duncraig castle on the other side of the harbour. Calum spotted Gregor instructing a couple of school kids, presumably on their lunch hour, in a small dinghy. He watched him with interest and thought what a great way it was for them to spend a school lunchtime. Gregor was talking to them, joking and getting a spirited response. Calum could feel the good nature filling the boat, even at a distant of fifty yards or so.

Suddenly Calum saw something in the boat that caused his flesh to tingle.

He said nothing but his mind raced like lightning through the possibilities of what it meant. He looked at Jenna. She appeared serene and happy. Maybe she hadn't seen what he had.

'He loves teaching kids you know. One day he'll love teaching his own.'

Calum looked at her, wondering how much to read into that statement, then turned away, munching on the ham sandwich.

After a couple of silent mouthfuls, and with an eye on Gregor still, he took a deep breath and looked at Jenna.

'So look, I've been meaning to say these last few days. I think you did a great job on the Muir case. In fact you always do a great job. I know you're harbouring thoughts of going to university but I'd like to give you more money, a rise - and a bit more license to roam with your thoughts - so maybe you'll stay a while longer?'

He looked away, not wanting to see a disappointing response in her face. There was a little more silence. He caught sight of her out of the corner of his eye, gazing out at Gregor's boat. He knew Gregor was all part of her decision - he was happy to play on it.

'Gregor will be pleased if you stay of course.'

'For heaven's sake, you couldn't be more obvious if you tried Neuman,' she replied, struggling to contain her grin around a mouthful of sandwich.

'I'm flattered thanks. I'll think about it. I really will. I need to talk to Gregor for sure. I actually have a course place offer from Edinburgh to start this October and I've kept that all to myself. I need to make my mind up I guess.'

She turned to Calum and smiled warmly. He felt somehow that she had signalled she would stay; but he would leave her to say that in her own good time.

Gregor's boat turned shoreward, flying a flag of white seagulls behind, as they hovered hopefully over the childrens' lunch bag remains. The boat crunched against the sand and pebbles on the shore and the two boys jumped out, running off to make the bell for afternoon school. As he approached the road, Gregor spotted them, took off his cap and veered towards them.

'Any sandwiches left?' he shouted cheerily as he approached their spot on the wall.

Jenna picked out a cheese roll from her lap and threw it hard at him. He caught it in front of his chest, spraying some of the filling sideways at Calum. They all broke out laughing as he simultaneously plunged the roll into his mouth and sat down on Jenna's lap and her remaining sandwich. 'That one's mine too!' he spluttered as he fought cheese, laughter and Jenna's knees pushing sharply up into his crotch.

'Come on, I've something to talk to you about. I'll buy you another sandwich and you can get rid of the one stuck to your bum.'

She smiled again at Calum as she rose to walk away.

'Hang on Gregor. I've something to ask you first,' said Calum.

'Just pass me what you have in your hand there.'

Gregor instantly looked sheepish and handed his cap to him.

'Were you wearing this in the bar on the night Jenna met Glenda?'

'Well yes, I did put it on for a while. Not at first, I just put it on later out of boredom.' He glanced, apprehensively, sideways at Jenna. She looked quizzically at him and the cap, then the reason why Calum had asked suddenly fell into her mind.

'Ok look, before you ask any more - I was just worried Jenna, about who you were meeting and - well - I was jealous. I suppose I just wanted to be the person with the cap you were meeting. I guess I was trying to be sarcastic by putting it on and walking up to you in the bar with it on and now I feel completely stupid about it.'

She looked at the cap. 'I don't remember you having one like this?'

'Well no, I pulled the logo off it to match the description he gave you: it was the old dolphin conservation one you gave me ages ago.'

Calum sat quietly as the conversation unfolded. He wondered whether his previous confidence in Jenna staying had now been blown apart - he hoped not.

She glanced at Calum again. 'No, look I understand you were worried... I know. That's what I wanted to talk about. Come on, let's leave Calum to finish his sandwich in peace. See you later boss.' She threaded her hand through the crook of Gregor's elbow and pulled him up towards the road.

As Calum watched them chattering earnestly, walking away from him up towards Jenna's stone cottage, he turned back towards the sea and leant back with his elbows on the wall behind him.

All done then.

62

DI Johnston pulled up outside the hospital, parking completely irresponsibly on double yellow lines, telling himself it was warranted given there were no regular parking spaces and he had a busy day ahead of him. He couldn't waste public time and money looking for a space outside of the hospital grounds.

He was feeling in a pretty miserable mood, which was not far from his normal demeanour. An hour or so of re-questioning Butler lay ahead and he knew it was unlikely to help him much; Butler was a smart cookie and probably wouldn't give anything away that he didn't mean to. It had been a few days since they were last allowed to talk to him, so he'd have thought more about his story, what he'd told them already... what he wasn't ever going to tell them.

He nodded at the guarding officer and flashed his ID mechanically as he walked, almost apologetically, through into the private room.

Alan Butler was sat up in bed, propped up by two regulation pillows with starched white cases. He greeted the detective with a sigh that resonated with his cynical hubris.

Johnston ignored the dubious greeting and nodded curtly to him, drawing up a chair alongside the bed.

'Don't get too close, you might catch whatever I'm suffering from,' Butler said with heartfelt venom.

Johnson again took no notice and calmly opened his notebook, pulling out the engraved pen his wife had given him on their silver wedding anniversary.

He made a heading in the notebook and then looked up at Butler, who realised he was going to have to suffer a lot more questioning before this was over. Whatever "over" actually meant.

'So, we do need to pursue the question of how you and Glenda came to form this sort of unholy alliance against Calum Neuman.'

'I've told you before about all of this. She helped me with some therapy sessions in prison. She was doing some research for a post-grad degree. We sort of got on well. I had an issue with Neuman, you know why, I told you that as well. She helped me get started outside of prison. She's a good woman.'

Johnson found himself suddenly cynical, after the last utterance.

'But why exactly did she help you? Assisting a murderer is a serious thing for her to have contemplated. I'm sure she wouldn't have done it lightly. We believe she tried to kill Mr. Neuman's assistant too. Any idea on why she would want to kill both of these apparently innocent people?'

'Heh, you police have a very blinkered view of who's innocent. By what measure is Neuman innocent? He helped convict me, I was always innocent. So who is *really* innocent here?'

Johnston mentally shrugged him off. The 'attack is the best form of defence' patter he often got from the more capable criminals was typical behaviour and he ploughed on. He used to wonder if it was a conscious tactic on their part or whether it was driven by total delusion. Either way, it didn't matter to him. All that mattered was the plain truth, so he'd never considered the reason important.

'Did Glenda ever talk to you about John Coulson?'

'No.'

'But you know him.'

'Well, yeh of course, he was part of the team that sent me to jail.'

'Have you been to the Isle of Skye over the past few weeks?'

'No, again, no I haven't. I'm not going to remember all of a sudden I went there. For god's sake!'

'Did you travel to Italy during the past few weeks either?'

'Also a fairy tale destination for me.'

'Tell me more about what you were doing in the period between leaving jail and your arrival at Plockton.'

'I stayed in my flat a lot. Ate pizzas, watched TV, drank beer, that kind of thing. The things you don't get much of in prison. I've no family, well none that I keep in touch with. My friends haven't been rushing to get in touch since I got out. So like I told you before, I've got no alibi really, but nothing to confess either.'

'Where did you get the rifle?'

'I've had it for years.'

'And a licence?'

'You know the answer to that one. Why ask?'

'Did you have the revolver for years too?'

Butler checked himself briefly.

'I don't have a revolver.'

Clever. That was close. He had to stay clear of any linkage to the Italian incident. No need to increase the impending sentence.

'Did Glenda ever mention her children?'

Butler's heart struggled to contain a skipped beat and he looked away from Johnston momentarily.

'Nope. I didn't think she had any.'

'So why did you actually tell us about Glenda treating you?'

'Because she encouraged me to get to Neuman. It wasn't just me, it was her as well. I don't know *why*, I didn't ask questions. She just did.'

Johnston sat back. He thought he had begun to be sure about Butler's motivation to provide information about Glenda now. He suspected she somehow wanted to claim she carried part of the blame for the attempt on Neuman's life. The lawyers could argue over that one.

The detective was also pretty sure there was more he'd chosen not to tell. He needed to continue to whittle away with the questioning, looking for little mismatches, gaps, inconsistencies between versions over the last few rounds of interviewing. So far, there weren't any.

He threw in his last trick for the day.

'I need to tell you that Glenda Muir is dead.'

Butler fell silent for a few seconds and Johnston sensed a frenetic brain operating behind his frozen face.

'What? Why do you think I should believe that?'

Butler's voice betrayed his shock. Johnston thought it also leaked some tightly reined in emotion.

Butler was ashen white underneath his bluster and ruddy visage. He couldn't believe or understand how she could be dead. Now his whole world had changed its axis within a few short seconds.

But he knew they were playing a game of spotting the mistake. He was smart enough to think carefully about his answers and keep them as brief as possible: the less he said, the less could be pored over and pulled apart by the police. In the end, they would falter beyond the fact he had shot at Neuman. He couldn't really argue that one: the ballistics would be conclusive. But beyond that - well, if it was true that Glenda was dead - no-one else knew about what they had done. He was pretty certain of that.

Johnston continued repeating similar, probing questions over the next thirty minutes. He found himself met with a consistently solid defence and left feeling even more dispirited then when he arrived.

*

A little later, a nurse entered the room and Butler turned his gaze onto her. That was something he needed to help himself to before this case led him back into prison too. A woman or two. He wondered if he'd left it too late.

'Need anything?' she asked innocently.

'Yes and no.'

He laughed. 'Actually, no.'

She met his gaze with a tight grimace and walked away with the remains of his lunch tray.

*

The nurse returned half an hour later. She was carrying an envelope in her hand.

'Actually you meant yes. You wanted this morning's post all along. You are allowed letters, I think. I'm sorry, it arrived a few days ago but it got mislaid at the nurses' desk station.'

She winked and left him poring over the envelope she'd handed to him.

He waited until the door had closed and carefully opened the letter. He noticed there was no stamp or postmark. It appeared to have been hand-delivered. He was surprised he'd been allowed to receive it: maybe the nurse had been bribed in some way. The handwriting which he recognised on the front of the envelope confirmed that suspicion. He wondered what she'd meant by "mislaid" - the envelope showed no signs of tampering with though, not even a steam open since it was sealed with sticky tape as normal.

Inside there was a single, hand-written sheet and a copy of an old photograph clipped to the back of it.

He read slowly.

My Dear Alan,

Why???

Why did you make a sacrifice over Neuman? I was sure that I'd dealt with him in my own way. There was really no need to go after him. Anyway, what's done is done.

I was there on the lochside in Plockton when you shot at him. I wanted to make sure his assistant was taken care of but I abandoned that

once you started firing. In any case, I think that by the time you get this I'll
have succeeded in removing that threat. At least Coulson is out of my life. He
ruined mine. A life for a life eh? Let me tell you, watching his blood flow
down that ridiculous witch's robe was the most exhilarating thrill.

I'll tell the boys about my illness now. The adoption people will pass
it all on I think. I'm glad we decided all those years ago that they would take
your name, it may help them to identify with you eventually, even if you are
going to be absent from the free world again for a while. I'm sure one day
they'll want to know who their father is and come looking for you. Don't be
down about the possibility they'll find out where you are. Remember, we just
couldn't have looked after them all those years ago: it was the right thing to do
then and I still believe that now.

Look at their picture, remember them.

I'm still going to keep the illness from my parents. Not sure that
they'd care anyway: if they ever get in touch with you, you don't know anything
OK? They didn't help all that time ago, don't think they'll suddenly try now.

I'll be there in court. Just see I'm there. I'll start writing to you again.
Don't forget, we are and will always be in this together.
Be strong,
Glenda. X
(Remember to rip this into small pieces and flush it away!)

He folded the letter up and put it back into its white
sheath. How had she found out he was here? The woman was
devious.

He grinned, without a trace of humour, and leant back
onto his pillows, blowing his cheeks out. It had all started with a
dance. Didn't it often?

He used to go to the university Friday night discos: more
fun and better educated women there. It had been intense at first,
then - she got pregnant.

The last thing he'd expected was a child and when it
turned out to be twin boys, that really sounded the death knell for
their relationship: Glenda didn't want them at all and yet didn't
have the heart to abort them. Looking back, it seemed that was

out of character with the hard-hearted way she dealt with most things in her life, at least those that he'd been party to. But she'd always been kind to him despite not wanting to stay with him. Well, prison kind of killed that off didn't it?

She'd dumped him, before the children were born and then adopted by a local couple. Glenda had then started the relationship with Coulson, the man she became obsessed with for the rest of her life. She had loved him to bits and according to Glenda he'd felt the same about her – until, apparently, the day she caught him in bed with another undergraduate, when she'd turned up at his room unexpectedly one lazy summer's afternoon.

What a damn weird twist of fate that Coulson had also been part of the case that took him to prison. It must have been almost his first professional case. He'd never blamed Coulson though, it was that bastard private investigator, that PI, Neuman, who had been the start of it all. It was *him* that needed to suffer. And besides, Glenda had always been so convincing about Coulson's lack of malice. She always convinced him. It was like being under her spell...

She didn't know what else he'd been up to before their relationship and that he was essentially bound for prison. But for some reason she'd stayed in touch with him, wheedling her way into his prison, years later, with the pretext of a research project. He'd always wondered if she was just attracted by dark people, intensity, some sense of adventure however misplaced. His semen had *definitely* been misplaced.

Would he ever understand that woman and his own relationship with her, whatever that really was? He thought not. Now, it seemed, that would remain a lifelong enigma.

He held the copy photograph above his face at arm's length. Those two boys had been the source of so much trouble in Glenda's head. He knew that she should have had them with Coulson, then this eternal tension in her would never have arisen.

It seemed extreme to have killed him because she was entering a steep decline in her health. Glenda was an extreme woman though. No wonder Coulson ditched her. His mistake though. Now, finally after all these years, she'd got her retribution, despite his best efforts to hide his whereabouts.

Brilliant idea, to locate him by asking a PI to find his non-existent children by searching him out first. Choosing Neuman was just bizarre: but he wondered if she had done it knowing she would try to kill him afterwards to erase the trail? Her letter implied *something* like that.

The really stupid thing though, was that she'd encouraged him to go after Neuman. So what did she mean by having *dealt with him*? Had she meant him to be caught trying to kill Neuman? He suddenly felt totally without reference points. Maybe he'd just been duped. Was she really dead now? He'd resisted the strong urge to ask the DI more about how she'd died but was burning up to know. Maybe he could get access to a phone, perhaps tomorrow... maybe another day. Probably pointless.

More definitely, he was going to be losing his freedom fairly soon. One thing and one thing only was starting to fill his mind. The thought that had lain there for so many damned years, was now burning brighter with Neuman's escape and Glenda's apparent death.

The need for revenge.

He would, once again, have to wait.

ACKNOWLEDGEMENTS

So many thanks to:

Jill for endless inputs and support throughout

Dad (Ken) for his meticulous proof reading

Charlotte & Tori for their critiques of earlier drafts

Macclesfield Writers for their advice and help

Nik Perring for being my editor

Front cover photography: Karl 'SneachtaPix' Bergin.